# SERPENTINE

C. Dietz

# ADVANCE PRAISE OF *SERPENTINE*

This alternate future history centered on Esther reflects so much of the rhetoric we hear in these hot political days, it adds a fearsome tone. It's almost too real. Letters left by her resistance leader parents and flashbacks to her experience in the Catholic orphanage provide a running memoir for a back story. Love, betrayal, loss, young romance, and dystopian survival. What more could you ask for?

GUY L. PACE
author of the *Spirit Missions* trilogy

# SERPENTINE

## CHRISTY DIETZ

Ambassador International
GREENVILLE, SOUTH CAROLINA & BELFAST, NORTHERN IRELAND

www.ambassador-international.com

# SERPENTINE

ISBN: 978-1-62020-729-1
eISBN: 978-1-62020-748-2
Library of Congress Control Number: 2021940944

Cover Design by Megan McCullough
Interior Typesetting by Dentelle Design
Edited by Daphne Self and Katie Cruice Smith

AMBASSADOR INTERNATIONAL
Emerald House
411 University Ridge, Suite B14
Greenville, SC 29601, USA
www.ambassador-international.com

AMBASSADOR BOOKS
The Mount
2 Woodstock Link
Belfast, BT6 8DD, Northern Ireland, UK
www.ambassadormedia.co.uk

*The colophon is a trademark of Ambassador, a Christian publishing company.*

*For my dad, who taught me to dream*

# 1.
# PRESENT DAY

"Hey! Watch where you're going!" I trip over the foot of a man . . . I mean woman. It's so hard to tell these days. I'm breathless and clumsy as I stumble to evade the paunchy baker running after me. The intersex looks at me with half pity and half disdain as she turns back toward her lover. The lover peels his eyes from his phone just long enough to cast me the same look of scorn. He knows what I represent. I notice the couple is surrounded by the most recent propaganda of the Federation. Flyers grip the wall with slogans of "Uniformity is Diversity" and "Peace Will Come with Acceptance." I usually try to rip a few down on my way through these elusive alleys, but there's no time for that now.

The baker is falling too far behind. I catch his words as I round the corner. "I knooow who you are, Blondie!" he heaves. "I'll report you!"

I knew he was too fat to catch me, one too many loaves of bread consumed in a world that's starving. What I am counting on is that he doesn't know my name. I will have to find another area of the city to steal food, though. I pull my long, straight hair into a ponytail and run. I'm even less concerned because I know that the Federation doesn't care anyway. If anything, they promote stealing, as they promote all forms of chaos. It helps them to hide. Yet, I am relieved to have avoided a confrontation as I unlock the door to my small apartment and take a large bite of my hard-earned baguette.

I'm lucky to have this apartment—part of a boxy, one-story building, run down by years of disrepair. Most apartments are under government surveillance in Headquarters, but I managed to find something through the Resistance. It's a happy accident that the Federation hasn't caught up to the fact that it's vacant, but I'm sure that's only a matter of time.

"Finnick?" I call as I walk through the dark, another perk of being poor. My fingers fumble on the table for some matches. I light a candle and open the blinds. Slowly, the meager furniture in the room is illuminated, and I gasp as I see Finnick lying on the floor.

"Finnick!" I scream, as I run toward his motionless body. I lean down and shake him.

"Ugh, get off me, Esther. I'm just sleeping." It's an effect of living in a dystopian world; you're constantly fearing the worst.

"Well, wake up. I need to talk to you." I glance toward the door, anxiety rising within me. "Here, eat some of this."

I rip off a portion of the bread and place it into his hand. He looks up at me groggily, keeping his muddy green eyes partly closed. He sighs and pulls the blanket over his head, taking his bread with him. I do understand why he's tired; I mean, I am, too, but this is important.

I hesitate. "I was seen." These three words are enough for Finnick to leap up and rip the blanket off, pushing his hand through his wavy, brown hair. Well, that got his attention. I'm briefly reminded of how much I envy his hair. It isn't right for a man to have that kind of hair. It's such a waste.

"What do you mean, *seen*? What did you do?" Panic floods his eyes, and I can tell he's thinking the worst.

"First of all, I didn't do anything. I was placing flyers about our meeting under the doors of the apartment building on Elm when the traitor, Ezra, came out of nowhere." I feel my upper lip tighten just saying his name. "He yelled at me to stop, and I told him to go crawl back up President Alastor's . . ." Finnick's eyes convey disappointment, and I pause before continuing, "Okay, so, in retrospect, I probably could have chosen my words better, but I wasn't about to let that conniving backstabber bring me in."

Our acquaintance with Ezra dates back to our time in the orphanage as kids. The three of us were actually friends until Ezra betrayed us.

Finnick sighs. He seems to sigh a lot around me these days. "You have to learn to keep your mouth shut. It just fuels their incentive to find and arrest you. Besides, I thought we promised to lay low for a while after what happened at Barron Creek." The pain is there again, in his face and his eyes, and I immediately feel remorse for not being more careful.

"I'm sorry." And I really am, but the words fall flat between us.

"So, what now? We move again? Does he know where you're staying? Did he have you followed?"

"I ran . . ." My voice trails off as I consider his questions. It has been a couple of hours now, so maybe I am in the clear, though, the nagging tug on my insides says otherwise. I fight to keep my voice steady, to fill it with more assurance than I feel. "I circled through several places in case I was being followed. I didn't notice anything or anyone suspicious, but who knows?" I pause and take a breath. "Then, I stole this bread." I look down sheepishly. I sense the flush of my cheeks, the shame and realization of what I have done.

"Well, great," Finnick responds, his voice sarcastic, bitter. "You know we can't take any chances. Pack up your stuff. We'll walk toward Emporia and stay in the woods on the outskirts. We'll have to camp again until we can find somewhere to stay."

"But what about the meeting? We have to go . . . "

"For all we know, they'll be there ready to arrest you." He pauses before continuing, his brow creasing with anxiety. "But you're right." He pulls his old canvas bag out from under the bed. I have a flashback of the last time I saw him packing but quickly shake it off. There's no time to dwell on what I can't change.

Finnick is staring at me as I stare at the bag, his features converting from anger to resignation. "Es . . . " He trails off, and there's just silence, the words neither of us want to say falling between us. When he does continue, he avoids my eyes altogether. "We'll go to the meeting and update everyone before . . . " I shift uncomfortably when he stops. His eyes survey the room like he's listening for something, his head tilted to the left. I can't see his eyes, but I know the defeat that swims there. "We disappear . . . again." The last word comes at me like a dagger, and I shrink away.

## 2.

Finnick and I didn't always live in Headquarters. And we didn't always travel alone. We came here to make a difference, but sometimes, the danger we face makes me question our decision. I've heard stories of days long before this life of when there was no United Federation of Acceptance and people were allowed to think differently from the robotic masses. Sometimes, I find myself longing for my childhood, when I was sheltered from the way things really were. I don't allow myself to dwell too much on what was, though, because I recognize it will never be that way again. But I have to try. If for no other reason, I have to do it to honor my parents. They died for this cause.

"We'll stop back here and grab our stuff after the meeting. Just have it ready to go," Finnick says as he looks at me impatiently and roughly pulls his arm through his coat.

"I'm ready." I swing the strap of my backpack over my shoulder and grab my keys. I follow Finnick outside and make sure to lock the door. The chill of the air hits me like a tsunami, and I pull my scarf tighter around my neck. The temperatures have plummeted this week, and it's only November. I fear it'll be a bad winter, and bad winters never end well for us.

The small park where we're holding the meeting appears up ahead. With a sigh of relief, I see that the coast looks clear, and there's no sign of any UFoA officials. There are a few people milling around the pavilion but not many.

"What time is it?" I look at Finnick, my eyes watery from the wind.

"Ten 'til two." He's rummaging through his backpack, looking for his notes. He always runs the meetings. I have many gifts, but oration in front of large crowds is not one of them.

I take a seat on the edge of a bench and tap my foot. My head's on a swivel, and my heart's pounding out of my chest. After today's confrontation with Ezra, I'm fearing the worst. There's no way he got his grubby hands on a flyer, unless someone in the apartments gave him one. But knowing Ezra, he terrorized and threatened people until he learned what was going on.

I hear Finnick clearing his throat. I guess we're starting. I look around and see a crowd of about twenty, not nearly as many as I had hoped for after spending all morning recruiting.

"Thank you all for coming on such short notice," he begins. "I know it is a danger for you to be here, and we greatly appreciate your support and loyalty to the cause. I will try to be quick. I'm sure, by now, you have all heard the news of President Alastor's adaption, to put it mildly, to the national anthem. We cannot and will not stand idly by and allow such a violation to occur. We must fight back. Esther and I are proposing that you post copies of the original national anthem of our forefathers everywhere you can. We must remind people of what was. We must awaken the voices of those not changed by the propaganda that is being shoved down their throats. We must stand—"

"You, boy!" Oh, no. I turn and see one of Alastor's goons sprinting at us, his arm outstretched in outrage.

"Disperse!" I yell at the panic-stricken faces of the people whose lives I've endangered. Suddenly, it's chaos. People are heading in every direction as they try to avoid the officials who are chasing them down.

Finnick and I exchange glances, and I see him mouth the word "clock." I immediately understand that is where I should meet up with him as I throw my backpack over my shoulder and take off. I round the corner, praising myself for at least managing to put dozens of copies of the original anthem into the hands of resistors, when I forcefully collide with none other than Ezra himself, doubtlessly the trailblazer of this dispersal.

"Ha!" Ezra smirks and grabs my arm.

"Let go." I stare coldly into his dark, gray eyes, as I try to pry off his rough fingers.

Not breathing a word, his steely eyes lock into mine as he drags me by my arm. Fingers dig into my skin when I squirm, and his grip tightens. The rapid, hard beat of my heart fills my ears when I realize he's dragging me toward the long block of governmental offices.

"Get your hands off of me," I hiss. He's forgotten the years of friendship we spent wrestling. I pinch his arm, right above his elbow, and as I hear him yelp, I give a swift kick to his groin.

He yelps again before doubling over in pain, and I allow myself a moment to enjoy this small victory.

"We-we're building a c—c—case against you, Esther," he sputters through his discomfort. "It's only a matter of time." His body hunches over, his hands between his legs, as I bound away from him. I look back with a smug smile.

But it's only a few seconds before a familiar regret returns, and I feel the unwelcome remorse for our friendship. I never would have imagined that Ezra would become the enemy.

# 3.
# ONE YEAR EARLIER . . .

The hazy, blistering sun cascaded over the fields behind St. Mary's orphanage. Prior to being an orphanage, St. Mary's had been a penitentiary, sitting on a hill in the suburbs of Pennsylvania. The caged yards from the building's former use enhanced the perception of the orphanage as a prison. Since we were rarely ever allowed to leave, we often felt the zeitgeist of the incarcerated past. St. Mary's housed just under five hundred orphans, an average size for this type of residential institution, which had started to spring up like wildflowers throughout the country. Many parents had been dying at the hand of the Federation's changes or by those resisting them. Peaceful protests quickly turned into violent riots, and cities fell. The Catholic Church considered it their duty to take in the orphans and the abandoned, and a new generation, who were being raised by nuns, faced a life far different than the generations of the past.

The day when my current life was set in motion started as any other had at St. Mary's. It was the middle of August, and the heat had been unbearable. It was the kind of day where I could taste the humidity on my tongue, and the sweat returned to my face faster than I could wipe it off. Sister Margaret was yelling at us to come in for dinner. Finnick, Ezra, and I had been playing Capture the Flag with some of the other kids, and we were exhausted.

The three of us had been close since the day I first arrived there, three days after my thirteenth birthday. They had both lost their parents younger than I did and had less memories to hold onto. I was never sure if that was a blessing or a curse, but, perhaps, in retrospect, it was both.

As we walked into dinner, I tried to hold tight to the moment, make it a photograph in my mind—the three of us with our arms strung lazily over each other's shoulders laughing at the way Finnick face-planted into the mud. It was a rare day of innocence, a moment where we could just be teenagers, a fleeting instant my mind fought to retain.

"He totally had you." I laughed playfully and gently shoved Finnick into Ezra. Ezra had led his team to victory, barely beating Finnick back to the base with their team's flag raised in triumph. Right by the base, Finnick tripped and ate a mouthful of mud. I was on Ezra's team and relishing the win. I was also quite enjoying rubbing it in Finnick's face.

"If you weren't so clumsy, your team might have had a chance." I dodged Finnick's fist coming at my arm.

"Yeah, yeah, Esther. Next time, you're going down, and I'm gonna bust on you for a week," he retorted. He laughed then and pushed me away. Finnick had never been a sore loser.

"Who's that?" I looked up ahead to see a black Cadillac parked on the circular gravel drive in front of St. Mary's main entrance. We never had visitors, at least not the good kind. Since we were orphans, there was barely any family left to come see us.

"It's probably just someone meeting with the nuns. C'mon. I heard there's lasagna for dinner, and I'm starving." Ezra ran ahead. He looked back over his shoulder, beckoning with his hand.

We were breathless when we entered the main hall and saw a tall stranger who had that whole "cloak and dagger look." He was looming over poor, little Sister Margaret, who barely reached a height of five feet. I felt the hairs on my arm stand up.

"I'm guessing he's the driver of that car." I didn't know why I was whispering. Maybe it was because Sister Margaret's face was all furrowed up with anxiety.

She saw us and quickly hid her nerves with a look of feigned pleasantry. "Oh, Ezra, I am so glad you're here. Come with us. Finnick and Esther, you go on to dinner." Ezra shot us a confused glance as Sister Margaret put a gentle hand on his shoulder and steered him toward her office.

"What was that all about?" I glanced over at Finnick, who looked as uneasy as I felt.

"No idea. Let's just hope it's nothing. I'm sure he'll fill us in later. And, anyway, maybe it's good news?"

I could tell he didn't think so, but neither of us wanted to say what we were thinking. After growing up in the type of world we had, where nothing but an endless stream of misfortune arrived at our doorstep, it was hard to put words to our fear.

I allowed Finnick to lead me to the cafeteria but, despite how hungry I was, I barely touched my lasagna. My thoughts were overrun with memories of conversations Ezra and I had had over the last year. The unsettling feeling in my stomach compounded with the reminder of the turbulent emotions associated with my and Ezra's past. I was looking over my shoulder every five seconds in hopes that he would join us. "Maybe we should go look for him," I suggested. Just sitting here was killing me.

"Not yet, Esther. Let's get our homework done, and if he isn't here by bed check, we'll ask Sister Margaret. We don't want to seem paranoid."

I knew he was right. The last thing we needed was more attention from the staff.

But we let two hours pass, and there was still no sign of him. "Can we ask now?" I gave Finnick an exasperated look as I spat my toothpaste into the sink. I didn't know how much longer I could bare not knowing what was happening.

"Okay," Finnick agreed, "we can try to see Sister Margaret before we go to bed. C'mon." He clasped my hand and pulled me through the main bath toward the hallway to the staff's offices. We were both in our pajamas and bare feet as we tiptoed up to the door and listened.

"It was for the best, Sister Margaret, and besides, it's out of our hands. We have our duties, and we must remember our place." I gasped at the sound of Mother Maura's voice. Finnick elbowed me hard in the side, and I grunted.

"Shh." He rolled his eyes and put a finger to his lips.

"Yes, Mother, but where do we draw the line between morality and uniformity?" Sister Margaret's voice was muffled, but I could tell she had been crying.

"Ezra is one young boy among many in our care. We cannot put the future of one boy ahead of the lives of so many. He has every right under the law to take him. I know you understand this, Sister, and I know it's unfair. But we must be cautious and guard St. Mary's from the upcoming evils. There will be many more difficult decisions to come."

My eyes were saucers as I turned toward Finnick. We both knew instinctively that Ezra was not coming back. The idea of not seeing Ezra again came down on me with the weight of a storm, and I reached for Finnick's hand, clasping it hard against my own.

The months ahead would only grow darker for St. Mary's. We would pour our efforts into finding out what happened to Ezra, but that day was the last time we saw him until almost a year later.

# 4.
# PRESENT DAY

The town's old clock reigns high in the middle of Headquarters' square. It's been there for as long as anyone can remember, which gives me an irrational attachment to its mechanical dials and moving sculptures. The clock is at least two miles from the park, and I'm out of breath as I approach the area where the streets coincide. I hide in the shadows of the buildings to avoid a soldier patrolling, so I see Finnick before he sees me. His hunter green beanie is pulled down low on his head, and his jacket, torn in two spots, is zipped up tight over his neck. His languid body is leaning casually back against the clock's outer surface, and President Alastor's book, *The Integration of Gender Alliance*, is being held open in front of his face. I stifle a laugh as I let out a low whistle, our signal of arrival. Finnick is a master charlatan when it comes to deceiving the Federation.

At the sound of my whistle, he doesn't miss a beat. He waits the appropriate couple of minutes before standing up. He heads over to the kiosk near a tall building of offices and buys a black coffee. I sit in the shadows waiting. Once I see he isn't being watched and has made his way down a contingent alley, I cross over to meet him.

"Hey," I whisper, even though there's no one around us.

"Hey back." He takes a long sip from his coffee and offers me the cup. I take it gratefully as I study his handsome face, his eyebrows turned down to match the grim shape of his lips.

We don't say anything for a few minutes, lost in our own thoughts. My mind is racing about what we should do next and where we should go.

I place my hand on his arm and say softly, "We should go get our things and head out." I toss the empty coffee cup into a trash bin and turn toward our apartment.

"To go where?" he asks but follows me.

The idea comes to me suddenly, yet I know instantly that it's a good one. "We can go to Solomon. He'll know what to do next." Solomon was our philosophy teacher at St. Mary's. He took an interest in Finnick and me, and over time, we began to trust him. He is a peace-seeker, much like his name suggests, but he understands the importance of foregoing peace when your morality is at stake.

Finnick seems to think about this for a minute before responding. "The last contact we had with him was in that old church near St. Mary's; the Federation may have converted it by now."

The Federation has been converting all the churches to posts where they can carry out their mandates, while indoctrinating the masses to think like them. Soon, there won't be any churches left, and with each generation, more people will forget there ever was a basis for virtue. Which, of course, would mean the Federation wins.

"Oh, no." Finnick picks up his pace as we turn onto our street.

"What?" But as soon as the word's out of my mouth, I see that the door to our apartment is ajar. "I know I locked up, Finn; I swear I . . ."

He's inside, and there's no use explaining myself. Clearly, someone has broken the lock. I heave a sigh that shudders my whole body as I walk through the door. The place is a mess. What little furniture we had is either broken or turned over onto the floor. The mattress has been flipped over, and our suitcases, with the few belongings we own, are gone. Tears burn my eyes as I approach the cracked floorboard where I keep the letters from my parents. I realize as my hand clasps them that I haven't been breathing. I take in gasps of air and hold the letters to my chest. The room spins. I search for Finnick and find him, sitting on the floor with his head in his hands.

"Who do you think it was?" I ask, but I already know the answer.

Finnick looks up, his eyes cloudy, heated. "I think we can safely assume Ezra was behind it since he saw you and raided the meeting. You really shouldn't antagonize him, Esther; it only makes things harder for us. If he didn't hate us so passionately, we could contribute much more to the cause and maybe even keep a roof over our heads!" He is angry, but it's more than that. I can see that he is on the brink of giving up.

"I can't let it go, Finn." I look down guiltily. "His betrayal is unforgivable."

"Who do you think is suffering the most from your inability to move on? It's certainly not him! Look at us. We have nothing now but the clothes on our backs. What are we to . . . to do?" An angry sob escapes his throat as he puts his head in his hands. "I just want an easier life, Esther. Will we ever have that again? A life where we can laugh and love, a life where we aren't hungry and tired?"

I walk over and kneel beside him, taking his hands in my own. "Look at me." He looks up, and I see his eyes swim with indignation, regret—and I'm probably imagining it, but I think there's something softer there as well. "We'll go see Solomon, and I'll make an effort to avoid Ezra at all costs. But if I do see him, I promise to keep my mouth shut. I know I've caused us more trouble, Finn. I'll try harder."

He rips his hands away from mine and stands up. I feel like I've been slapped. "We need to leave before whoever was here comes back." He zips up his jacket, turns away from me, and walks out the door.

"Okay," I whisper to myself. I try to hide my hurt as I follow him to the street, where the wind smacks me in the face and covers my tears.

# 5.
# THREE YEARS EARLIER . . .

"We're going to the lake today!" My mom smiled at me as I poked my head out from under the covers, rubbing the sleep from my eyes.

"Happyyyy birthday to youuuu, happy birthday to youuu," my dad came in bellowing, and I couldn't help but laugh at his loud, screechy voice. "Get up; get dressed, Birthday Child!" he said as he grabbed my arms and playfully pulled me out of bed.

I laughed and shoved him and my mom into the hallway, so I could throw on a pair of jeans, a t-shirt, and a zip-up hoodie. I struggled to pull a comb through my long, tangled hair. The smell of homemade blueberry scones baking in the kitchen permeated my senses, and I was practically drooling as I ran out of my room.

"Do I look older?" I stood as tall as I could muster, shoulders thrown back and chin up.

"What are you now? Twenty? Twenty-five?" My dad smirked, and I softly punched him in the arm, laughing. I could barely contain my excitement. My parents promised not to work today, which meant I had them all to myself. It was my day.

"All aboard. Everyone in the car!" Dad made the whistle-blowing motion with his hand, and I giggled. He was always pretending to be a train conductor, ever since I was a toddler. Some of my friends thought it was cheesy, but I found it endearing.

We packed up a basket with my mom's homemade scones, some fresh fruit and cheese, and a few baguettes. I threw our big picnic blanket into the trunk and, at the last minute, had another thought.

"Can we grab the tent, too, Dad?" I looked at him hopefully.

"The birthday girl wants a night under the stars?" He grinned and nodded as he looked over at my mom to ensure it was okay. I saw her smile, and my heart surged with love. I never took the love I had for my parents for granted. I knew how lucky I was.

The morning sun warmed my face as I hopped into the Jeep, buckled my seatbelt, and leaned forward to fiddle with the stereo. I scanned through my dad's playlists on his phone and found what I was looking for as he and my mom closed the trunk and got in. I stifled a laugh in anticipation of my dad's singing, which I knew was inevitable.

"Youuuu really gotta hold on meee," my dad squawked. The Beatles had been our band. If there was a game show titled "Name that Beatles' Song," I'd have spent my entire existence trying to be on it.

"Really, Caleb." My mom rolled her eyes, but I could see her fighting a grin.

We pulled into the state park and parked the car. I jumped out in a flash, picnic basket in hand. I knew I would be given my birthday present soon and was anxious to open it. I chose a spot under two maple trees and laid out the quilt we used for picnics. My eyes squinted at the sun as it cascaded over the dense grass, and I dug in my bag for my sunglasses. It had rained the week before, which prompted the flowers, grass, and trees to come out of hibernation. I took a deep breath of the fresh air as I plopped down on the quilt and stared out over the lake. My mom scooched up beside me, and my dad started laying out the food, still whistling the Beatles' tunes.

"So, Monkey, what's been your favorite part of this last year?" My mom loved calling me Monkey, a name I derived as a baby when I would climb up my parents and sleep on their chests. She also loved asking these types of questions. I always acted annoyed by them, but I secretly enjoyed answering.

"Umm, I'd say that hike we took last summer, I guess. The one where Dad slipped and fell on his rear end." I giggled shamelessly as he passed me an amused look.

"Glad I could be a source of entertainment for you."

My mom smiled as she spread Brie over a chunk of her baguette. "That was a great day. I couldn't believe we actually made it to the top. That had to be a record for all of us."

"My knees are still paying the price," my dad grumbled.

"I think today might be my new favorite, though. It feels like it's going to be a good one." I bit into my apple and smiled widely as juice dribbled down my chin. "I mean, after I get my present, of course."

"Uh-huh. Now we're getting to what's really on your mind." My dad laughed as he dug into the bottom of the canvas bag he brought and pulled out a small box, wrapped flawlessly with sea green paper, my favorite color. My eyes lit up with excitement. I was rarely given presents. My parents had always felt that gifts were only for special occasions.

So, I took my time to carefully unwrap each side of the box while relishing the anticipation and folded the paper neatly beside me. My parents watched me quietly as I lifted the lid off the box and pulled out a rose gold chain with a cross pendant. I ran my fingers over the pendant, turning it around to see Romans 12:21 engraved on the back.

"'Do not be overcome by evil, but overcome evil with good.'" My mom said the words aloud, and my dad squeezed her hand.

"It's perfect . . . and beautiful," I whispered, recognizing that there was more to this choice of gift than I was able to understand. "Why this verse?" I asked as I looked up at my parents' now somber faces.

My mom gently reached out and took my hands. "You are still young, Esther, but you're a teenager now, and although there is much you don't understand . . . " She paused, and her face furrowed in uncertainty before she continued, "What I'm trying to say is that we try to shelter you from the evil in this world, but you need to be aware that this life is not what it appears." She stopped, shifting uncomfortably. "There will come a day—soon—when we will tell you more, and you will have to decide some things for yourself."

"But you can tell—" I was interrupted by my dad tossing me up into the air and onto the blanket.

"Fortunately for you, that day is not today!" He bellowed as he tickled my sides, coercing me into a fit of laughter.

"Ohh! Daaad." I fell onto the blanket in surprise, swatting at him with one hand and gripping my stomach with the other.

"Oh, Caleb," my mom murmured in resignation. She knew that the moment of seriousness had passed. But as I lay on my back, struggling not to laugh, I was shaken by the disquiet of her eyes. I looked to the sky as ominous clouds rolled in, a thunderstorm on the horizon.

"To the tent," my dad said as he jumped up and packed away the remainder of the food. We made it under cover just as the sky opened up, pellets of rain battering the tent's canvas. My dad took out Monopoly, and two hours later, I had taken all four railroads for the win. I told my parents stories from school while we ate our scones and fruit and my dad read us poetry by Whitman, Frost, and Bryant.

The rain was still coming down, and I shivered, pulling my sweatshirt tighter around me. "Here, Monkey," my mom said, passing me a blanket.

"Thanks, Mom," I said as I wrapped it around myself and inched closer to my parents. I looked at her affectionately, softly rubbing my new cross pendant with my thumb and index finger. I bit my lip before speaking. "What you said before, about telling me more . . . I can handle it, you know. I'm not that naïve; it's obviously been weird for me that you and Dad are always away."

"We'll tell you when it's time, Esther," my dad responded, placing a hand on my arm. "Until then, just try to enjoy your childhood. You only get one."

I yawned and nodded, accepting that they didn't want to tell me and wanting to enjoy the rest of my birthday. "Can we put the Beatles on again?" I asked sleepily.

"Now that I can do," my dad said with a smile, choosing "Yesterday."

I felt a sense of contentment and love as I drifted off to sleep.

I had let it go. My parents would be taken from me two days later, and I had just let it go.

# 6.
# PRESENT DAY

It feels like we have been walking for weeks. The old church where we're headed, close to the remains of St. Mary's, is at least a three days' walk from headquarters. My legs hurt, and my feet are blistered. I'm afraid to say anything because I know Finnick is still mad at me, and I don't want to fight anymore. We have been walking for seven hours today, and I haven't gotten more than a "this way" or a "hurry up." For the most part, we've stuck to the woods in an attempt to camouflage ourselves from anyone. Other than a brief stop at a stream of water three hours ago, we have had nothing to eat or drink. Every ounce of my essence wants to complain, but I keep my mouth clamped shut.

"Should be getting close." Finnick's clipped tone cuts through me.

"Okay," I whisper, and I hear him sigh heavily. I can't seem to breathe without upsetting him. We continue walking a few more feet when he stops abruptly, and I run into his back.

"What—"

"Shhh! Listen!" He spins his head around. I hear it now, too. It's a rustling in the trees maybe a hundred or so yards ahead.

"Over here," Finnick whispers and points toward a large area of undergrowth. I follow him, and we duck down, peering cautiously over the top of the shrubbery. A short intersex, who has reconstructed to the male form but still has a feminine stature, appears next to a tall, robust man. The tall man has dark, greasy hair that he's slicked back into a tight, low bun. The intersex is wearing a Mets baseball cap and hoodie, and the casualness and athletic devotion of his attire briefly reminds me of the days before all this began.

"This is ridiculous, Charlie; it's going to be dark soon." We hear the disdain in the taller man's voice as he draws closer to us. Finnick and I are both holding our breath.

"Ezra said it starts at the Divine Covenant. And it's only the beginning, Man. You better get used to it." He pauses before looking suspiciously up at him. "That is, unless you want out?"

"What? Nah, that's not what I'm saying. It just seems like Ezra's on a rampage for these people. He claims it isn't a personal vendetta, but I dunno . . ."

"Yeah, well, he's our boss, and I want to get paid. So, I really don't care what his motives are."

"I just don't see why a tattoo is necessary."

"How else can he hold people accountable? How will we know the people who aren't following the Federation? I think it's smart. We can weed out those who aren't loyal."

"I guess." He is obviously less sure of this new mandate than his counterpart. I feel Finnick squeeze my hand, which is clammy and shaking.

"C'mon, we better hurry, or Ezra will be angry," Charlie says. They take off in the direction of the Divine Covenant, the old church where we were hoping to meet up with Solomon.

"Oh, no, Finn—" I feel a wave of panic rise in my chest, rebuking myself silently for the way my mind always goes to the worst possible conclusion.

"Breathe, Esther, it's fine. We will get through it. Deep breaths, in and out." He is holding both my hands now, his brow creased in concern, his eyes earnest. We breathe in tandem until my heart rate returns to normal.

I fearfully bring my eyes up to meet his. "What if Solomon is still there? They'll kill him."

"Then we have to find him before they do." Finnick's tone is anxious and determined. He scans the woods to ensure there's no other members of the Federation before pulling me forward. "C'mon. We need to move."

Solomon had once told me the history of the Church of the Divine Covenant, which is centuries old. Once a colonial meeting house, with a steep pitched roof and large oak doors, it is an apparent landmark in such a rural area. As we approach the church from the woods, we can see that the doors are propped open and a large stream of people are filing in from the street. The parking lot is overflowing, and cars have spilled over onto the grassy hillside.

"There's no way we can get inside without anyone seeing us." I bite my lip in frustration.

"We may have to wait it out." He sighs before taking a seat at the foot of a tree, leaning his back against the rough bark.

"Do you think Solomon got out before they came?"

"Who knows. He may still be in there hiding. I'm hoping he is because we could really use his help. Hey, look, there's that guy, Charlie." Finnick points toward him, and we see him confidently stroll outside. He's holding a clipboard and appears to be recording names.

"What do you think this tattoo is all about?" I ask, while still watching Charlie's stony face.

"It sounds like some way to ensure people are pledging their devotion to the Federation. What worries me is what they're planning for those of us who refuse."

As he says this, we see a man being dragged away from the line by one of the Federation's officers. He seems to be trying to explain something, but the officer is ignoring him. A moment later, we see Ezra appear, carrying a gun in one hand and a clipboard in the other. I gasp when we see him. Despite hating myself for it, my heart still stops at the sight of him. We watch as he approaches the man, who is now near tears, and says something to him while pointing at the clipboard. The man's hands start flailing wildly, fear streaking his face, yet whatever he is saying is only making Ezra angrier.

"I wish we could hear what they're talking about," I whisper. I'm about to move closer to try to make out some of the words, but the sound of a gunshot freezes me in place.

Finnick jumps up and protectively grabs my arm. "What the . . . " he starts. My mouth drops open. The ground under me seems to shift, and I put a hand to my head in an attempt to quell the dizzy sensation. Cold sweat creeps over my body.

"He . . . he . . . he just shot him," I stutter. "How could he do that?"

I feel sick, but I can't pry my eyes away from the pool of blood surrounding the man's head. We watch as chaos breaks out. Several women are screaming in confusion, the children around them crying. The officers are swiftly channeling people through the doors before anyone can run away. Ezra is calmly wiping off his gun with a handkerchief, his face set hard in arrogance, a dare to anyone who might confront him.

"Oh, Ezra, what's happened to you?" I hate that there are tears in my eyes. Tears for him. All he ever brings to my life is misery. Why do I still care?

"I'll tell you what's happened to him. He's bought into it. All of it. Their propaganda. The lie of all lies. I can't believe what a spineless, cowardly traitor—"

"Finnick."

"What? I didn't want to see it, okay? I thought maybe he just needed to come to his senses. I never imagined he'd—he'd—"

"Become a murderous psychopath?"

"Yes!" he says in exasperation before his eyes meet mine, his expression sheepish. "Man, I'm sorry, Esther. I was too hard on you."

"Eh. I may have partially deserved it." I give him a half-smile. We stare at each other for a minute, and I feel the tension that's been between us dissipate. I let out a breath of relief. I need Finnick. But even more importantly, I need him to realize he needs me.

We both sit down on the grass, and I lay my head against his shoulder. We watch as the proceeding continues and see that no one has bothered to take the man's body away. At some point, I must have fallen asleep because I wake to Finnick lightly shaking me, and I see that it's dusk. My stomach rumbles. When did I last eat?

I look toward the church to see that people are beginning to clear out. The parking lot has dwindled down to only a few cars, and the officers are loading up utility vehicles with what I assume is the equipment they used to execute the markings. "Did you get a good look at any of the tattoos?" I ask sleepily.

"Yeah, looks like they're all the same, an emblem of some kind. My thought is that they're going to make it the mark of the Federation. It looks like the plumed serpent but with only one large eye and feathered wings. The wings are spread out within a triangle."

"Creepy," I say. "I bet we will start seeing it everywhere. The plumed serpent dates back to Mayan times, right?"

"Yeah. It's supposedly the bringer of civilization, a symbol for rebirth, and a way for the UFoA to push the idea of a prosperous new era."

I shudder, laying back on the grass. I think about all the conspiracy theories over the years surrounding the end times. Maybe there was some truth in them after all. I lay there for several hours until we're sure everyone is gone and no one is coming back. They did finally take the body away, after leaving it there all day. Whatever point they were trying to make, they made it. Every face I saw leaving the church looked terrified.

"Be careful," Finnick whispers as he reaches back for my hand to help me down the steep hill. Cautiously, we approach the doors of the church, only to find them locked.

I sigh in exasperation. "Of course."

"It's okay; we'll get in," Finnick says, his eyes searching the perimeter. "I also saw a back door and a door to a basement."

We find the back door locked as well, but there is an old, rusted lock on the door to the basement that we easily break off.

"Let me go first." Finnick pushes me behind him. I swallow my annoyance. Truthfully, I'm still pretty shaky from seeing that man shot.

My heart is pounding loud in my ears as we make our way down the dark stairs. Each creak of the stairs makes me jump.

"Esther, relax," Finnick hisses back to me.

"Sorry."

We reach the bottom, and I'm holding onto the back of Finnick's shirt as he guides us through the darkness, his hands outstretched in front of him. We reach the top of the stairs that lead into the sanctuary where we find the room illuminated by moonlight. The beams of light shine through the large, stained glass windows.

"It's beautiful in here," I whisper, looking over at Finnick. We pause to kneel before the large cross where I say a quick prayer for our safety and the strength to continue. *And please, God, let Solomon be safe, wherever he might be*, I silently plea.

"I hope you'll add a blessing for me."

I whip around. "Solomon!" I exclaim, running into his open arms.

Laughing in delight, he embraces me in a warm hug. "Esther," he says tenderly, "I can't tell you how glad I am to see you." He looks up over my shoulder at Finnick. "And you, my boy."

Finnick gives him a wide smile. "Hi, Professor. We've certainly missed you. But how did you avoid the enemy invasion?"

Solomon smirks. "I was hiding in the utility closet. It was quite uncomfortable. But I was able to acquire some useful information. We have much to discuss. I think, though, we can hold off on all of that for now. Something tells me you kids are hungry."

Both of our eyes light up as we nod vigorously. "I'm starving!" I practically yell.

Solomon laughs. "This way—the church has a kitchen from when they ran a daycare here. I'll make you some of my famous pasta from a box," he says with a chuckle.

We follow him into a large room, a broad stove on one wall and an old refrigerator and utility sink on the other. Finnick and I pull up two chairs to the long island in the middle, while Solomon pours water from a jug into a pot to boil. I lean back and examine him more closely. I see that he's aged since we were last together. He's dressed in ripped cargo pants, a faded gray t-shirt, and old work boots. His graying hair is pulled back tightly into a ponytail, enhancing the dark bags under his large, hazel eyes. There are more defined wrinkles on his face and dirt underneath his fingernails. The toll of war. My mind flashes back to him in his dark suit and short, set hair at St. Mary's.

"What are you thinking about, my Esther?" Solomon looks at me curiously.

I smile sadly. "Just how much things have changed and are continuing to change."

"Yes, they have." He sighs. "But we must put our best foot forward, especially now. To focus on the bad will only deter from achieving our purpose. And our purpose, dear children, is very important." He smiles broadly as he pops the top off of a jar of sauce and pours it over three bowls of steaming pasta. "Now, though, we feast!"

# 7.
# THREE YEARS EARLIER . . .

I had been at St. Mary's for about a week when I first met Solomon. Sister Margaret was taking me to each of the classrooms to introduce me to my teachers. To say that I was severely depressed would be an understatement. The loss of my parents had ripped through my soul like a storm. Moments in life define our existence and create a demarcation that firmly establishes a before and an after. The day my parents died, my "after" began, and I knew that I would never be the same. Those first few days at St. Mary's were a blur of darkness. They had me in intensive counseling and kept trying to sedate me on various uppers to numb my pain. I refused what I could, afraid that the numbness would become a crutch that I would never be able to shake. Meeting Solomon somehow helped; call it an instinct, but I just knew that he was going to play a role in my life. From that first moment, his raw perception had spurred me, at least for a moment, out of my grief.

"Professor Solomon, I'd like you to meet our newest student, Esther Warder." Sister Margaret smiled at me in encouragement.

"Esther? The biblical heroine?" I immediately noticed the kindness in his eyes. He reached out his hand to shake mine.

"Hardly," I whispered and softly shook his hand.

He examined me kindly for a few seconds before speaking. "I don't buy that. It is my understanding that you are capable of great love, for

35

the pain we suffer from loss is often a reflection of how much we have loved. In his book *Three Edifying Discourses*, Soren Kierkegaard tells us that 'when the heart is filled with love, then the eye is never deceived.' I bet no one has deceived you, have they, Miss Warder?"

He looked at me keenly, and I was briefly taken aback. Who was this man? And how much did he know?

Before I could respond, Sister Margaret cut in, giving him a disapproving look. "Thank you, Professor; that's all. We're going to meet Professor Darci now."

"I'll see you in class tomorrow, then." I nodded at him before shyly looking down. I turned to walk away, but he continued, "And, Miss Warder?" He paused. "I was very sorry to hear of your loss." He said this as if he knew my parents, but I had never seen him before in my life.

"Did you know—"

I felt Sister Margaret's small, steely fingers on my shoulder. "Come along now, Esther. Professor Darci is expecting us," she said firmly, steering my shoulders out the door before I could finish the question. I might have imagined it, but I could have sworn I saw him nod.

*I walked in from school and threw my backpack in a heap next to the coat closet.*

*"Take it to your room!" I heard my mom yell from my parents' office. I jumped slightly before picking it back up with a sigh.*

*I peeked into the office to see her bent over her desk with her head in her hands. She pulled her head up to write furiously on a piece of paper. "Hey, Mom, everything good?"*

*"Yes, yes," she said distractedly. "I just don't want there to be anything I forget."*

*It was obvious she was frazzled. A flutter skipped across my heart. "You're scaring me, Mom. What's up?"*

As if she was just then fully realizing that I was there, she looked up, her hair falling in her face. Her eyes were wide as saucers. "Oh, Esther, I didn't realize . . . But it's just as well." She sighed. "Take a seat here next to me, Monkey. I need to tell you something."

I approached her desk and sat down with my legs crisscrossed next to her feet. When I was a little girl, I used to sit next to her like that as she worked. I couldn't bear to be away from her, so I would bring my dolls and play there while she made phone calls and answered emails. My mom's job had always confused me. She said it had to do with missionary work, but she never wanted to talk about it.

"See this lockbox?" my mom said as she gestured toward a box in the bottom drawer of her desk.

"Yes," I answered in confusion.

"The key is hidden in an aspirin bottle in the medicine cabinet upstairs. If anything were to ever happen to me and your father, you need to open the lockbox and take out what's inside."

"Mom, you are seriously freaking me out." Panic rose from my chest to my throat as I fought back tears. "I don't understand what is happening."

"Esther. It's okay. We are fine. God willing, nothing will ever happen to me or your father, but there are precautions we have to take on the chance that something does. Do you understand?" She looked at me with both love and severity.

I nodded slowly. "I understand," I said. Although, I didn't actually understand, but I could tell it's what she wanted me to say.

"Good. Now come here," she said as I crawled up on her lap and let her embrace me. "I love you so much, Esther Rose."

I wrapped my arms around her, breathing into her chest. "I love you, too, Mama," I whispered against the fear in my throat.

# 8.
# PRESENT DAY

After we finish eating, Solomon leads the way to what used to be a Sunday school classroom, and we take a seat on child-size chairs. Seeing Finnick's long legs awkwardly flop on the floor would have been comical in other circumstances. Solomon takes out a pocket-sized memo pad and reads over what he wrote down as he nervously runs a hand through his graying hair.

"I wish I could shelter you kids from all this," he says regretfully.

"Professor, it wouldn't do us any good. Besides, we are older than our age after all we've been through." Finnick frowns and squeezes my hand. My heart lifts with the gesture. He hasn't shown me this much warmth since before Barron Creek.

"I suppose you're right. The days of innocence are in the past," he says, sadly. "I was able to write down what I heard during the administering of the tattoos, if you're sure."

"Go on," Finnick says, and I hold my breath.

Grudgingly, he continues. "It's pretty bad. They plan to execute the application of these markings on everyone in the territories controlled by the United Federation of Acceptance. The Federation's icon, the winged serpent, is becoming a symbol, much like how the Nazis used the swastika. As so many scholars have pointed out throughout time, history merely repeats itself, and patterns are renewed through modernization. These markings are said to give people absolute freedom, and they are pushing them through the propaganda that you are showing loyalty and support to all those who have had their rights previously jeopardized. They put a spin on the concept of equality and acceptance, insisting that the marking gives more rights, not takes rights away. Those who refuse are, therefore, bigots, anarchists, freedom haters . . . They aim to leave us behind."

"What do you mean, 'leave us behind'? How are they pushing this propaganda?" I ask fearfully, realizing what that will mean for our future.

"I mean the worst, my dear; we will not survive this war. The push is through the distribution of brochures and numerous officers who sat with families and 'counseled' them on the Federation's ideals. And then, of course, through the dispersion of advertisements on cable channels and social media outlets. The truth is, it's everywhere now; society is being emerged in their ideals."

I try to take in what he's telling me, but I have so many more questions, things I don't understand. "Wait, what are the rights they are claiming to give?"

"Well, for example, it will become nearly impossible to maintain a job, get married, apply for governmental assistance—"

Finnick intervenes. "The man who was shot . . . Did you hear anything about it? Did he refuse?"

"I heard the gunshot, and then it was chaos. I could not make sense of what was being said afterward."

"We saw who shot the man," I whisper, more to myself than aloud.

"What was that, Esther?" Solomon looks at me quizzically.

Finnick glances at me, and I nod. "She said, 'We saw who shot the man.'"

His face grows red, and through gritted teeth, he continues, "It was Ezra."

"Oh, dear." Solomon's face conveys both anguish and regret. "I am sorry to hear that, but I can't say I am overly surprised." Finnick and I look at him in confusion. "It may be time I told you more about Ezra."

"What's to know?" I demand. "He's a two-faced snake."

"Perhaps, but maybe it will help you to understand why he is that way if I tell you about his family."

"Let me guess, they worked for the Federation, too?" Finnick asks.

"Well, yes, they did, but they were killed by our side. The Resistance shot his parents when protecting several children who refused to adhere to the New Order's dress code, the unisex uniform promoting gender indifference. His parents were delegated with the job of arresting the students and bringing them to Headquarters for prosecution."

Or execution, more likely.

Solomon takes a breath and continues, "The children were in hiding, and when Ezra's parents found them, the Resistance was waiting. It is my understanding that Ezra didn't know the full truth surrounding his parents' deaths until the day *he* came for him."

"That's true," I say. Finnick and I exchange glances, contemplating how much we should tell our professor. I think back to that day at Barron Creek and shudder before I continue. If Solomon notices, he doesn't say anything. "Before Ezra disappeared, he found something out about how his parents died. Something that made him—"

Finnick interrupts me. His eyes rest briefly on mine, and I shut my mouth like a clam. "The Resistance is told not to murder. So, what happened?" he demands with the implication that there must be an explanation. I shift in my seat, attempting to hide my discomfort.

"We aren't entirely sure."

"Wait, who came for him?" This was information I didn't know.

"His uncle."

"Do we know his uncle?" Finnick senses his apprehension and urges him to continue.

"You do," he says with a sigh. "His name is Alastor."

I jump out of my chair with a gasp. "Alastor? As in President Alastor?"

Finnick's eyes find mine as both of us go back in time to the night Ezra disappeared. What was it that Mother Maura had said? *"He has every right under the law to take him."* That was why the sisters had allowed Ezra to leave without asking any questions. They wouldn't have dared to challenge Alastor's authority, especially when St. Mary's was under such scrutiny as it was. And Ezra would have been so relieved to realize he had family who was alive. The reasons Ezra betrayed us begin to make more sense in my mind, although my heart can't reconcile the deception.

The image of Ezra with the smoking gun emerges, and I look down at my trembling hands. Who knows what lies Alastor told him about resistors, about God, about my parents to pull him into the darkness. The fear that Ezra will forever be lost to that darkness falls over me like a shadow, and I pour my heart into a prayer.

# 9.
# THREE YEARS EARLIER . . .

The first time I laid eyes on Ezra, I was walking out of therapy. His voice made my blood course like rapids through my veins. He has always had that effect on me.

Counseling at St. Mary's was mandatory for most of us. The nuns felt that the trauma we had experienced in relation to our parents' deaths should be discussed ad nauseum. The session prior to meeting Ezra was exhausting, and I sat biting at my thumbnail until there was nothing left.

"Is there anything else you feel you need to talk about today?" Sister Mary asked as she stared at me expectantly. I knew that she meant well, but I was done with all the counseling. There was nothing about my parents' horrific deaths that could be talked out. There were too many questions surrounding that night for me to ever feel like I would have closure.

"Can you tell me what happened that night?" I asked her for the fiftieth time, knowing she couldn't but unable to resist the antagonistic nature of the question.

She made a brief note in my file before answering. "Esther." She took a deep breath, then spoke as if she was talking to a young child. "Sweetheart, you know very well that—"

There was an abrupt knocking, and Sister Mary's secretary, Glenda, popped her head through the door.

"Your next appointment, Sister."

I started talking before she could say anything. "It's okay, Sister; I know you can't answer that question. I think I'm good, and I do really appreciate your being here for me." I told her what she wanted to hear in hopes that I could leave. She seemed satisfied with this remark and began to close my file.

"All right, Esther, I will see you next week, then. I will be assigning you Professor Solomon as your mentor. Here, at St. Mary's, we feel every student should have a trusted adult to support them. You will begin meeting with him once a week. And remember to keep writing in your journal. I recommend Revelation 21:4 for inspiration this week."

I knew the verse well. "For the old order of things has passed away." How appropriate. I jotted it down in my notebook and looked up at her with a smile. The key was to appear as well-adjusted as possible, so these sessions could end. I was intrigued that she had assigned me to Professor Solomon. When we had first met, I was left with the strong sense that he had known my parents. I shoved my notebook into my bag and stood up to leave.

"Thanks again, Sister," I called over my shoulder as I walked through the door. I stumbled as I bumped right into a boy; he was of medium height with large, robust shoulders. What thirteen-year-old had shoulders like that? Aloud, I murmured "sorry," avoiding eye contact.

"No worries." I could feel his eyes on me, forcing me to look into their dark, gray mist.

"Oh—oh," I stuttered. I was taken aback by his confidence.

"I'm Ezra," he said with the grin of the Cheshire cat, "and you are?"

"Esther," I answered and allowed myself a timid smile.

"I think you're in my science class; you sit close to the back, right? By that massive cactus?" He laughed as he continued, "I gotta wonder why Professor Graham has that thing. It's a hazard. Seriously, it could take a finger."

I giggled. "It is pretty ridiculous."

Sister Mary came to the doorway and looked at me in surprise. "Oh, Esther, did you need something else?"

"No, no. I'm leaving." I looked down shyly and started to walk away. Ezra grabbed my shoulder and turned me back toward him.

"Sit by me in lab tomorrow."

I was again surprised by his forwardness but also intrigued. "Okay," I said with a shrug. He smiled, and I felt a flutter in my stomach. Now, I was being ridiculous.

# 10.
# PRESENT DAY

After spending the night in the church, I feel oddly renewed. There is even running water, since the Federation had been there and paid the electricity. I had all but sat in the sink in the bathroom trying to bathe myself last night. Finnick and I wait patiently in the chapel to hear what Solomon wants us to do next.

"This is the best I've felt in weeks," I say in exhilaration. "My stomach is full, and I smell good."

"I wouldn't go that far." Finnick snickers, and I stick my tongue out at him.

Solomon enters the doorway where we're standing, and he looks as though he, too, feels better. "You kids ready to take on the day?" he says affectionately, but there's an unease behind his smile.

"What do we do now?" I ask.

"I have been contemplating how to best proceed. I heard the Federation discussing their plans." He gives a half-smile before continuing, "And the next two churches they're planning to occupy are in Shades Run and Lawrence. Shades Run is too far by foot, but I bet we can make it to Lawrence in time to warn people to leave or go into hiding."

"Okay," I agree with a nod. "But how do we do that?"

"There's only three of us, so door to door isn't going to accomplish much. We need a way to reach a large number of people."

Finnick has been standing quietly with his back against the wall while we talk. "Penny for your thoughts?" I ask.

He frowns in concentration. "I was just thinking that I've been to Lawrence before. My dad used to be stationed there." I remember then that Finnick's parents were both military, killed in combat. "What about the radio station? It's on Pine Avenue. We could enter through the back after hours—you know, pick the lock or something?"

Solomon contemplates this for a minute. "It could actually work. The radio is the best way to reach a lot of people, but I'm not sure many will be listening after hours. What if we create a distraction while one of us sneaks inside to make a broadcast? It would be dangerous—"

"That's expected," I cut in. "I volunteer to sneak inside."

"No, absolutely not. I'll do it," Finnick retorts.

"No way! I said it first; I'm doing it. You always think I can't do anything."

Solomon looks at us in exasperation. "You would think this was the opportunity of a lifetime or something."

I cross my arms and bite my lip in frustration. "It's just that he is always treating me like I'm too fragile to do anything, Professor, and I'm just as capable of taking down our enemies as he is," I whine, scowling at Finnick.

"Okay, Finnick, Esther can make the broadcast. You and I will create a diversion."

"Ha!" I smirk at Finnick.

Solomon frowns. "Don't gloat, Esther; it's not becoming."

"Yeah, Esther, it's not becoming," Finnick mimics in feigned annoyance. But he's over it already and rushes to the church's podium to find something he can write with. "We need a plan!"

"Relax," I say with a smile. The truth is I'm just as excited as he is to ruin the Federation's plans.

*My Darling Daughter,*

*I can only assume that with the reading of this letter, your dear, old dad didn't make it. I hope you're not dwelling too much on the loss but instead on the time we had together. For "the grass withers, and the flower falls off." Take comfort in the knowledge that we will be together again. If I know my daughter, you are doing quite a bit of pouting. Give yourself some time but remember that we raised a strong girl with a great purpose; you must go live and make a difference while you can.*

*I apologize that your mother and I did not share everything with you while we were alive. It's a precarious life in this current world, and you are still so young. We wanted desperately to keep your childhood free of the danger that comes with knowledge. That meant hiding a number of secrets, which will come as a shock for you. So, take your time with these letters and cry if you feel it necessary, but then move on. You must move on, for we are counting on you. I have great faith in you, my daughter. And God is with us through it all.*

*With love and affection always,*

*Dad*

# 11.

We approach the town of Lawrence cautiously. It's early in the evening and several hours before curfew. The sun is low on the horizon, and there's a brisk breeze that chills my face and hands as we walk. A dusting of snow has painted the trees and the ground with white sparkles. The snow is untouched by footprints, and the only sound is the birds' banter as they share their stories.

"You could almost forget it all, couldn't you?" I say.

"Hmm?" Finnick asks.

"This beauty—it's just hard to believe that evil exists within so much beauty."

"The same could be said of people," Finnick muses. "The most beautiful people can be the cruelest."

I consider his observation, and my mind flashes back to Ezra, a gun in his hand and a pool of blood at his feet. "Microcosms for the world at large . . ."

"Exactly."

Solomon has remained relatively silent throughout our walk, lost in his thoughts. He's been leading the way and has now stopped to look at a notice posted just outside of town. I frown as I read it.

**Show your loyalty to our great cause!**
**Acceptance for all!**

**The officers of the UFoA expect to see you at the following time and location:**

**Saturday, November 18th**

**1-4 P.M.**

**Church of the Divine Truth**

**38 Oakland Drive**

The poster is marked with the symbol of the serpent we saw being tattooed on people at the last church.

"It makes me sick that they're using churches to implement their deranged agenda," I mutter angrily. "It'll confuse some into thinking their cause is the right thing to do."

"I'm sure that's exactly what they're hoping," Finnick retorts. "Hopefully, we can get to some of the people who don't understand before it's too late."

Solomon sighs quietly, his eyes sad as he looks from the poster to us. "I'm afraid this is going to be happening everywhere and is much bigger than us. I need to reach out to my contacts in the Resistance to inform them of what's going on."

This idea seems to spur Finnick's enthusiasm. "Yes. We need to generate a mass movement; the more resistors who can intervene, the better. We'll first need a list of when and where the Federation is executing markings." He looks over at Solomon anxiously. "How might we get that?"

"Good thinking, Finnick," he pauses. "By hacking into the Federation's main system, I suppose."

"Do you know someone who can do that?"

Solomon allows himself a small smile. "Actually, yes—several men. I can likely have us a list by the end of the week."

Finnick looks pleased before looking over at me in concern. Embarrassed, I find that I have tears running down my face. I wipe at them furiously.

"What is it? Are you scared?" he asks.

"No, it's nothing," I whisper. "Just something my mom wrote in a letter."

"Share it with us, Child. It may help." Solomon places a hand on my shoulder, urging me to continue.

"The whole thing reads like gibberish. She called the end 'a storm by fire.'" I pause and consider my words before going on. "When I read it, I didn't entirely understand what she meant. Like I said, the whole thing was so confusing, a conglomeration of thoughts she rushed to get out. It was the last letter she would wri-ite," I choke on the last word, thinking of how afraid she must have been.

"'A storm by fire . . .'" Solomon ponders this thought. "Perhaps the first trumpet?" he wonders aloud.

"I thought of that, too. But she also wrote something about a man named David? She said his soul would be the one ignited." They both cast me a puzzled look. "I know that doesn't make any sense." I sigh, wishing I had just kept that last part to myself.

Solomon mulls this over. "There is no David that I know of, and I've kept tabs on all of Alastor's cronies. I'm not quite sure what to make of the ignited remark, either."

"Maybe it's a metaphor?" Finnick asks. But before we can consider it further, we see a line of officers marching toward us. "Act normal," Finnick hisses.

I fight the urge to roll my eyes at him. "Obviously."

A short, heavily built officer approaches us with a sense of authority. "What are your names?"

Solomon responds without missing a beat. "I am Bart Smith, and these are my children, Sara and Jacob Smith. We aren't from here; I was recently put out of work and was hoping to find something—"

The officer holds up a hand, interrupting him as he looks us up and down wearily, his interest waning. "I'm sure once you attend the assembly at the church tomorrow afternoon, the Federation will be happy to assist you with work." He looks at us smugly and continues, "I'll be sure to have them add your names to the list."

"We really appreciate it, sir," Solomon replies. And even though I know it's a façade, I silently cringe at his respectful tone.

The officer nods and goes on his way. When he's out of earshot, I ask, "How much time do we have?"

"Not long," Finnick answers. "We need to get things started."

We had come up with the plan of tying a large banner across the front of the townhall with the original ending to the national anthem. President Alastor hadn't been in office more than six weeks when he changed the once-great hymn. His version reads:

"And this be our motto: 'In the people we trust':

And the serpent of the Federation in triumph shall soar

O'er the land of the accepted and the home of those who conform."

It is now being sung every morning in every school across the states of the United Federation of Acceptance. The banner we intend to tie to the columns of the Federation's post in Lawrence will use the original words:

"And this be our motto: 'In God is our trust':

And the star-spangled banner in triumph shall wave

O'er the land of the free and the home of the brave."

If we can pull it off, it will hopefully remind some people of how things used to be. It also might as well give me some time to put out a broadcast.

"Ready, Es?" Finnick looks at me expectantly as he pulls the banner and rope out of his backpack.

"Definitely." I glance toward Solomon to ensure he's with me. He nods, and we start walking toward the radio station. It's a single, brick building connected to a parking lot by a narrow strip of sidewalk and two patches of newly cut grass. The lot is only a quarter full, which I see as a good sign. I leave him to go toward the back entrance and slink quietly up to the rear door. I gently crack the door open, slip inside, and wait. I whisper a small prayer of gratitude that there's still limited surveillance in smaller towns.

The main area for transmission is in the larger room close to the front of the building, and within minutes, I hear Solomon's voice shout from that direction. "Quickly, everyone, come see what's been done to the townhall!"

I hear bouts of confusion, and one of the broadcasters responds, "What, Old Man? Just tell us. We don't—" It's a woman's voice, and it sounds rough, conveying her irritability and impatience. A man's voice interjects, "We aren't leaving our station." He sounds young, maybe twenty to twenty-five.

Solomon continues in a high-strung, jumpy tone as though he can't believe what he saw. "You have to see it for yourselves!" he screeches. "They should be arrested!"

I stifle a laugh as I hear them scurrying around. Curiosity always trumps reason. They are muttering to themselves and following him outside. I prepare to move forward. *The clock's ticking.* I know I don't have much time. I open the door to the production room slowly, take a timid step inside, and give a cursory glance around to ensure no one is there. Upon discovering I'm alone, I go over to the main microphone and radio headboard. I flip the "on the air" switch and talk as clearly and articulately as my nerves can muster.

"My fellow citizens, I'm interrupting your nightly broadcast with an imperative message. Please listen. The gathering at the Church of the Divine Truth tomorrow is not what it seems. It is a ploy by the Federation to conform you further. They will mask the idea of marking your bodies with their emblem with the lie that you are showing your love of equality and freedom. This tattoo of their emblem is a trick! You do not have to believe what they believe! You do not have to accept what you feel is morally wrong. We can change our nation if we stick together and do what is right. Please run, hide, or fight, but do not take the mark."

I realize I haven't been breathing and take a deep breath. Beads of sweat line my forehead. Steadying my hands, I flip the off switch.

## 12.
# THREE YEARS EARLIER . . .

When I wouldn't talk much about my trauma in therapy, my counselor, Sister Mary, wanted me to write about what happened to me. I was sitting in her office, my hands underneath my thighs as she told me to relay the events of the day my life had changed.

"I can't talk about it," I said, my voice quiet, raspy. She nodded. Her eyes stared at me with a pity that I scorned. She reached in a drawer then, giving me a journal. I wanted to resist, to tell her there were no words to convey the kind of emotions that ripped through everything I was, everything I'd ever been. But, of course, she wouldn't have understood. The words, like so many others before them, would be wasted.

I stared at the journal in my hands. It wasn't that I didn't remember the day. I remembered every minuscule detail as if it had been carved into my mind like a piece of engraved wood. As though trauma and memory were friends, they whispered secrets to each other, embracing the experience and etching its nightmarish details into the psyche of my mind. The trauma had accentuated my senses, brought the mundane to life. Of course, when I had awakened that morning, I didn't know any of that, for it had started like any other day.

*I had been sitting in math class on a Tuesday as Mr. Hawk droned on about negative coefficients. I was sitting in the second row, third seat back, and the room smelled like a mixture of cafeteria food and cologne. The boy next to me had apparently bathed in it. Mr. Hawk had on a blue floral tie that was slightly crooked. The sound of the door opening interrupted his explanation of how to simplify a problem. The school counselor, a middle-aged woman named Mrs. Walters, with long, dark hair, came in to retrieve me, and I innocently wondered if she wanted to discuss the interest I'd shown in going to science camp that summer. But then, it became clear that she was upset, the feeling of my heart in my stomach growing as I realized that something was horribly wrong.*

I pulled myself out of the memory and looked up from my lap to meet Sister Mary's eyes. I tried to communicate the difficulty of what she was asking of me. She maintained eye contact but didn't say anything else, a refusal to back down from what she thought I needed.

"Thanks," I finally muttered, and pushed the journal in my bag. "I'll try."

*Hi, Monkey,*

*You're okay. Tell yourself that continuously and let yourself grieve, then be okay and move forward. I'm watching you swing right now and relishing the sound of your carefree laugh as you go higher and higher. We're at the local park, and it's a beautiful day. I'm sitting on a bench near you, treasuring the moment and reflecting on how deeply your father and I love you. You are the light in our otherwise dark lives.*

*Throughout these letters, you are going to learn things about us, many of which I hope will make you proud, but I'm sure you will feel an array of emotions, including anger that we kept such secrets and fear over what's to come. These are normal reactions; I want you to feel whatever you need to in order to understand. But at the end of the letters, you must understand.*

*I'll begin by explaining what we do. I know you think we work in missions. That is not entirely untrue. Your father and I are part of a resistance movement. You can't see who we're resisting now because they're doing such a good job of hiding their agenda, but there is an organization—an underground, evil organization—that is gaining ground. They'll be indiscreetly taking over soon if we aren't able to stop them, and I've begun these letters because I fear that we may have failed in stopping them. If I'm right, my darling girl, there will be much worse things to come.*

*All my love,*

*Mom*

# 13.
# PRESENT DAY

I've barely stepped outside of the doorway to the radio station when I'm spotted.

"Hey, you!" It's one of the radio broadcasters, the woman with the coarse voice. *Oh, no, run!* I take off and head toward a back alley. My mind is on Finnick and Solomon. I need to know how it went in town and if they're all right. *Why didn't we discuss a fall-out plan?*

"Look out, Girl!"

I scream as I'm hit in the shoulder by two men racing by me. "What's going on?" I ask anxiously.

"There's a church on fire!" one yells over his shoulder.

I realize immediately that it has to be the Church of the Divine Truth. I knew the broadcast would bring results, but I never imagined they would happen so quickly.

"Es!" I feel Finnick's hand as it grabs my arm and pulls me back onto a side street.

"Kneel down." He pushes the top of my shoulder behind a dumpster and crouches beside me. He's drenched in sweat, despite the freezing temperature outside.

"How bad is it?" I ask as I feel what is now an accustomed sense of fear rise in my throat.

"Bad," he says, trying to catch his breath. "I can't find Solomon. Your broadcast had more of an impact than I thought it would. I bolted as soon as I hung up the banner. I caught sight of Solomon as he was running outside of the station. Those who worked there were right behind him. I figured I'd be able to catch up with him in the center, but then things just got crazy."

"Crazy, how? What happened to the church?"

"Moments after you were on the air, the church was on fire. There are obviously other resistors, many of whom we don't even know about, who are anxious to retaliate against these new regulations. Officers were suddenly everywhere, and I had to get out of sight before one of them questioned me. I didn't have time to find Solomon again." His eyes fill with concern for our professor. "I should have waited for him when I had the chance. I'm such an idiot."

"You're fine. You didn't know." I scan the perimeter. "Where would he go?" My thoughts come out clipped, and I put my hands on my head as I try to clear my mind and think. I look up and see clouds of billowing black smoke in the distance. The angry sounds of a mob, cries of anguish and hate, resound from the street.

"He'll want to know that we're okay. He won't leave here until he does," Finnick says as he looks around a dumpster toward the chaos. "We have to wait this out a few minutes. If we go out there now, we'll just get caught."

I nod before responding. "Solomon will know to do that, too. I'm sure he knows to stay out of sight until things calm down." We both hear the uncertainty in my voice as we lean against the wall to wait.

# 14.
# THREE YEARS EARLIER . . .

My first official day in Solomon's class, we were learning about religious epistemology. Solomon was gearing kids up for a debate. His aim was to have us think about the uncertainty of what we know and understand while considering our perceptions in a broader sense.

Solomon was standing at the lectern as my classmates sat in rapt attention. I slipped into class late and stood quietly in the back as he spoke.

"James Madison, a former president of our nation, rejected the existence of God, citing religion as bondage that hurts reason. He was certainly not alone. Many great philosophers and historians throughout time have had these same notions and thus considered themselves atheists. On the other hand, men like the philosopher Aristotle and many of our nation's presidents have rejected the idea that there is not sufficient evidence to support God's existence, citing examples such as the impossibility of infinite time to support their beliefs. So, what I'm asking you to do today is to pick a side. Does God indeed exist? And if so, how can you support such a notion? What concrete evidence and theistic arguments can be used to support your claim? Alternately, if you are going to take the stance of an atheist, how will you refute the many generations of people before you who have believed in God? Do you only believe what is within your mind's capability? How will you combat the idea that there may be much we do not understand?"

Silence ensued as everyone took in the magnitude of what he had said, each student considering where they stood.

I slipped back out the door and into the hall without being noticed. Tears were burning my eyes, and I was ashamed to go sit down. I missed my parents, and I was so angry at God.

"Esther?" I turned around to see my professor standing there in concern. A sob escaped my throat, and he reached out to hug me.

"I'm s-s-sorry," I sobbed. "You barely even know me."

"Oh, Child." He exhaled and continued sympathetically, "I know much more than you think."

# 15.
## PRESENT DAY

Finnick stands up and brushes off the back of his pants. "The coast looks semi-clear. If we're careful, we can avoid the officers still out there. I can't sit here any longer; I'm too worried about him."

"Okay." I nod as I stand up next to him. "Let's go." With our backs against the wall of the alley, we cautiously head toward the center of town.

Finnick peeks his head around the building of an old insurance agency and looks toward the townhall. The banner has been ripped down, and in its place, there's a sign that reads: "THOSE WHO DEFY ACCEPTANCE, DEFY EQUALITY AND WILL BE PROSECUTED."

"Ha! What a joke. I'll take my equality with a slice of free-thinking, but thanks," Finnick snaps.

"Solomon!" I scream in horror. I recognize his St. Mary's ring, which is on the index finger of his right hand, now visibly outstretched from behind a bush. He's lying motionless in the park parallel to where we're standing. Finnick and I stumble over each other as we run to his side. "Please, God! No one else," I beg and fall on my knees next to him.

"Move over; let me feel for a pulse," Finnick says as he gently pushes me aside. He places his fingers to Solomon's neck, and I hold my breath.

"Well?" I ask.

"I feel one, but it's weak."

We look Solomon over and see he has a cut above his right eye; his left eye is swollen shut; and there are bruises forming on his face. His shirt has been torn from his abdomen, which looks discolored and distended. I look up at Finnick. "I think he has broken ribs."

"He needs medical help," he answers, looking around as if a doctor will appear.

"You know that's impossible," I say in frustration.

"Maybe not . . . " Finnick stares pensively at the officer patrolling the park. "If we could just get his uniform and badge . . . "

"You have to be joking."

"Do you have a better idea?"

"Fine, but hurry up, and don't kill him."

Finnick reaches into the back of his pants and takes out the gun he keeps with him. Weapons of all kinds have been banned for months, but we managed to keep a few.

We have no intention of actually killing people with these weapons, but we have to protect ourselves. I watch him now as he creeps up behind a tree, near where the officer is monitoring. Finnick once confided in me that his parents trained him in mortal combat before Alastor gained power. He said they raised him to be both reticent and combative, and he always had the feeling they were preparing him for something. What that something was seems pretty clear as I watch him sneak up behind the officer, who is obliviously whistling the old tune, "Here Comes the Rain, Baby."

I shudder as Finnick slams the butt of his gun against the back of the guy's head. The officer drops to the ground, and I look around to ensure no one saw. His movements fluid, Finnick slides the body over to the bushes.

He motions to me with his hand to come over and puts a finger to his lips. I hate to leave Solomon's side for even a moment, but I grudgingly creep, hunched over, to where Finnick is taking off the officer's pants and jacket. He throws the pants at me. "Check to make sure his badge is in his pocket."

I pull out his wallet and flip it open to see a picture of three smiling, dark-haired children. I feel a punch of remorse before remembering that they did this to Solomon. I'm done letting them take people I love.

"It's here," I say and zip it into my own side coat pocket. We both go carefully back to Solomon and dress him in the pants and jacket. "It's pretty tight," I protest, yanking his arm through the hole of the jacket. "That guy is a lot smaller."

"It's fine, the best we can do. Here," he continues, picking up his legs. "Take his feet, and I'll lift him under the arms. The hospital is about a kilometer north of here."

I inhale a deep breath to gear myself up for the walk, nod to Finnick, and take Solomon's legs in my hands. He lets out a moan, which I take to be a good sign. We head as discreetly as possible, while carrying a two-hundred-pound man through the park and toward the main road. We're about halfway to the hospital, when a jeep full of officers sees us and motions for us to stop.

"What's this about?" the driver, a burly young man who is not much older than Finnick and me, asks us suspiciously. I notice the mark of the Federation on the front of his hand.

"This officer was working when that resistor gave the broadcast. It looks like he was attacked. We're just trying to get him some help," Finnick responds.

"Let me see his papers and yours."

"Sure, sir, of course." Finnick pulls his false ID card out of his pocket as he gently lays Solomon down, then gestures for me to do the same. I take the badge and my own false identification out of my coat pocket and try to remain calm as I place them into the driver's hand. I can feel the eyes of the other officers on me, and I try not to squirm.

The driver glances at them skeptically, but then, like he can't be bothered, hands us back our IDs. "Go on, then. Make sure he gets help." He turns his head sharply back toward the road, dismissing us.

Finnick doesn't move. "If I might just ask you a quick question, sir?"

I stare at him incredulously. The driver just scowls and waits.

"We were planning to attend the church to receive our marks today, and we were wondering where we might go instead."

"Hmmph," the officer smirks, raising his eyebrows. "There's still markings today in the next town over. Chester. At the Methodist church." His tone is clipped, condescending.

"Chester. Got it. Thank you," Finnick replies hastily, and we turn to continue toward the hospital. The man watches us as we go; he's typing into his smartwatch, and a wave of anxiety washes over me.

"He's reporting us," I whisper, adjusting the weight of Solomon's shoulder to relieve the cramping in my arm.

"It'll be fine. Come on. The hospital's just up there." He tries to sound confident, but I see his cursory glance back at the officer. I take another deep breath and keep walking.

*Esther Rose,*

*Do you know why we chose your name? Yes, it's the name of a book in the Bible, and certainly, the fact that Esther became the queen of a great empire is reason enough. But the main reason for our choice was not her power as much as her secret. For, you see, she had to pretend. She was forced to conceal her heritage and gain great favor with the king, even marry him. Her steadfast ability to maintain this secret identity led to the opportunity to save her people from death. And save them, my girl, is exactly what she did.*

*In Your Heart Always,*

*Mom*

When we arrive at the hospital, Solomon is only semi-conscious, letting out moans of pain every few minutes. His uniform gains him the attention we hoped, and he is rushed off to surgery. Finnick follows me into the waiting room. I sit down on the edge of a chair, unable to relax. Finnick sits, then stands, then sits again. He runs his hand through his hair and bites his lower lip. There is a woman and a small child, maybe six or seven years old, sitting across from us. She looks upset, and the child has clearly been crying.

To my right is a middle-aged couple. The man is tall with brawny shoulders. He is clean-shaven and well-kept. The woman is of medium height with a gentle, sad face; her hair is pinned back softly in a loose bun. They seem to both hold important positions, their uniforms adorned with several medals. The man has "Commander Sergeant Major" stitched in black lettering on his jacket. There is blood on the woman's face.

A young doctor appears and addresses the couple, "Mr. and Mrs. Hawthorne?"

"Yes," the man answers. "That's us."

The doctor's face furrows with concern. "I'm so sorry to tell you this . . . " He trails off as the woman starts to scream. She is shaking her husband.

"It's your fault! I hate you!" Tears cascade down her face, smearing the blood and dripping reddish drops onto the linoleum floor. The man is trying to soothe her, but she is pushing him off, her eyes filled with rage. The doctor is clearly uncomfortable and takes a step backward.

"Ahem." He clears his throat before interjecting, "I'm very sorry, but when you're ready . . . she is in room 247." I watch him turn and walk back down the hall. Finnick and I exchange glances. The man has taken a seat, and his shoulders are shaking with sobs. The woman is hysterical.

"Someone, do something!" she yells, her eyes bouncing frantically around the room.

I know that they're the enemy in this war, but my heart is bleeding for them. "Can we do anything?" I whisper to Finnick.

"No, shhhh," he returns. "We're not going to put our identities and Solomon's life at risk." He pauses before continuing, "And anyway, it sounds like it's too late for anything to be done . . . You can pray."

"Yes . . . " I trail off. "Pray."

# 16.
# THREE YEARS EARLIER . . .

Chapel at St. Mary's was every Wednesday morning at 7:00 a.m. At my orientation, they had told me that Mother Maura would choose a student every week to open in prayer before Sister Margaret led the singing. The morning of my first chapel, I didn't know anyone but my professors, so I didn't know where to go or who to sit with. I tried to inconspicuously take a seat in one of the back pews; but Professor Solomon saw me, laid a hand on my shoulder, and guided me toward the front. I sighed.

He pushed me gently down in a seat next to a boy who looked about my age. The first thing I thought was, *His hair is gorgeous.* His eyes were a unique shade of green, the color of seaweed, and his dark black hair was brushed perfectly back from his face, two tendrils falling parallel with his eyes. He turned toward me and smiled. I was about to introduce myself when Mother Maura tapped the microphone.

"Good morning, Scholars! Today, I would like to ask Finnick Draven to open us in prayer." Mother Maura smiled toward the boy next to me, and he stood.

"Excuse me." He looked down at me amiably, and I moved my legs over, so he could walk through the aisle. I watched him curiously for a second as he made his way up to the podium. I pulled out my economics notebook and began nervously doodling on the front cover.

"Good morning, St. Mary's! I am Finnick Draven, a freshman in high school here at our beloved orphanage and home." At his charismatic tone, I looked up with interest from my notebook. "I've been here for the last four years after tragically losing my parents, who died while on a military operation in the heart of Iran."

Okay, I wasn't expecting that. There was a thick silence as Finnick paused. Did people usually go into depth about their personal lives? I looked around to gauge others' reactions; they seemed sad, but unphased, as he continued.

"The power of prayer is what has enabled me to deal with this incredibly difficult thing that has happened to me. I have felt a sense of peace that I know I would not have experienced without God's intervention. He has helped to bring me closure through a close family friend who fought beside my parents, and I now understand what He wishes for me."

*I want closure*, I thought. I stared at his confident demeanor, overcome with envy, not only because he had had time to process his grief, but also because he seemed so sure of who he was now. I couldn't help but think how far I was from reaching that point. The people around me were bowing their heads, and I realized he was praying.

"Help us as we go about the business of our lives and education to see through the falsehoods that face us. Help us to see things for how they really are and to rise above the evil of this world. And may God bless us as we educate ourselves and try to find our place and our purpose." He looked up and smiled. "Amen."

"Amen," the student body repeated. Finnick stepped down and walked back down the aisle toward his seat. I moved my legs over again, so he could get by me.

I turned toward him as he sat down. "My parents just died." Why had I just come out with that? My cheeks turned crimson, and I looked down uncomfortably.

"I'm sorry," he said and waited for me to look up. When I did, I saw him studying me curiously. "You haven't accepted it." It took me a moment to realize he was asking me.

"No," I whispered, still embarrassed. "I never will."

"I felt like that too—because I didn't understand. If you . . . never mind, it's none of my business."

I looked up at him then and saw from his expression that he was genuinely concerned. "Go ahead. I'm the one who blurted out my business in the first place." I gave him half a smile.

"I was just going to ask if you know what happened," he asked warily.

"Oh," I breathed, and my eyes filled with tears. "They were murdered."

*When I first heard of my parents' deaths, my whole body went numb. My eyes glazed over in an effort to distort my new reality. Since I was in school when I heard the news, the administration took immediate action to rid themselves of their obligation in the matter; and before I knew it, I was in the hands of social workers.*

*"Esther, this is Mrs. Meyer; she's the social worker assigned to your case. She'll be going over some things with you now," the school counselor informed me sympathetically.*

*I didn't respond. I was staring vacantly at a picture of a vase of flowers on the wall. Their vibrant colors seemed inappropriate and cruel.*

*"Hi, Esther. It's nice to meet you, dear. That's a very pretty ring you're wearing." Mrs. Meyer smiled at me as she looked down at my hand.*

*I absently twirled the ring my parents had given me for Christmas around my finger. I stared again at the picture of the flowers. I thought about how*

*I had learned of abstract art in school last year; it was visual language or something like that. Mrs. Meyer realized I was not going to respond.*

*"There are just a few things we need to take care of regarding the funeral services and the will. Your parents, of course, left everything to you but with the instructions that all their assets be sold." She was right in front of me, but her voice felt so far away. "So, we'll allow you to go retrieve a bag of your things, and then, since you're so young, we'll take over the estate."*

*There was a faint alarm bell inside of me and the memory of my mother's voice. I remembered a day in her office and something about a medicine cabinet.*

*I looked up abruptly. "I want to go home now."*

*Mrs. Meyer peered over her glasses at me in alarm. "In a few minutes, dear."*

*"Now, please. I won't sign anything until we go." She looked annoyed with me but seemed to realize she couldn't be rude to a girl who had just found out she was an orphan. We sat in silence for a few seconds. I maintained eye contact to ensure her I wouldn't take no for an answer.*

*"All right," she agreed reluctantly. "But we're headed right back here to finish this paperwork." I nodded at her and stood to leave.*

*As we pulled up to my house about twenty minutes later, Mrs. Meyer stepped out of the car with me. "I want to go in alone," I said firmly.*

*She looked uncomfortable. "I don't think that's a good idea, Esther. I was told to watch over you . . . You're in a, um, a fragile state."*

*My eyes spat daggers at her; my whole body was fueled with anger. I didn't care that none of it was her fault. "Look, I'm fine. You people are all about dealing with your emotions and finding closure and all that, so let me say my goodbyes." I walked ahead with my head held high in determination. I glanced back briefly and was grateful to find that she wasn't following me.*

*I unlocked the door and quietly went inside, hiding the unsettling anxiety that was squeezing my insides until I was out of eyesight. I closed the door and* took off toward the upstairs bathroom. I threw open the medicine cabinet to see a row of pill bottles . . . . What had she said? What had she said?

"The aspirin!" I practically shouted. I felt like my heart was going to pound out of my chest as I ripped off the top and found a small, silver key. Clasping it in my hand, I raced back downstairs to the office. I stopped at the doorway, taken aback by the familiarity of the room. Everything was how my parents had left it. My dad's reading glasses were folded gently on his copy of Brave New World. My mom's favorite sweater was hung casually on the back of a chair. Overwhelmed by emotion, I sat at the desk and pulled open the bottom drawer. With trembling fingers, I inserted the key into the lock of the box. I took a deep breath before slowly opening the top.

I saw the letters first. They were packaged together in a stack and tied carefully with a black ribbon. Tears blurred my vision as I realized I still had pieces of my parents, words and thoughts that I had not yet heard. I swiped at my eyes, so I could see what was underneath. My chest tightened when I saw a small revolver. I checked and found that it was loaded. I put it in the back of my pants behind my denim jacket and turned, again, toward the box. Laying on the bottom was a single picture that looked to be taken somewhere important. There were crowds of people in the background holding banners and signs. It must have been a protest.

I immediately recognized my parents' faces, but they were definitely younger. But I didn't recognize the other couple pictured. All four were smiling, but they were apprehensive smiles, forced for a camera. Their arms lazily strung over each other's shoulders. There was a sign in my dad's free hand, leaning against his leg; it was turned around, so I couldn't make out what it said. I flipped the picture over to look at the back and inhaled so sharply, it hurt. There were two words written in black, block lettering. My palms started to sweat as I ran my fingers over them and read, "YOU'RE DEAD."

# 17.
# PRESENT DAY

We've been in the hospital now for two long hours, and there's still no word of Solomon's condition. My stomach growls loudly, and I look around, embarrassed.

"I doubt you're the only hungry one here," Finnick says supportively.

The woman and child who were beside us have left with whom I presume was the husband and father. He had a broken leg. The Hawthornes are still sitting next to us. They have not yet gone to go see whomever it is that they lost. The man has not stopped crying, and the woman has been verbally berating him off and on since the doctor left.

"I don't know how you plan to live with yourself." Here we go again.

I let out a loud sigh to remind the woman that other people are here, too. The husband seems to pick up on my cue and, for the first time, responds to his wife.

"She was trying to help someone."

"What?" the woman responds in confusion, and I look over at Finnick and narrow my eyes as a signal to listen.

"She tried to help this older man. Officers were beating him; they said he was responsible for the banner or the broadcast; I can't remember which. It all happened so fast." He puts a hand on his head as if to remember. "A sergeant, a young one . . . he must have been trying to feel important. I think he meant to shoot the man . . . But she was there . . . She tried to help . . . " He trails off, his cheeks wet with tears. I look at his face. I know that expression—the one of desperation for it to be anyone's fault but your own.

"Why would she do that? Why would you let her?" The woman stares at him in confusion and pain.

"I tried to stop her. I shouted, 'Sara! No!'" He begins to sob. "But then the shot rang out. There were so many people and so much shouting."

"Did the man live?"

"I don't know . . . We left him there. He was unconscious."

"Why would she help a resistor?"

"I told you; I don't know."

Finnick and I meet eyes, silently acknowledging that the older man must have been Solomon. I'm amazed by the smallness of the world, especially in times of such considerable chaos. This girl, whom these people clearly loved, made a choice that saved our Solomon's life.

It's a war of souls. I stare at the couple, deep in their grief, and am reminded yet again of the ramifications we face.

"Excuse me." I turn to see a young, female doctor holding a clipboard and looking at me expectantly. "Are you here for Officer McClaren?"

Was that the officer's name? I hear Finnick answer.

"Yes, is he all right?"

"He suffered a head injury. We did an MRI and then rushed him into surgery. He's in the clear now, but we'd like to keep him under observation for a couple days. Our officers are our first priority here at Health West." She looks over at the Hawthornes as if seeking their approval before continuing, "I assume you're family?"

"Yes," Finnick lies. "May we see him?"

"As long as you have recorded your credentials at the desk, you may go back. He's in Room 243."

"Thank you, Doctor," I say. She smiles tiredly at me and nods. We wait until she's out of sight to speak.

"We need to get him out of here before they realize," I hiss under my breath. Hawthorne examines us curiously, spreading goosebumps over my arms.

"I know. I'm thinking," Finnick replies. I see him look down the hall where Solomon is. "There's an exit stairwell at the end of that hall."

"Yes, but if he's not conscious, I—"

"We'll have to roll him as close as we can and then carry him."

"Are you insane? There are people everywhere. You don't think that might look a tad suspicious?"

"What choice do we have?" Finnick snaps, and then, as though realizing it's not my fault, he continues in a calmer tone. "We can grab lab coats. I saw a couple hanging up in the X-ray room next to the bathroom. That should at least help."

"Where will we take him?"

Finnick looks at me exasperatedly. "Why do you always think I have all the answers?"

"Well, I certainly don't," I mutter. "We need sanctuary."

"The Federation has done a pretty good job of eliminating that."

"Yes, but Solomon said something about having contacts who could help us get the word out. We put his real wallet in his pocket, didn't we?" I think about how dumb that was. Why didn't we just hold onto it? I bite my lip in frustration. "Do you think they took it out of his pocket? He may have an address or phone number of someone who can help us."

"Now you're thinking, Es. We'll check. Walk with me and keep your eyes straight ahead like you belong here. I'll grab the coats, and then we'll head to his room."

"Got it." I say, and we start to make our way toward the restrooms next to x-ray. I go into the bathroom where Finnick meets me three minutes later.

"I never thought I'd be grateful bathrooms are unisex." He sighs as he passes me a lab coat. I pull my arms through and catch a glimpse of myself in the mirror.

My blonde hair looks straggly. I try to pry a couple fingers through it to smooth it out, but it's hopeless. The bags under my eyes are dark and my skin bloodless. The hours of daylight have diminished rapidly, replaced by the smog of industrialism and an abused environment. Everyone is a bit paler these days.

Finnick pokes his head cautiously out the door to make sure no one is paying us any attention. He nods at me to signal the coast is clear. As we step out into the hall and make our way toward Room 243, I remember what Finnick said and keep my eyes straight ahead.

I take in a breath as we enter Solomon's room. He looks so frail and much older than his fifty-three years. He's dressed in a hospital gown, and his head is wrapped in white gauze. I notice immediately that he's hooked up to an IV. "We'll need to take this out," I say and begin to take the tape off of his wrist.

"Be careful. I'm going to check his pants." Finnick goes over to the chair where the staff has folded his clothes. "Bingo," he says with a smile and flips open his wallet. After leafing through its contents, he sighs heavily. "Nothing."

"No way. Check again." *Please God*, I pray, *we need a break here.* I've carefully pulled the IV out of Solomon's arm and pressed on the area with a tissue. "Wake up," I whisper.

"Here's something . . . " Finnick says as he holds up a business card.

"A business card?"

"It's all we have. We'll go to this address. It's for a plumber in Chester."

"So, we're just going to go to some random plumber's house?"

"At least we know he knows Solomon. It's one of his contacts if his card's in his wallet, and if you have a better idea, I'm all ears."

"Wasn't Chester where that officer said to go for markings?"

"Oh, yeah, it was. That could work to our benefit, if there's time." He hands me Solomon's shirt, and we dress him together. He begins to roll the gurney forward toward the door. "Check the hallway."

I look out and see the Hawthornes standing in the hall with a doctor. The doctor's shaking his head. "Hold up," I tell Finnick as he steps up behind me. We both peer out and listen.

"She will not wake up. I know this is hard. But keeping her hooked up to machines is not the answer," the doctor tells the Hawthornes solemnly. He looks like he wants to say more but stops himself.

"We need more time," the man responds. "Was she conscious at all before surgery? Did she say anything?"

The doctor looks around uneasily. "There was something."

"Yes?"

"She said she had changed her mind." The doctor avoids meeting their eyes.

"Changed her mind about what?" the woman demands impatiently.

"She was praying, and she, um, asked for forgiveness." He fidgets from one foot to the other uncomfortably. "For you."

"I can't hear this," the man says as he walks back into the room.

"I don't understand. Our Sara didn't believe in God." The woman looks at the doctor quizzically.

"I'm not sure, ma'am. That's honestly all I heard. I'm really very sorry, but if you'll excuse me, I have to run my rounds. I'll send a nurse to sit with you shortly." The doctor looks relieved as he walks away, leaving the woman stupefied in the hall.

"Yikes," Finnick says behind me.

"Yeah. That's heavy. Maybe her death will make a difference, at least . . ."

"We can't wait around and see. They've gone back in the room. It's time to move." He begins pushing Solomon on the gurney toward the door. A few feet away, we stop and lift him off, each holding up a shoulder.

I have a hand on the door to the stairwell when we hear, "Hey! You can't move him." A nurse is shouting at us, and I see Mr. Hawthorne come into the hall.

He stares at us for a moment, and I watch in dismay as recognition washes over his face. He begins to walk toward us briskly.

"Move!" Finnick shouts, and we push our way through the door. Latched together, we hobble down the stairs as quickly as we can. We shove the door open to the outside and fall onto the pavement, barely keeping Solomon upright. "Over here!" Finnick motions toward the back door of a restaurant's kitchen.

There's steam billowing out into the street, filling it with the smell of rotting garbage and seafood. I gag and cover my mouth with my free hand. We collapse inside the restaurant and pull Solomon behind a row of trash cans. I feel bile rise in my throat from the smell.

"I'm going to be sick," I say in disgust.

"Shhh! Breathe out of your mouth," Finnick hisses. We hear footsteps in the street outside the door.

"Who were those people?" Mr. Hawthorne demands angrily.

"The patient was an officer, sir; the only way they should have been in his room is if they were family." The nurse speaks hesitatingly, as if realizing there may have been a mistake in protocol.

"Do family members typically break their unconscious loved one out of a hospital?" he demands furiously.

"No, sir," the nurse whispers.

"I'll need that officer's file. I want to know why he was here and the circumstances of his injury."

We hear the nurse respond as the back door to the hospital opens, "Yes, sir, of course."

Simultaneously, I wretch on the floor at Finnick's feet.

*Hi, Monkey,*

*Today's been a difficult day. Your father and I are protesting the rise of a man named Alastor, who is gaining power in a party he calls the Federation of Acceptance. He's gaining support through the propaganda that conformity is diversity. It's contradictory, but it's working, particularly with those who embrace free love or who feel their rights are in jeopardy under the current administration. His speeches urge that equality cannot come without the acceptance of all people and that solely because we are human, we are all the same. But there's much more at play that many don't understand. We can't live in a world where everyone "lives and let's live." It'll be Sodom and Gomorrah all over again. We must consider our souls.*

*Character, morals, beliefs—these are what's at stake. And I fear, my sweet girl, that we will be fighting for the right to keep them.*

*All my love,*

*Mom*

"Gross! Esther!" Finnick leaps backward, knocking over a trash can.

"Sorry, I couldn't help it," I sputter, still reeling with nausea. "Can we please get out of here?"

"Yeah, they're not coming back out here," he answers, looking queasy himself at the sight of my vomit. "Let's get some distance from the hospital, but I don't want to make the trek to Chester until Solomon's awake. There's no way we can carry him that far, and we'd look way too suspicious."

I nod in agreement and follow him out onto the road. Solomon's arms are slung over our shoulders. We walk cautiously along the street, staying close to the buildings. My stomach stops churning and is replaced with the familiar pangs of hunger.

"Look, Es, there's a library over there." I look across the intersection where he's pointing toward a large, brick building.

"Sounds good to me," I say in relief. We make sure no one is watching us as we cross the road and walk toward the front entrance. We scope it out and immediately determine that the twenty stairs leading up to the wide oak doors are not an option, so we head toward the back. On the way, we see a fire escape door on the side of the building and a stairwell leading up to it.

"I'll go in the front first, show them my papers, and then let you in the side with Solomon. Can you get him up that stairwell?" Finnick asks.

"Yeah, I got it," I say with more surety than I feel.

"Okay. See you in a few."

Finnick runs out of sight, toward the back, and I grab Solomon behind the arms. I slowly begin to pull him up the stairwell. "For the love of all things holy, Professor, can you wake up, please?"

I carry him halfway up to the middle landing and have to take a break. I set him softly against the wall and wipe the sweat off my face with my arm. My vision clouds up for a second, and I feel like I might pass out. I take a seat next to him and put my head between my knees but immediately jump up again when I hear Solomon groan.

"Professor!"

"Where am I?" he moans, opening his eyes slightly to look around.

"Well, right now, on a stairwell. It's a long story. We'll fill you in once we get inside the library. I was trying to carry you, but I had to take a break. I'm so tired, and you're kind of heavy. Finnick went inside through the back; he's going—"

"Esther."

"Yes, Professor?"

"If I could just have silence for a moment . . . " He closes his eyes again, while still holding his head with his hands.

"Oh, of course, of course, my bad." I look down sheepishly and dig the pain pills I took from the hospital out of my pocket. "Here you go," I say as I place them in his hand.

He murmurs gratefully and swallows them dry, even though I know he must be even thirstier than I am. I give him a couple minutes to gain his bearings and am about to suggest we try to make it up the next flight of stairs, when I hear the door at the top of the landing creak open.

Finnick pokes his head out and looks down at me. "What's the hold up?"

"Solomon's awake!" I exclaim. He grunts next to me. "C'mon, Professor, let's make our way up. I'll help you."

He attempts to rise but sways to the left, and I grab his arms before he tumbles down the stairs. Slowly, we all but crawl to the top of the stairs and come through the door. Solomon is panting; his eyes lack focus as he teeters back and forth.

Finnick grabs one of his arms, and I take the other. We gently walk him behind a row of bookcases and lean him against the wood paneling of the side to sit down. Finnick unscrews the cap off his canteen and puts it to Solomon's lips. He drinks greedily, then sighs.

Taking a deep breath, he speaks with relief and gratitude. "I thought that was it for me. I owe you a great debt."

"Don't be ridiculous, Professor. It's a fragment of what you have done for us," I respond.

"Yeah, honestly, Professor. And, anyway, what would we do without you?" Finnick smiles, and I laugh softly.

"Seriously, we're helpless," I affirm with a grin.

"You don't see your own strengths, Children; you've dodged many mishaps to reach this point. You joke, but I'm quite proud." His eyes tear up, and he gives us a pleased smile. I feel a rare warmth of belonging in my heart and squeeze his hand. The three of us sit there silently for a few minutes, allowing ourselves this limited comfort.

It is Finnick who brings us back to the present. "We were going to go to an address in Chester on a card we found in your wallet. We didn't know where else to go."

"Arthur Grant, the plumber?"

"Yeah, I think that's his name."

"That would have been all right, if he's still there. He has played a minor role in the Resistance efforts. He would have tried to help."

"Where do you suggest we go now, Professor, if not there?" I ask. "We came across a few UFoA officers who said the next markings were in Chester. But we may have missed them by now."

"It is worth the trip there. One of my contacts who may be able to hack into their system lives just outside. He keeps a low profile, residing in a shack of sorts in the woods."

"How does he have internet?"

"He is a hacker, Esther."

I give a small laugh. "Oh, right. Gotcha."

"How far do you estimate it is from here to Chester?" Finnick asks.

"I'd say at least eight or nine miles. I'm not sure I could make that right now; you may have to go without me."

"No way!" Finnick and I respond in unison.

"Even if it takes us days, we will go together. We're not splitting up again," Finnick says decisively, his face confirming the resolution of his words.

"As you wish, but I will only slow you down." Solomon takes a few deep breaths and closes his eyes. "A cat nap may help me to regain my strength. You children go scope out the propaganda on the shelves. See what you can find out. I'll be rested and ready when you return."

# 18.
# TWO YEARS EARLIER . . .

I had been at St Mary's for over a year the night the ear-splitting sound of a bell jolted me upright in bed. What was that? I rubbed my eyes and quickly looked around, seeing the clock. It read 5:42 a.m. My first thought was that there was a fire, an evacuation of some kind. I heard movement in the hallway outside of my room.

"What's going on?" I poked my head out of my door and asked the girl running down the hall.

"Emergency meeting in the chapel," she yelled over her shoulder.

I quickly threw on my uniform, splashed some cold water on my face, and grabbed my shoes. St. Mary's never had emergency meetings. There had been only one in the year that I had been there, and it was because two kids were caught snorting lines on the roof. Needless to say, Mother Maura thought a reiteration of school rules was in order.

"Hey," I said as I collided with Finnick at the end of the hall.

"I was just coming to find you. Do you know what this is about?"

"No clue."

"Hey, Guys," Ezra said as he ran up behind Finn.

"Hey," I said, happy that all three of us were together. "Any idea what's going on?"

"I heard it's pretty bad, but not sure why," Ezra responded as he led the way toward the chapel.

Students were packed into the main hall, and I looked anxiously around at the sea of faces; their expressions were contorted in confusion and fear. Many were still in their pajamas with bleary eyes and disheveled hair. Sister Margaret and Professor Darci were trying to corral everyone into the chapel. Sister Margaret was being barraged with questions as she ushered students along.

"What's happening, Sister? Should we be concerned? Is it related to the president?" This last question sent my mind back to my parents' letters. Many of them mentioned Alastor, who had just recently been elected to the presidency. Unlike any president before him, his election had come with the integration of a new party. People had grown tired of the uncompromising practices of the Republicans and Democrats and had seemingly embraced the Federation of Acceptance, a party whose ideology claimed to accept all of humanity as equal.

"This way, Students," Sister Margaret urged. "Nice to see you three," she said toward us and smiled. My eyes caught the unease in Professor Solomon's, who was standing behind Sister Margaret. He gave the three of us an encouraging nod.

"Go on, then," he said. "It's all right."

We walked past him and took a seat near the back and waited anxiously for everyone to be situated. Mother Maura walked up to the podium and cleared her throat. Complete silence disseminated over the room. For perhaps the first time, she had the attention of every adolescent in St. Mary's.

"I've called you here today, Students, to share difficult news. Religious institutions that believe and practice the teachings of the Bible are being asked to either change their views or be shut down. Bibles and all religious figures and symbols within government-funded institutions are now forbidden. President Alastor and his allies feel that the Bible rejects the acceptance of all people, and he, therefore, does not see a place for the book in society or our schools. He and his administration argue that the Christian and Jewish God are not accepting of the practices of humanity. The board has not made any definitive decisions yet as to how we will proceed here at St. Mary's, but we will inform you once we have. In the meantime, please direct all questions to your dormitory leaders, and they will bring them to us. Thank you, Children. You may file out of the chapel by pews beginning in the back."

I started to stand up before realizing that she hadn't moved from the podium. My eyes stayed on her, waiting to see if she would continue.

"And, Students . . . " Everyone stopped moving, and she waited to ensure we were listening. "Be careful."

## 19.
# PRESENT DAY

I've been scanning the shelves of the library for about ten minutes, finding nothing of value. "Hey, Finn, check this one out." I hold up a copy of *Modern Day Brothels* and scrunch my nose in disgust.

"Any pics?" he teases, a mischievous smirk on his face.

"You're sick. And anyway, I don't think this is the stuff you'd be into. It's talking about intersex brothels, bestiality houses, free love lodges . . ."

"Those are things?"

"Apparently." I sigh. I never told Finnick, but I've actually known about them. My dad mentioned them in a letter he wrote from Dematra, a city out West that's known for its violence and crime. He was appalled to find a street there where such things were going on. In a later letter, I learned how many more cities have followed suit. "They're growing. These types of establishments—they're, um, part of the Federation's policies for creating acceptance. Alastor claims they'll increase revenue for lower income cities."

"How do you know what Alastor claims?" Finnick narrows his eyes at me suspiciously.

"From the letters . . . I don't have to tell you everything."

"I wish you'd let me read them."

"They're private. And all I have left." I roughly push the book back into the shelf, closing the subject. Finnick gives me a wounded look, but I pretend not to see it and walk over to the religious section. I stare at the shelves silently, but my mind's still thinking about the letters.

"What's there?" Finnick calls over from periodicals, where he's reading the daily paper.

I start reading some of the titles. "Looks like there are books here on evolution, atheism, scientology, Buddhism . . . obviously there are no Bibles. Hmm, come look at this one." I pull out a book entitled *Religion for a New Age*. I briefly skim through the pages, stopping on a chapter entitled, "Why There's no Room for a God." I feel a wave of sorrow as I look at Finnick and read a section aloud. "Humanity has long depended on themselves for survival. We have had to use our instincts to persevere through hard times and watch as people suffered. Wars, violence, and persecution have been brought on for generations under the guise of a supreme being's will and intentions. Thus, peace can only be found when one defies the root cause of such strife, which is God himself." I stop reading, unable to continue.

I look over at Finnick sadly. "It's growing worse; younger generations will not know of any other way of thinking. They'll be conditioned to believe life is better without God. Sometimes, it's so defeating. How can we possibly change this or keep these ideas from growing?"

He hands me today's newspaper, returning my gaze with a look of resignation. I read the headline: "PEACE AND SAFETY FOR ALL! UFoA Approves Mark of Acceptance Law."

My jaw drops, and I find myself mumbling a verse I've known since childhood: "While people are saying, 'Peace and safety,' destruction will come on them suddenly . . . " I trail off and look up at Finnick fearfully. "What will it mean?"

Finn's eyes mirror my apprehension and disbelief as he skims the article, muttering the words aloud. "Those who refuse are prejudiced. The mark symbolizes freedom for the oppressed . . . Rights and power will finally be given to the sexually free . . ." Finnick stops, his mouth forming the next words, and I barely make out what he says. "Examples will be made of those who try to take away our rights." He looks up then, and we lock eyes.

"It's only going to get worse, isn't it?" I ask as I grab Finn's hand. "I need you to know that no matter what's ahead, I'll stand with you."

He squeezes my hand, his eyes searching mine. "Me, too, Es, until the end."

## 20.
# TWO YEARS EARLIER . . .

"Did your parents think there'd be war?" We were in our tenth grade chemistry class, and Ezra was pouring our glue into a mixing bowl for a science experiment where we had to make slime.

I measured out the water, added it in with the glue. "Yeah, I believe they knew."

"What side would they have been on?"

I was taken aback by this question, having assumed it would be obvious. "The Resistance, of course. Wouldn't yours?" *They were already part of it,* I thought to myself but was hesitant to share what I knew of their involvement aloud.

"I'm honestly not sure. They never told me much." He seemed regretful of this, as though he wished he had asked them more.

I gave him a look of understanding. "I get that. My parents kept me in the dark about a lot of things. It bothered me sometimes, but, perhaps selfishly, I mostly enjoyed being able to live without having to worry about anything. Of course, I never imagined one day they'd be gone." I paused, remembering the wave of nausea and desolation I had felt that day and the sense of longing for my parents that had never gone away. "Though, in retrospect, the loss was much more damaging because of my ignorance of the truth."

My words evoked the heaviness of the burden of knowledge I had carried since reading my parents' letters. The familiar pang of guilt that I was not doing more about it returned with a vengeance to my gut.

"At least you know where they stood. My parents left me with nothing. They kissed me goodbye as I left for school one morning, and I never saw them or heard anything about their lives again." He looked down, his voice conveying both sadness and anger. "I just have so many unanswered questions." He took the cap off our green food coloring and counted out six drops.

I felt sorry for him. At least some of my questions had been answered. "What do you know? Maybe we can try to fill in some of the holes."

He looked at me doubtfully. "They worked in the private sector for education. They considered themselves anti-political. I remember that only because my dad once commented that he hated the party system."

"How did they die?"

"They told me it was a car accident, which I've never believed. Just the way they said it, not looking me right in the eyes. I asked to see the car, but they kept putting me off."

"Who is they?"

"The social workers assigned to my case. They're who brought me here. I was only ten." He handed me the liquid starch to add to our mixture. I added it in and began playing with the blob absentmindedly.

"So, you think they were murdered?" I asked cautiously as I thought about my own parents' murder and the lack of answers I was given.

"I don't just think it, Esther; I know. It's like a hunger pain or a headache when you're dehydrated—the feeling isn't always there, but it creeps up on me, reminding me I have to figure it out." He looked up at me then, and swimming in the gray sea of his eyes were loss, confusion, and regret. "When I'm out of here . . . when I'm able to leave, I'll get answers." His tone was determined, and I could feel the gravity of this need that weighed on him standing forcefully between us.

# 21.
## PRESENT DAY

We race back to where Solomon is resting, my hand grasping the newspaper. I practically thrust it in his face.

"What is it, Esther?" Solomon asks as he bolts upright and wipes the sleepiness from his eyes.

"The verse in Revelation—the one about peace and safety. Read the headline!" He takes the paper from my hand and scans the page.

"So, it begins," he whispers.

From the corner of my eye, I see a rigid, middle-aged woman with graying hair walking toward us. She is scrutinizing Solomon's bandages, her eyes scrunched in disapproval.

"Excuse me, what's going on here? This is a library, not a hospice," she says with disgust. "I must ask you to leave," she continues. "And return the paper."

Without flinching, Finnick flashes her his most charming smile before he responds. "Of course, we don't mean any trouble, ma'am. Don't mind my uncle here; there was an accident, but he's all right. We were just looking up some information for a project I have due for the Youth for Acceptance. Actually, I bet you could help." He smiles again and runs his hand through his hair. I fight the urge to gag.

She looks at him warily but slowly starts to relax under his friendly gaze. Leave it to Finn to win over every woman he comes across. Part of me is annoyed that Finn's charm seems to always work on women, but I have to admit that it has helped us to gain information.

Finnick's now next to her, practically touching her shoulder as he continues. "I'm writing a biographical account of our president, whom I just idolize, don't you?" She smiles slightly, and he continues, "And, anyway, I need to find more information on his upbringing and family. Might you be able to steer me in the right direction?"

Solomon and I watch as she walks with him over to the history and current events section. "She was literally just kicking us out. He's unbelievable," I say with a sigh and shake my head.

Solomon chuckles. "You have charm, too, my girl, just of a different variety."

"Yeah, a variety no one understands." Finn always makes me feel wounded. Is that my fault or his? I meet Solomon's eyes and smile. "But thanks just the same, Professor."

## 22.
# TWO YEARS EARLIER . . .

"Finn has a girlfriend; Finn has a girlfriend." Ezra was dancing circles around Finnick's chair and mocking him in what had to be the most obnoxious tone I'd ever heard. The three of us were eating lunch in the cafeteria, and Ezra was using the opportunity to taunt Finnick about the upcoming winter dance St. Mary's was holding for the underclassmen.

"You're a child, Ezra. A jealous child, at that," Finn answered with feigned contempt. I saw him glance over at me briefly. I took a bite out of my apple, looking down with a sudden fascination at my biology notes.

"Sooo, how did you ask her?" Ezra asked. "She's been crushing on you for, like, a year. It was so obvious," he taunted, smiling broadly. It was true. The whole orphanage had known this girl, Rachael, was into Finnick. Her annoyingly wide, emerald eyes were always staring at him as if in adoration that he simply existed.

"It wasn't a big deal. I just walked to her locker with her after econ and mentioned that if she were free, I'd like to take her to the dance," Finnick answered, smiling playfully. "At least I have a date, unlike you two losers," he finished. Ezra flashed me a shy glance. I pretended not to notice.

"Hey, leave me out of this. I'm not the one making fun of your newest conquest," I said as I wrote a note in the margin of my biology practice test. "I'm trying to study, if you hadn't noticed." The truth was that I had felt some jealousy; but I hadn't worked out the why of those feelings yet, and I certainly wasn't going to share that confusion with either of them.

"Go with me," Ezra practically demanded, his arms folded as he leaned across the table toward me.

"What?" I said as I looked up, surprised, yet again, by his abrasiveness.

"To the dance." He looked at me with his intense, confident eyes, and I almost squirmed. Finnick flashed me an ear-to-ear grin.

"Um, okay," I responded hesitantly.

"Sweeeet. My two best friends dancing the night away," Finnick said as he looked at each of us, unable to stop smiling. His reaction immediately bothered me. But what had I expected? He liked Rachael, clearly. And, anyway, isn't that what I had wanted? I'd had feelings for Ezra for months. At least, I thought I had.

"What's going on in that head of yours? Dress shopping?" Ezra beamed at me, and I tried to shake away my thoughts with a laugh.

"Oh, yes, plotting my sultry makeup and voluptuous dress," I teased.

He laughed as he responded, "You know I love it when you talk dirty."

"Okay, you two, save it for later," Finnick said, jumping up and gathering his books, "The moment of truth is upon us. Time to ace that biology exam."

I closed my notebook and stood up to follow them out. "I better get a higher grade than you two. You never study for anything,"

"Born geniuses, Es," Ezra said as he slung his arm over my shoulder.

"Right," I said with a sigh as I smiled up at him. We walked out of the cafeteria, and I pulled my arm up around his waist.

## 23.
# PRESENT DAY

I'm just about to ask Solomon if we should go save Finnick from the draconian librarian when we hear what sounds like raindrops on a tin roof.

"What is that?" I ask as I go over to the window and peer out. I squint my eyes and look down at the scene below. "No, it can't be," I whisper in horror.

Solomon walks up beside me, and I hear his intake of breath. I clasp his arm as we helplessly watch what unfolds. On one side of the intersection below the library is a courtyard that links with a former YMCA, likely abandoned, its dark windows broken in. The courtyard has two ancient-looking benches and several trees. After blinking what feels like a thousand times, I am certain that I see two UFoA officers shooting machine guns at what appears to be three bodies tied to trees. The hands of the bodies are tied behind their backs, their faces covered by shirts pulled up over their heads. The gunfire feels endless, going on much longer than necessary.

People are peering out of their offices along the adjoining streets, and I lock eyes with a man in a building cattycorner to us. His eyes are filled with the same confusion and terror I feel, and my stomach is sick upon realizing how bad things have become. Thoughts race through my head. I suddenly remember history class where we did projects on the Holocaust of the Jews. I remember learning about the terror of the Jihadi in the Middle East and the suicide bombers who preyed on people's freedoms. I remember reading about the countless number of mass shootings. Mass shootings that went on for years, and no one did anything to stop them. Our predecessors failed us, and now we are here, stuck in this apocalyptic nightmare, where people shoot people tied to trees in the middle of a street, and no one does anything about it.

How did we not see this coming? How was no one able to stop it from getting this far?

"What's going on?" Finnick asks, coming up behind me. I can't bring myself to form words to answer his question. I just stare, and he walks up next to me and looks down to the street. I hear his intake of breath, my eyes still on the bodies. "Did they just . . ."

The same disbelief that radiates inside me is in his voice, and he's unable to complete his thought. His voice becomes firmer as he continues, "We need to leave. The librarian's patience with us has run out, and I think she's about to call the authorities." There's necessity in his voice, the need to rush, but he's still staring down at the street.

"We'll go to my friend's house in the woods outside Chester," Solomon answers.

"Is it safe?" I ask.

"It'll never be safe again," he says, and the three of us look back out the window one last time. We watch as the November wind blows against the bodies, still tied to the trees. The officers are gone but have left the remains as ghastly reminders to those of us who are against Alastor's plans.

*I had always been consumed by the idea of memories. They were mere shadows that were just out of my reach, yet they defined my reality. In the first weekly meeting as my mentor, Solomon described them to me as "the guaranteed existence of our identities." For months, I shared every memory of my parents I could think of with him—spewing them into the world like smoke from a fire. My hope had been that saying what they had done, articulating what they had said, would somehow make them alive again. It didn't, of course, but the process had helped me to heal.*

*I closed my eyes and tried to grasp those memories, to remember the once-uninteresting details of my day-to-day, of the life I had once lived. Each day, those details slipped farther out of my reach, and I was afraid of losing what I loved most about my past altogether.*

*I remembered Christmas morning—the smell of cinnamon rolls in the oven, and my father's laughter when I gave him the side eye for wearing his "Merry Christmas Ya Filthy Animal" t-shirt. Or the first day of middle school, when I had a fresh haircut, my nails painted, and an on-point outfit I had spent hours picking out. And one of my favorites, the first time I went sledding. I spent hours going down the hills with my mom, her blonde hair flowing behind her out of the knit wool cap she was wearing, her cheeks rosy with the cold as she turned to smile broadly at me and said, "Again!"*

*These moments in time were so fleeting. Had I only known that in the near future, I'd be holding onto them for dear life.*

We've been walking for so long that I've completely lost sense of time. This thought dawns on me as I watch the descent of the sun through the trees.

"What I would give for a car right now." I sigh in exasperation and stop to readjust my shoes in hopes of minimizing the growing number of blisters on my feet. I immediately feel guilty for complaining and pass Solomon a look of pity. His head dressing has started to deteriorate, part of it hanging down off the side of his head, making him look more like a disabled hobo than a wise professor.

"Almost there," he says quietly.

I'm amazed at how the man never complains. I stare at him admirably, wishing I had his courage, his unwavering faith.

I turn from Solomon to look around at the dark, barren trees that surround us in every direction. The ground is hard, frozen even, and the leaves are all dead. The last bit of sun slips away, and I can feel the temperature dropping. Shivering, I look ahead at Finnick to see how he's faring as the pack leader. His walk has always reminded me of a gazelle. He's become so slender over the last few months that the resemblances are even more glaring.

"How's it going up there, Boss?" I yell out to him. He's about two hundred yards ahead as he keeps his head moving back and forth to assure that he doesn't miss any sudden movements. "I don't want any surprises," he had told us sternly before we left.

"I'm good," he says now. I wait for more, but his words fall into the silence of the woods. The familiar pang of guilt forms a cloud in my stomach. After spending years, days, hours, and endless minutes together, it's easy for me to know what he's thinking. It didn't used to be that way. I used to spend hours trying to figure him out, to read his thoughts. Trauma connects us now, and I know that the woods reminds him of Rachael, which then reminds him that he's not sure whether he can really forgive me for what I did, and he certainly can't forget.

## 24.
# TWO YEARS EARLIER . . .

The night of the Winter Dance, there was a circus of butterflies fluttering through me. Goosebumps covered my arms as I took a few long, deep breaths to steady myself. On nights like those, I wished I had girlfriends and silently punished myself for only hanging out with Finnick and Ezra.

The dress I had bought gracefully draped to the floor and hugged all the right places; it was made of smooth satin with two thin spaghetti straps. The color, a rich, dark red, contrasted well with my long, blonde hair and light eyes. My mom had always loved me in red. I did my makeup for once, carefully applying black eyeliner, mascara, and a touch of bronzer that brought my pale skin to life. Sister Margaret had taken me and a few of the other girls shopping for our dresses. The whole time, my body had ached for my mother, from the tips of my fingers as I brushed the fabrics of the dresses to the deepest consoles of my heart.

I sat on the edge of my bed to put my strappy sandals on when there was a knock at the door. "Can I come in?" Rachael, Finnick's date, stood in the doorway looking nothing short of breathtaking. Her gown was an emerald green that perfectly matched the color of her wide, almond-shaped eyes. Her dark hair cascaded in waves down her back, and her plump lips were red, breaking apart as she smiled widely at me.

"Wow," I said before I could stop myself. My face went crimson.

She smiled wider. "Thanks! Your dress is beautiful," she said warmly. I just nodded, still embarrassed that I had given her the satisfaction of knowing she looked as good as she did. I didn't want to like Rachael.

As if reading my thoughts, I heard her say, "I hope we can be friends, Esther; I really care about Finn, and I know how much he cares about you."

A wave of contempt washed over me, and I knew it was wrong, but I just couldn't allow her to walk that easily into our lives. It was the three of us; four was a crowd.

But I just feigned a smile as I replied, "Of course we're friends, Rachael." I stood up then and wobbled for a second on the thin heels of my stilettos. I caught myself as I reached back to the bed for my wrap and pulled it tightly around my shoulders. "We should get going, though. The boys will be waiting."

She looked like she wanted to say more but just nodded and turned to follow me into the hall. We didn't talk much as we walked to the stairs, both of us lost in our own thoughts about the night ahead. The Sisters had gone all out and even decorated our dormitories with snowflakes and garland, so that as we began our walk down the stairs, it felt like something out of a movie.

Finn and Ezra were standing by the front door, dressed flawlessly in tuxedos, their hair freshly cut and gelled. It was hard to decide who was more handsome, and I felt my hands grow clammy as my heart started to race. Next to me, Rachael's breathing was unsteady, and I could tell she was just as nervous as I was.

Both boys looked up at the same time. I locked eyes with Ezra as his mouth dropped open, and he let out a low whistle. I smiled broadly at him, and he grinned back at me and winked. I cautiously walked down the steps until we were face to face. The rest of the world around me was fading, and all I could see were his gray eyes twinkling with excitement. I had the sudden urge to grab his face and kiss him. Without thinking it through, that is exactly what I did. He hesitated for only a second before he had his arms wrapped tightly around me, kissing me back.

"Whoooaa!" Finn shouted, his tone shocked. And maybe I imagined it, but it sounded like there was a hint of envy in it as well.

Rachael giggled and shrugged. "I guess she couldn't resist."

"That's enough, Children!" Sister Margaret came running at us, pushing us apart with her small arms.

"Sorry, Sister," Ezra and I muttered, but we were staring at each other, still reeling from the kiss.

"My goodness," Sister Margaret continued. "The book of Proverbs tells us that 'like a city whose walls are broken through is a person who lacks self-control.'"

"Yes, Sister." But I bit my tongue to keep from giggling.

"My sincere apologies, Sister Margaret; please know I have nothing but respect for our dear Esther Rose Warder," Ezra said charmingly, and I coughed back a laugh as Sister Margaret practically swooned.

"Unbelievable," Finnick whispered, but he was grinning.

Ezra clasped my hand in his, and we followed Finnick and Rachael outside, still laughing and smiling. There was an electricity in the air, the kind of anticipation when a night was just beginning, when I felt and looked my best and when I was with people who made me love life. It had been a long time since I had felt that kind of joy, and I allowed myself to relish in it. Nothing was going to break my spirit that night.

Or, at least, that's what I had thought.

# 25.
# PRESENT DAY

There's finally a clearing up ahead, and I can see the outline of a chimney. I'm so excited at the prospect of warming up and eating something, I practically start running. I'm side by side with Finn now, and he looks over at me. We make eye contact, and I smile. He lifts half of his mouth in a lopsided grin, and I feel the sense of relief that comes when he stops thinking about our past.

A robust man with a long beard is outside the cabin chopping wood. He is wearing an old flannel shirt, jeans, and a red plaid hat with ear flaps. A true lumberjack. His head jerks up when I step on a branch, and he lifts his axe in defense.

Solomon calls out to him, "Sanctum." Finn glances over at him, a little perplexed. "An old code word," Solomon tells us, and I watch as the man's shoulders visibly relax.

"Old friend," the man says as he embraces Solomon in a tight hug. "You look as though you've seen better days."

"Haven't we all. It is good to see you, Abram." Solomon smiles weakly. I cringe as he puts a hand to his head, sensing how much it still hurts. "Abram, this is Esther and Finnick. They were students of mine at the orphanage and have become like family. They are true soldiers of our cause, and you can trust them with your life. I certainly have with mine."

I feel tears burn my eyes and self-consciously look down.

"I am pleased to meet you both. The cause is blessed to have brave, young minds working toward a greater good. Now, please, all of you, come inside where it's warm. I am careful about making fires in fear of our enemies seeing the smoke; but it's almost dark, and we'll be safe." Abram smiles at us encouragingly, and we follow him through the door of the cabin.

As I walk through the door, I already feel better. I can smell bread and grin at Finn when I see cheese set out on the table. Abram catches my eye and nods. I cut hunks of cheese off, handing a piece to each of us. "How do you get food out here?" I ask in admiration.

"I'll fill you both in regarding our operation but know that you will not have to go hungry any longer. The network is ever-growing; we remain hidden, but powerful."

Solomon locks eyes with Abram. "This is Esther Warder. I'm sure you remember her parents." He says this as a statement, not a question, and my eyes whip from the bread to them.

"What? You knew my parents?" I practically yell, and Solomon looks at me disapprovingly. I lower my voice. "Sorry, I mean, it's just that I don't meet many people who knew my parents. How did you know them?"

"Oh, Esther, their names are quite popular with the Concealed," Abram answers.

"The Concealed?" Finn asks.

"Yes, that's the name of the operation. We felt the word 'underground' had enough of a history."

I let out a small laugh. "I like it . . . " I pause and then continue nervously. "Can you tell me about my parents; did they help the Concealed?"

Abram looks uncomfortable as he answers, "I would have thought you knew." He looks over at Solomon, who softly nods, before turning back to me. "It was your parents who started it."

*Our Esther,*

*We're writing this letter together, for it may be the most important one you read. There will come a time when you must rise up. You will know when this time is, for you'll feel the calling in your heart, just as we did. When that time comes, be brave. It is not this life, but the next, that endures, and it's so important for you to remember that. Please be careful who you trust; keep everyone at arm's length, for there are snakes behind every door. Remember that Second Peter warns us not only of false prophets but of false teachers. When times are trying, people will change. They will become selfish, cruel, and underhanded, caring only about their own needs for survival. Be wary of all these things.*

*We must confess something to you now that may change your perception of us. We are fighters who believe in the cause of righteousness. We do not condone or promote violence in any way, but there were times when we have had no choice but to resort to it. We will have to face God with what we have done. If and when you hear things regarding our actions, please know that we felt we had no other choice, and there was always a reason for the decisions we made.*

*Our love is with you now and always,*

*Mom and Dad*

I take a moment to digest what Abram has just told me before responding. I cast a look at Finnick, whose mouth is slightly open in both surprise and awe. "That actually makes a lot of sense," I finally say. "Their letters, which were often vague, hinted at things they were led to do that were difficult for them. I imagine that starting and then leading a resistance, such as this one, comes with some risks."

"You have inherited your parents' wisdom, then," Abram says solemnly.

"Hardly. They were far braver than I am and far less selfish." I avoid eye contact with Finnick as I say this, knowing he's been hurt by my selfishness more than anyone.

"You have never seen the light in yourself that others see," Solomon says. He lays a hand on my shoulder, and I look up at him. "The time has come for you to join us. We will prepare you to step up and take your parents' place."

"I was afraid you were going to say that." I smile at him weakly and shakily sit down on a stool next to the fireplace.

"Abram, we will need you to hack into the Federation's main system and locate a list of the locations being used to execute markings." Solomon continues as he keeps his eyes on me, "I will gather the council members, but Esther, I'd like you to speak to them on how to best proceed."

"The council?" I ask, swallowing the lump in my throat. Finnick is sitting against the wall in silence. He hasn't looked at me since Abram revealed who my parents were.

"Yes, Abram can send out a secure message that informs them of when and where to meet," Solomon replies. He seems to suddenly remember that Finnick is there as well and turns toward him. "She will need you now, Finnick, more than ever."

"She knows I am with her until the end." He stares at me compliantly, and there's a twinge of doubt in my heart. My mind goes back to the first time I saw Ezra after he left the orphanage and the hurt and distrust I felt when I realized whom he had chosen to become. I loved him, and he left me. There are now so many unspoken words that fall between Finnick and me as I return his gaze, and I silently pray he won't leave me, too.

# 26.
# TWO YEARS EARLIER . . .

"Punch?" Ezra asked breathlessly after we had shouted our lungs out dancing to Usher's "Yeah!"

"Please!" I shouted over the music and grabbed onto his hand as he weaved through the masses of people and hanging snowflakes to reach the refreshments. He poured us two full glasses of punch and handed me mine with a smile. I took a sip but sputtered when I realized it had been spiked. Ezra laughed good-naturedly.

"A bit strong, eh?" He smirked and gave my shoulder a soft push.

"I'd say. Someone's in a rush to get drunk."

"What's a high school dance without a little booze?" He laughed again, tipping up his cup and finishing the punch in one long gulp.

"I guess," I answered.

"Hey . . . wanna get out of here for a bit? I want to tell you something."

"Sure," I said with a smile, glad to have the chance to break away from all the other people. Large crowds had never really been my thing.

Ezra took my hand and laced my fingers with his own. I felt a ripple of warmth go through me. It was what I liked most about Ezra; he made me feel safe.

We sneaked out through the side door of the gymnasium, giggling as we walked briskly down the hall. I looked back over my shoulder to make sure we hadn't been seen.

"This way," Ezra whispered and pulled me into our science lab. "I thought it only right to come spend some time with our cactus." He chuckled and pulled two chairs together for us to sit next to it. I dissolved into giggles.

"He has been part of our relationship from the beginning," I confirmed in mock seriousness, hiding a smile. He was still holding my hand, facing me now, and I could feel his warm breath, fragrant traces of peppermint gum and alcohol, on my cheek. His dark gray eyes caught mine, and my heart literally stopped beating. Any doubts about my feelings for Ezra were gone now; he had me captivated.

"You're into me, right, Es?" He looked so vulnerable in this moment, and I felt the clamminess of his hand under my own.

"Unequivocally." I breathed the word softly, my heart pounding in my chest.

Ezra's shoulders relaxed before a look of passion washed over his face. "I was hoping you'd say that," he murmured, and suddenly we were kissing, his mouth hot on my own.

I ran my hands through his dark hair, yielding to his touch. I breathed him in and clasped his head to my face.

"Ezra," I whispered.

"Be my girl?" he asked, breaking away from me softly. He gently placed soft kisses on my nose, head, and cheek.

Before I could answer, we both looked toward the door at the sound of men's voices and rhythmic marching in the hallway.

"What in the . . . " Ezra jumped up and ran to look out the window of the classroom door.

"What is it?" I stood and brushed down my now-disheveled hair.

"Officers . . . How odd. They're in uniforms I don't recognize."

"Oh no. Do you think it has to do with Mother Maura's announcement about banning Bibles?"

"Could be. They look pretty serious." I peered over Ezra's shoulder as he said this and saw the humorless faces of two men who had paused to talk to Mother Maura. "I'm going out there."

"What?" I said in surprise. "You are not." But he was already opening the door and walking toward the men. My palms started to sweat in concern, and I kept the door open a crack to listen.

"Ezra," Mother Maura said, clearly caught off-guard by his presence, "What are you doing here?"

"I thought I might be able to help." He turned toward the officers and reached out his hand. "Ezra Lodge," he said with assurance.

A tall, burly man with sandy hair returned his handshake. "Nice to meet you, young man. I'm Officer McCaskey. Perhaps you can answer a couple of questions for us."

Mother Maura looked visibly uncomfortable. I watched as she wrung her hands in front of her and looked at Ezra nervously.

But before Ezra had the chance to answer, the officer next to McCaskey cut in. "You look familiar, Son; have we met before?"

Ezra took a moment to consider his question, looking over the Hispanic man of medium height. "I don't think so, sir," he responded.

The man continued scrutinizing Ezra with his eyes. "McCaskey, a word please," he said severely.

"Excuse us," McCaskey said, bowing slightly to Mother Maura and nodding at Ezra.

My eyes, wide open, watched as the men walked to the side, whispering conspiratorially and casting glances at Ezra. What was going on? Ezra looked as confused as I felt.

"You should go now, Ezra," Mother Maura told him sternly.

"But . . ."

"I said go."

"Yes, ma'am." He threw a quick glance my way before heading obediently in the opposite direction. I let out a breath but didn't move as I watched the men come back toward Mother Maura.

"That boy," Officer McCaskey began. "How long has he been under your care?"

"Ezra? Let me think. He's been here since he was ten years old, and he's about sixteen now, I think. Why do you ask?" Mother Maura looked at the men quizzically.

Ignoring her question, McCaskey looked at the other officer. "Six years ago would be the right timeframe." The other officer nodded in agreement. McCaskey turned back toward Mother Maura. "Come along, Sister. We'll talk further in your office. There is paperwork to fill out."

Poor Mother Maura. She looked so distressed and confused. And why were they so concerned about Ezra?

I waited a few minutes to be sure the coast was clear before slipping out the door of the lab. I was about to slide through the gym door and return to the dance when a hand grabbed onto my shoulder. I gasped and jumped, letting out a small scream.

"Shhh! It's just me," Finn said hurriedly. Rachael was beside him, all doe-eyed and beautiful. "Where have you been?" he demanded.

"I, um, uh, nowhere. Why?" I stuttered, feeling my cheeks flame red.

"Where's Ezra? There's something going on. President Alastor's officers are everywhere. They have different uniforms than any other soldiers I've seen in this country. And they seem to be on a mission. All the sisters are frantic."

"Why would they care about an orphanage?" I asked.

"I think they're doing sweeps. You know, making sure the rules are being enforced. I saw them take down the crucifix leading into the East Wing. I even heard one tell Sister Margaret that her necklace was inappropriate."

"What was on her necklace?"

"A cross." Rachael chimed in now, nervously.

"Oh, man. The sisters didn't do much to comply with their requests; do you think they're in trouble?"

"Yes. I think they're in more trouble than they realize. I'm worried about a takeover," Finn answered.

"A takeover?" Rachael asked anxiously.

"Yeah, like, they'll be running this place soon, not the sisters . . ."

"Unless we don't let them." Ezra came up behind us and put a hand on my arm. My heart skipped a beat. "C'mon," he continued. "Let's get out of here. I say we all head back to the dorms and try to figure this out."

"Works for me," I said, and Finn and Rachael nodded in agreement. We walked outside, and Ezra allowed them to walk ahead, pulling my arm back to keep me next to him.

"Sorry I left you there," he whispered. "I wanted to help Mother Maura. I felt bad for her."

"No, I understand." I squeezed his hand. "So weird, though, how those officers were staring at you, I mean."

"Right? Like they knew me or something . . ."

"But that's impossible. You've been in the confines of the orphanage for the last six years."

"Do you think, Es, it is possible they knew my dad? I know that might be a long shot, but maybe I could try to contact them and see. I could find the answers I have been looking for about my parents' deaths."

There was a pit in my stomach at the thought of Ezra needing anything from these men, but I didn't want to dash this newfound hope he had. I knew the importance of a glimmer of hope. I turned to him and smiled. "I think that's a great idea."

A few months later, Ezra would be gone.

## 27.
# PRESENT DAY

Solomon arranged for the council meeting to be held in the basement of an old chicken processing facility in a very small town called Elkton, about an hour outside Headquarters and quite possibly the loneliest and most barren town I have ever seen. It's like zombies came through and killed everyone off. I look around at the closed down shops and the broken windows of the row homes and expect to see a tumbleweed blow past me.

"Nice place," Finnick jokes.

"It's like everyone died or something. Super depressing," I say.

"I heard the Federation has been taking people from smaller towns and moving them to larger towns and cities, so they have less areas to monitor. It works in our favor, at least," Solomon adds pleasantly.

I appreciate his positive spin on the situation, but the thought of millions of people being consolidated brings on images of ghettos and run-down barracks I can't erase from my mind. And I can't help but think of how much easier it is to kill people when they're all in one place. This is what my life has become, a mind pervaded by morbid images. I hide my concern, though, and force a smile for Solomon's sake, who is finally resembling the human race again. His head wounds have healed to the point where he was able to remove his bandages, and the color has returned to his face. After staying at Abram's for a week, eating full meals and sleeping through the night, we all feel better.

"How many council members are there?" I ask Abram now, who drove us to the factory in his pick-up truck. After parking in a wooded area outside of town, he's been stealthily leading the way to the factory.

"Eight in total," he answers. I nod, and he continues. "They each represent a different region throughout the country. Some have had to go to great lengths to be with us today, so we need to make it worth their while. The meeting will be lengthy."

I nod again. I don't feel like I can express my fears out loud, but in truth, I feel way out of my league and not at all prepared to help lead a room of avengers into the dark pits of an apocalypse. Yet how do you really prepare for that?

"Looks like someone beat us here," Finnick says as he approaches the back, metal door of the facility. It's been left slightly open, held that way by the support of a small rock.

"Let me go first and check things out. I'll come back out here and get you when I know the coast is clear," Abram tells us as he pulls a gun from the back of his waist band.

Finnick, Solomon, and I silently agree and back away from the door to wait. I kick my feet uncomfortably in the dirt, my heart racing at the thought of addressing the council.

"Did you prepare?" Finnick asks snidely. He's been giving me the cold shoulder all week.

I whip toward him, ready for a fight. "What's your deal now, Finn? Because they're training me and not you? Is that it? You've barely spoken to me since we found out about my parents," I snap. As I spit the words out, I feel all the pent-up anxiety I have about the meeting being spewed into the air.

But he doesn't miss a beat, like he's been waiting for this opportunity. "It's just unbelievable, really, that you didn't know who they were," he retorts angrily.

I bark out a sarcastic laugh. "You're too much, you know that? You think I want this? Please, take the reins, almighty Finnick; you always do know best."

"Maybe I will when you flounder in there and humiliate yourself."

He glares at me with contempt, and my eyes burn with tears.

"Enough," Solomon says firmly, placing a hand on both of our shoulders. Mine are shaking with sobs, and I silently berate myself for crying. "Whatever has happened between you two needs to be resolved. For good. There is far too much at stake to turn against each other. That is what they wish; don't you see that?"

"Of course, Professor, sorry," Finn mumbles but avoids both our eyes.

"I know," I say, wiping the tears off my face. "He just needs to forgive me, but he can't."

Finn grunts angrily. "How could I? You killed her."

"Finnick," Solomon's voice is steely. "That is enough."

## 28.
# TWO YEARS EARLIER . . .

After the night of the dance, Ezra and I had become official, but so had Finnick and Rachael. I was doing my best to accept Rachael, but I didn't entirely trust her. Maybe it was because of who her parents had been—two key players in the rise of Alastor, who were killed during a surprise attack on an underground resistance meeting. Rachael had shamefully told us this information when we asked, but your parents are your parents, ya know? I couldn't help but think that a part of her believed what they did.

But what was more important right now was that Ezra would not let things go. He had become more determined than ever to find out what happened to his parents. It was like those officers recognizing him that night ignited his resolve to know the truth.

"I'm going to do it. Tonight is the night. I'm sneaking into Mother Maura's office." The gray of Ezra's eyes swam in hope and trepidation as he looked at me for confirmation that he was doing the right thing.

We were sitting on one of the two homely couches in the common room waiting for Finnick and Rachel to join us, so we could all go to dinner. For the last couple of weeks, Ezra had been playing around with the idea of stealing his file from Mother Maura's office. She had a filing cabinet that contained all the secrets of our lives under lock and key. Honestly, I was scared of what he would find, but I knew I needed to be there for him.

"Okay," I said supportively. "Do you need me to go with you?"

He looked at me fondly for a minute before smiling. "I think I might be in love with you."

Both sides of my face lifted in a wide grin. The thought had occurred to me for a while. I had allowed the idea to grow in my mind since the night of the dance. But it felt good to finally hear the words. "Me, too," I said softly, moving closer to him and taking his hand.

"I don't, though. Need you to come with me, I mean. It's not worth us both getting caught. And I think it's something I need to do on my own." He ran a hand through his hair as he tapped his foot against the linoleum floor.

"I get it," I said, thinking of my parents' letters and how I had never let anyone else read them. "I'll be here when and if you want to talk about it." He nodded worriedly, and I continued, "No matter what you find."

"What are you two conspiring about now?" Finnick said as he plopped down on the couch next to me. Rachael stood awkwardly next to him.

"I'm going to take the plunge tonight and break into Mother Maura's office," Ezra said firmly, his mind made up.

"Cool. I mean, I was kind of sick of hearing about it, man. No offense," Finnick said with a laugh. "Just bite the bullet, you know." He paused. "Did you figure out how you'll open the cabinet?"

"I've been practicing picking locks," Ezra responded. "There are similar cabinets in the nurse's office for supplies and charts and stuff. I go there during her lunch."

"That's bold," Finnick said.

"I didn't know that," I said, a little hurt.

"It's not a big deal, babe." Ezra smiled over at me as he put a hand on my leg.

Rachael, who had been silent until now, said, "What will you do if you're caught?"

"I'll tell her the truth. That I know she knows more than I do, and I want answers," Ezra responded assuredly. "How can she, or anyone, fault me for that?"

"I agree. I think we all deserve the truth." I thought about all the questions that haunted me nightly about my own parents. Finnick and Ezra looked at me sympathetically, but Rachael's face stayed passive.

"They didn't tell you anything about your parents' deaths?" she asked.

"They told me they were robbed and shot while doing mission work in Brazil. They had left early that morning for a trip to South America, and I was supposed to go home with a friend after school. None of it made any sense; they wouldn't have even landed yet from their flight, but they were killed while there? I asked for more details, but no one knew anything. At least, nothing that they would tell me. I was so overcome with grief; it was hard to dig further. Now, though, I question whether they were even going to South America at all."

"Why?" Rachael asked.

"Just because of what they told me in the letters they left. I was pretty much lied to my whole life." I looked right at her as I continued, "So, yeah, the truth might be nice."

Finnick threw me a strange look. "It's not like Rachael would know."

"Yeah, but her parents might have," I said icily. Rachael's face went red, and to her credit, she looked embarrassed. "Okay, sorry, that's not fair," I added when I saw that Finnick was about to go ballistic on me.

"No, it's not," Finnick said, his eyes squinting at me angrily.

"I said sorry, okay? Let's just go eat and forget it." I stood to show I was done with the conversation. I heard Rachael whispering softly to Finnick and fought the urge to roll my eyes. Rachael was hiding something. I knew it. There was no way anyone was that naïve without some kind of agenda. Ezra gave me an understanding look, and I took his hand as we walked toward the cafeteria.

# 29.
# PRESENT DAY

"Everything looks good," Abram says as he comes through the metal door of the factory to meet us outside. Sensing the tension, he looks from me, to Finnick, to Solomon, and back to me again. "What'd I miss?"

"Nothing," I mumble. "Let's go."

I start to walk toward the door, but Finnick grabs my shoulder. My insides kick with the desire to shove him off of me, but I just turn my head slightly instead.

He looks at me now, the picture of sincerity. "You've got this. I know I'm a jerk. But don't let it stop you from being who you're supposed to be." He drops his head, and there's a flood of memories and emotions flowing through me—so much history that is both tying us together and pushing us apart.

"Don't worry about it. Another day, another fight, right?" I mean it as a joke, but there's too much truth behind it for either of us to laugh. I begin to wonder whether Finnick and I would have anything to do with each other if it wasn't for the disasters that link us.

I take a deep breath and turn away from him to push the door open. I walk through the warehouse wordlessly, letting Abram lead the way as I try to recenter my thoughts on the words I've prepared. The floor is still covered with feathers, and the room is filled with old cages. I feel sick at the idea of any living creature surviving in these conditions and shake my head to rid of the imagery of the country's former food crisis. Technically, I guess there is still a crisis; it's just that now the crisis is that there is no food.

We come upon a conference room at the edge of the building, likely used for the head honchos of the former chicken industry to count their money. I see a group of men and women, mostly middle-aged, sitting around the table, and the sensation of being in over my head overwhelms me all over again.

"You got this," Finnick says as he squeezes my shoulder.

I nod with what I hope is a sense of confidence and follow Abram into the room.

My eyes sweep the room, and I try to pause on each face for a moment, looking for any familiarities and memorizing their features. I look over at Solomon for guidance. He senses my apprehension and puts a warm hand on my arm as he addresses the council.

"Old friends," he says, his face lighting up in a broad smile, "It is with great joy and fond memory that I present to you the daughter of Caleb and Lucille Warder. I think you will find that she shares their courage, their strength, and, most importantly, their faith. Join me in welcoming Esther here today."

The council applauds; everyone is smiling at me as if they have known me my whole life. I fight off my nerves as I return a timid smile and clear my throat.

"Welcome, Friends. I'm so glad you are here," I start. Some nod their heads slightly, while others give me an encouraging smile. "There is much I want to go over with you today, and it is my hope that by the time we leave here, we will have a definitive plan of action moving forward. Many of you, if not all of you, knew my parents. As you also may or may not know, I lost them very young and have been left with a lot of unanswered questions. I look forward to the opportunity to connect with each of you to gain a better understanding of not just what happened to them but also their mission and presence in this life." I feel a sob begin in my throat and swallow hard before continuing. "The actions of the UFoA have escalated. There are now secret abductions and public assassinations of those who refuse to take their mark and follow their mandates. We cannot stand idle any longer. The measures we have taken up to this point are not enough. We must do more. I have come up with a proposal that groups us into various locations where the UFoA is planning to execute the mark. A kind thank you to Abram for risking his life to find this list."

I look over at Abram, and he gives me a reserved smile. Everyone applauds, and I see his cheeks grow pink as I continue. "I'm passing around copies of the proposal now; please look over it and arrange yourselves according to your Resistance group. I constructed them by the regions where you currently live; but if I've made any errors, let me know, and we'll work it out."

The council members stand up and move next to those closest to them in region, murmuring amongst themselves.

"Esther," calls out a man with graying hair who looks to be about forty-five. "It's nice to finally meet you. I'm Harry Peters."

"Hi, Harry," I greet him with a warm smile. "What can I do for you?"

"First of all, I want to tell you how much I cared for your parents. For years, their bravery kept the acts of atrocity we're seeing now from escalating. I wish there were more people out there like them."

A wave of emotion washes over me as I think about my parents. They were brave.

I see my dad holding the shirt on my back as I ride my first bike, my mom holding the strap to my harness as she teaches me to ski. All the while, they were fighting against forces I had no idea existed.

"Thank you, Harry; that means a lot to me. I miss them very much." I smile and continue. "What else is on your mind?" Out of the corner of my eye, I see Solomon look at me with pride, and I take a deep breath as I meet Harry's eyes.

"How will we go about destroying these centers you reference on the proposal?"

"Well, I was originally thinking we might try to plant bombs, but it may be easier to burn them down as was done at the Church of the Divine Truth after my broadcast. Speaking of that fire, does anyone know who was responsible?"

A young woman, not much older than me, responds. "I heard it was a Resistance effort from Harmony, once called the New England states; they were in the area recruiting when they heard your transmission."

Harmony represents a region President Alastor renamed when he took over; he coined various sections of the country with monikers synonymous with unity.

"We need to reach out to them and grow our efforts." I look over at Finnick, who is taking notes for the meeting. "Finnick, can you take care of that?"

He nods once, not meeting my eyes. "On it."

"Is everyone clear on their duties? I know it seems wrong to burn down churches, and it will hurt all of us, but the alternative is worse. We are out to save souls here, not buildings." I look around to make sure everyone agrees.

"I couldn't agree more, Child; we must remember when Jesus cleansed the temple. He will support us in our mission, as our intentions are pure," Solomon says, standing up beside me. The members of the council nod their heads, and there's a hum of agreement throughout the room.

"If that matter is settled, then there is one more thing that I would like to propose. Finnick, it involves you as well; so, if you aren't comfortable with going through with what I'm about to suggest, I'll go alone."

"Let's hear it," he retorts.

I inhale slowly and pause. Everyone is staring at me, including Finnick, who looks both annoyed and intrigued. I let out my breath, and the words come out in a rush. "I think Finnick and I should break into Alastor's headquarters."

# 30.
# TWO YEARS EARLIER . . .

I was on a bench behind St. Mary's, and my heart was racing as I waited for Ezra. He told me if he wasn't back in twenty minutes to go and get Finnick to find out what happened. It had been seventeen minutes and three seconds, and I was going to puke from anxiety if he didn't show soon.

It was May and had been months since our run-in with Officer McCaskey, but Ezra was finally taking steps to find out how they might be connected to him or his parents. We had been up until three that morning, hiding out in the janitor's closet in my dorm hall with a flashlight and a notebook. He couldn't work up the nerve to go the night before, so we had come up with a plan that we went over and over again; it consisted of Ezra picking the lock on the door and breaking into Mother Maura's office, pulling his file, and jotting down everything he could find out before anyone saw him.

There was a faculty meeting every Tuesday before lunch, so he had about an hour to get in and out. We had listed all the possible scenarios of what could go wrong, with the best being that the file spelled out exactly what happened to his parents and he escaped with no one seeing him, and the worst being that he got caught and was told he would be moving to a different orphanage before he had even read his file. I wished for a phone like I had back when my parents were alive. It would be so much easier for him to just take screenshots of the information from his file, but technology of any kind had never been allowed. The Sisters told us it would interfere with our education, but I always thought they just wanted to hide us from the world.

"Psst." I heard a hiss from the bushes and spun around.

"Ezra!" I jumped up off the bench.

"Shhh," he whispered. "I felt like I was being followed."

I looked behind him and around the quad but didn't hear or see anything but the birds singing and the hum of Old Man Larson, the groundskeeper, mowing the grass.

"Who would be following you?" I whispered back.

"I don't know . . ." he trailed off. "I'm probably just being paranoid." He scanned the area around us. "Let's go to the café. I want to grab something to eat, and I'll fill you in." He grabbed my hand, and I immediately felt calmer.

I stroked his index finger with my thumb as we started walking. He seemed far away, though; his mind was on whatever just happened in Mother Maura's office, and I was anxious to hear the details.

We grabbed chicken sandwiches, a plate of fries to share, and two chocolate milks before finding a seat in the far corner of the cafeteria by the windows. We saw Professor Darci and gave him a wave; he smiled as he headed toward the "grab and go" section. Most students had already eaten; it was the tail end of the lunch hour, and aside from a few stragglers lost in their notes or a book, it was just us.

There used to be a banner on the wall that displayed the verse of the week and a crucifix next to the bulletin board of weekly events. The banner and crucifix were gone now, the religious signs of the orphanage slowly diminishing at the hands of the new mandates.

"Did you hear how they fired Professor Rhoda?" I asked Ezra, taking a bite of a French fry. "Apparently, she refused to change her curriculum."

Professor Rhoda taught literature and always integrated sections of the Bible into our lessons to supplement what we were studying. There are so many biblical allusions in literature, so they were an easy fit.

"I don't know if I would say 'fired' as much as 'forcefully removed,'" Ezra responded. "My buddy, Thomas, told me he saw an officer putting her in a car. She looked pretty upset."

My stomach churned. I put the fry I was holding back onto the plate. "I'm scared, Ezra. I think it's only going to get worse."

"It's definitely going to get worse." He stared out the window distractedly, his face contorted with concern.

"So, what did you find out? Was there anything about your parents?"

"No, that part of the file just stated that they had died in an accident."

I reached across the table and touched his hand. "Oh no . . . " I trailed off. "I know how much you were hoping for something more."

"Well, there was something, though," he said, pausing to look around, ensuring no one was listening. I squeezed his hand, encouraging him to continue. "There was a log of phone calls."

"Weird. Who were they talking to?"

"The main headquarters of the United Federation of Acceptance."

"Super weird." I thought back to the officers' faces the night of the dance, their look of recognition as they stared at Ezra. "So, they probably know more than they said that night."

"Exactly, and I'm not letting it go."

"Okay, so what next?"

"I'm going to confront Mother Maura."

"Are you sure that's smart? She'll punish you if she knows you broke into her office."

"I have a right to know, Esther; it's my life. They were my parents. If there's more to their deaths than I was led to believe, which I know there is, then she should have told me. I mean, who does she think she is to keep something like that from me?" He raised his voice angrily, and I noticed a couple standing at the vending machine looking over.

"Shhh! Keep your voice down," I whispered. "She may not even know anything. Give her the benefit of the doubt."

Ezra was tapping his foot in frustration. "I just want answers." He sighed.

"I know. And we'll get some, I promise. Approach Mother Maura then, but just say that you haven't been able to forget about what happened that night. Don't mention the phone logs. Tell her the truth about your concerns. She's a good woman; she may be honest with you."

"I doubt it." He took a deep breath and met my eyes. "But I will try what you're suggesting. If it doesn't work, though, I'm going to contact Headquarters myself."

# 31.
# PRESENT DAY

My proposal to raid Alastor's headquarters is first met with silence before Solomon's voice projects his outrage. "Absolutely not! It's too dangerous."

Solomon is still standing next to me and grabs my arm as he speaks. I don't respond; my eyes haven't left Finnick's face. He's sitting in silence, and when I don't say anything in response to Solomon, that silence is deafening. The rest of the council members appear uncomfortable, tapping their pens absently and looking away from all three of us.

"If I might . . ." Harry speaks hesitantly, raising his hand halfway to be acknowledged. "I understand your fears, Solomon, but if we plan it down to every last detail and have people in place to protect them, I think it might actually be a good idea. If they were to succeed, think of how much we could do for the cause." The heads of the other council members nod around him, and I can see that gaining everyone else's support won't be the issue.

My eyes are still on Finnick, whose forehead is scrunched in thought. He's deciding—not whether or not he can take on such a dangerous plan, but whether he can do it with me. He doesn't trust me, and I can't even blame him.

It feels like everything that's happened since the day we met in the chapel of St. Mary's is standing in this room between us, a barricade keeping us apart. My insides shudder, and my mind goes back to his face on the day of Rachael's death. I would do anything to go back . . . But even as I think it, I know it's not true. I'd make the same choice again.

# 32.
# TWO YEARS EARLIER . . .

Just as we had feared, things at St. Mary's kept getting worse. Sister Margaret had made an announcement that there would no longer be any chapel service in the mornings. Teachers started randomly disappearing and were replaced by much more militant instructors, who gave us new uniforms and who seemed to discourage all forms of free thinking. We started reading literature on the rights of the paganists and the injustices brought on the world by Christians and Jews. We were strongly encouraged to embrace the new bylaws of the UFoA and employ their ideals in our words, thoughts, and actions. Alastor's adopted mission statement, "We are all the same. Conform for peace," had become our new motto, printed and posted in all our classrooms and common areas; it was essentially being shoved down our throats.

"Accept. Accept. Accept," our new teacher, Sergeant Hall, chanted as we streamed into class.

I cast a sideways glance at Rachael, who had world history with me, and we both grimaced as he continued. "We are all the same. Embrace unity and conform. World peace comes when we stand down." He looked around at the class as the second bell rang and smiled widely. "Good morning to you all. I hope the words I spoke as you came in ring true in all your hearts. World peace has been a long-time objective for many, and President Alastor is determined that it will occur under his term. What better goal can a president have? He is an admirable man."

I looked around to see if my classmates were as appalled as I was. Most were avoiding eye contact with Sergeant Hall, but I saw a few who actually looked excited and attentive. I turned back toward the front as he continued. "Now, we must then look at the forces that need to be squashed in order for this objective to be carried out. We have allowed Christians and Jews to discriminate against those who wish to live and love freely for far too long. They dare to cast their judgement on their fellow man. Make no mistake, they are our enemy in our attainment of peace."

My blood was boiling so hot; I could feel it rise to my face. I sat on my hands and bit the inside of my cheek to keep from making a scene. I saw my classmate, Judah, stand up. *Sit down; it's not the time.*

"Sir, with all due respect, you are asking us to not think for ourselves." Judah stood there confidently, and my insides deflated, knowing that his boldness would not end well.

"It's Judah, right?" the sergeant's face was placid, but there was a hint of condescension in his tone.

"Yes."

"Would you call yourself a Christian? Would you say that you adhere to the laws of the Christian God, Who says He will judge—how does He put it—'the depraved mind?'"

"Proudly, I am, yes; for I feel . . . "

The sergeant put his finger up to pause him and went over to his desk. He jotted down a few notes before looking back up at Judah in disdain, motioning with his hand to proceed.

Judah shuffled his feet anxiously as he continued. "It's just that I do believe, of course, that we should love our neighbors, but God is clear about sexual perversion and immorality. He didn't create us to love freely but wants us to love within the sanctity of marriage, as He intended, you know?" His confidence was diminishing, and his eyes darted around the room in hopes of some support. I wanted to stand up, too, and have his back, but it was like my body was made of lead. I looked over at Rachael, whose face was ashen.

"No, I would say that I certainly do not know. If you'll just come up front here, young man." The sergeant smiled bitterly and beckoned to Judah to come forward. "Judah's beliefs stand in contrast with the peaceful world we wish to create. What do you suppose we do about that, Class?"

No one said anything for what felt like an eternity. Then I saw a boy in the back raise his hand. His face was twisted in a sneer as he responded to the question. "I say we punish him. There is no room in this world for their self-righteous opinions. Love is love; your body is your body. Who is he to tell us what to believe?" There were a couple murmurs of agreement, and I felt bile rise in my throat.

Was this for real?

"A punishment? Yes, I think you are on to something there," the sergeant responded. "What do you propose?"

The question took up all the air in the room. I couldn't breathe. I could hear my parents in my head telling me to stand up for what was right. *Stand up, Esther.* I didn't move. My body was immobile. I gaped in horror when a student responded.

A girl with short, dark hair stood up and said, "He should be ostracized and humiliated like so many of our people have been because people like him made them feel inadequate or bullied them into submission."

The first boy shouted his assent. The sergeant nodded his head in agreement and went to the cabinet to pull out a piece of construction paper, a ball of yarn, and a black sharpie. Judah looked like he was going to pass out, or throw up, or both.

"Let me think . . . A word for one who finds themselves morally superior . . . Plaster Saint has a nice ring to it," the sergeant quipped, and a few students chuckled. We watched as he wrote out PLASTER SAINT in capital letters on the paper, punched two holes in the top, and laced through a piece of yarn. "You will wear this sign around your neck for the remainder of the week, or you will be put on the streets where I will personally ensure that your fate is not a pleasant one. Do you understand?" Judah gave a weak nod. "It doesn't have to be this way, Judah; we want to accept all who accept others. Let this change your heart. We will speak again at the end of the week."

Judah silently placed the string of the sign around his neck, his former courage gone and a look of resignation in its place.

## 33.
# PRESENT DAY

Harry's encouragement of my idea to break into Alastor's offices had changed the atmosphere of the room. I could feel the growing excitement.

"Okay, I'm in." Finnick looks at me decidedly, his lips a firm line. "What exactly do you have in mind?"

I reach into my bag and pull out blueprints of the main headquarters, spreading them out on the table. Finnick moves toward me in surprise. "How did you land those?"

I look over at Abram. "I have friends in high places," I say with a smile.

Finnick lets out half a laugh before he can stop himself. "Good one," he teases, while looking over my shoulder at the plans. "Let me check it out."

The tension between us dissipates slightly, and I want to capitalize on the feeling, to nurture its growth.

"I can work on getting you new identities and papers. You'll need security clearances," Abram says, briefly looking up from his laptop. "I also know a man on the inside, whose name is Elden Keillor. He'll help, but it will be a big risk for him."

"That would be really helpful, Abram; thank you. What is Elden's position?" I ask.

"He works in IT. One of my connections. It was how I was able to obtain those blueprints for you. He has two small children, and I frequently worry about his safety. But I guess that's the world we live in now."

I give him an encouraging smile. "Be sure to tell him how much we appreciate everything he's doing. We wouldn't have come this far without him."

The young woman whose name I learn is Mary and who spoke earlier chimes in. "You'll also need to change the style of your hair and dye it. I can help with that. I went to cosmetology school before the takeover."

"That would be great; thank you," I say looking over at Solomon, who hasn't said anything else since his previous objections. "Are you going to be okay with this?" I ask, holding his eyes with my own.

He watches me a moment, pursing his lips. "I still don't like it, but it would seem I am outnumbered."

"I promise we'll be careful, and it's not like we'll be alone. We'll have each other," I say with confidence, hoping to prove to Finnick that I want him by my side. He is busy taking down notes as he examines the blueprints. I notice where he's marked the location of Alastor's office and drawn a route there from the fire escape. He looks up briefly and nods.

"I'll look out for her, Professor," he says before turning his attention to Abram. "Can you show me exactly where Elden works on here?" He taps the prints with his pen. Abram comes over and points to a large room on the other side of the building.

"Hmm, that's not ideal is it?" Abram murmurs.

"No, not especially. But could he disengage the fire alarm on the escape door near Alastor's office without it being tracked?"

"Perhaps. It would be less risky than him having to let you in himself."

"Right," Finnick agrees.

"I'll see what he says."

I look at Abram in concern. "But how will we know when we won't be interrupted? We'll need to find out Alastor's schedule and that of his personal secretary. The office is bound to be heavily guarded as well." I start pacing back and forth; there is so much I hadn't thought through.

"You'll need a distraction, like what you did in Lawrence when you gave the broadcast," Harry interjects. He's been listening to our conversation, while planning the burnings of the centers with the other council members. "We can arrange to have a fire at a center nearby at the same time; that should help create a diversion."

"Terrific idea, Harry." I stop pacing and begin rummaging through my notes. "I have a record of where each of the centers are located, so I could distribute them to you all; they're here somewhere." I'm sifting through the folder when it slips from my hand, scattering papers all over the floor. "Idiot," I mutter to myself, leaning to pick them up. Finnick kneels down next to me to help.

"Take it easy, Es." His hand lands on mine as we reach for a paper. "We're pretty much the best team ever at this point, right?" He moves his hand to place it gently on the side of my face, his eyes imploring mine. "We got this."

My throat tightens, and I hear the waver in my voice. "Promise?"

"Have I ever let you down?" He smiles wearily, the bluish black of sleepless nights dark under his eyes.

No. That's my job.

# 34.
# TWO YEARS EARLIER . . .

It was about a week after the incident with Judah, and Ezra and I had planned to meet up at my locker before first period. I watched him now as he raced down the hall, his eyes dancing with fury and apprehension.

"Whoa." I put my hand up as if to stop him. "What's the big rush?"

I leaned in for a kiss. He kissed me back quickly, clearly distracted. "Sorry, it's just that I keep replaying what I'm going to say to Mother Maura." He lowered his head and lightly pounded his fists against the hard metal of the locker next to mine. "I don't want to freak out on her, but I feel so angry that she's keeping information from me."

"I get it. I really do. But you won't get anywhere by yelling at her. Did you schedule an appointment?"

"Yeah, it's at 8:45. Not sure how I'll focus through calculus," he said, sighing.

"Who can ever focus in calculus?"

"True." He laughed, holding the door for me.

We took our seats, and Professor Darci started talking about differential equations and partial derivatives, as my eyes glazed over. I looked over to my right and noticed that Judah, who had math with me the past two years, wasn't there. I had been hoping to tell him that I was sorry I hadn't defended him in world history last week. I shuddered thinking about his face, crimson with embarrassment.

"Psst," I hissed at Ezra. He raised his eyebrows in question, and I mouthed, "Where's Judah?"

He shrugged and looked back toward the front. I felt an uneasy pit forming in my stomach. He had worn the sign all week like Sergeant Hall wanted. I had seen him here in calculus and in the cafeteria, his face a mix of shame and indignation. In world history, he had kept to himself, never daring to speak when Sergeant Hall asked a question. Maybe he was sick. Or maybe he had to meet with another teacher.

I wouldn't let my mind go somewhere else because there was no way they would actually put him out on the streets, right? I shook my head to be rid of the thought.

Forty excruciatingly long minutes later, the bell rang, and Ezra and I dashed for the door like it was the last day of school. He kissed my forehead and headed for his meeting with Mother Maura.

"Good luck," I said over my shoulder, walking toward my locker to switch textbooks. I had English next, which used to be my favorite subject, but the new instructor, Sergeant Barnes, took away our poetic license. Now, we only write about compliance and read literature on non-traditional relationships.

"Es-Es-ther," Rachael panted, as she ran up next to me, her beautiful eyes full of horror.

I shut my locker door. "Oh no. What? Is it Finnick?"

"No, no, nothing like that. Come outside. It's so horrible, I can't even . . . I just . . . " She didn't finish her sentence, just pulled my arm toward the door, and my feet stumbled over each other.

"Okay, slow down; I'm coming."

She pushed open the doors, and we walked onto the concrete, five steps up from the ground. Rachael pointed over to a tree next to the tennis courts, and my breath caught in my throat. Judah was hanging from a branch, his mouth gaped open in surprise, his face a grotesque purple stemming from his swollen neckline. The sign screamed "PLASTER SAINT" across the school grounds, beating against his chest as his body swayed. I ran down the steps and dry heaved into the bushes, nausea filling my bloodstream as my pores filled with sweat.

"Di-d Sergeant Hall do this?" I sputtered.

"Everyone's saying it was suicide. That there was a note."

"No way, I'm not buying it," I said into my knees, the ground blurring around me. *Breathe, Esther.*

Rachael kicked the ground, her eyes filled with tears. "Me either. I feel so bad that we didn't stand up for him."

"It makes me hate myself."

"Finnick's in chorus; he's practicing for his solo at the concert tonight, so I didn't want to interrupt him."

"There'll be no keeping this quiet." I took a deep breath, the nausea having subsided to feelings of dread and disgust.

"It's already spreading all over campus. You should tell Ezra."

"He's meeting with Mother Maura right now, so I'll have to wait. Are they just going to let him hang there?" Large groups of students had gathered outside; everyone stood gawking at Judah's body. I caught whispers of "suicide" and "he was always strange."

How typical. People were already playing it off. It was a beautiful day, but I felt like I was choking on the air, like I might suffocate if I had to stand there for another second.

"C'mon," I told Rachael. "I'm late for English."

## 35.
# PRESENT DAY

Our plan to break into Alastor's office means a return to Headquarters. I can't help but think that it also means a return to where Ezra is. Abram's arranged for us to stay in what used to be a hostel but is now a popular brothel. Prostitution not only returned with Alastor's rise to power but is now one of the country's most lucrative forms of business. The economy is booming for those willing to sacrifice their souls.

Mary dyed my hair and eyebrows black and showed me how to apply my makeup differently. It's weird looking at myself in the mirror, like I'm seeing my doppelganger or something. It's just as odd looking at Finnick, whose once beautiful, dark hair has become a blond buzz cut.

"The loss of your hair is criminal," I say with a sigh.

Finnick laughs. "You were always obsessed with my hair."

"I think a part of me died as the locks fell on the floor."

Finnick just smirks as he fiddles with the lock on the door of our new room. A woman whose face looks tired and leathery, the deep lines portraying years of ill-treatment in a thankless industry, trudges by us in a nightie. One strap of her nightgown has slipped down over her shoulder, exposing part of her chest. She sees us but makes no effort to pull up the strap. I fight to hide my sympathy and disgust.

"Got it," Finnick says triumphantly, pushing the door open with a thud. We walk in to the smell of sweat and Chinese food. I cover my nose and mouth with my hand.

"Ugh, open the window," I say, and Finnick tugs hard on the handle. I hear paint crackle off as he yanks it upward. The cold, January air comes breezing in, making us shiver.

The room itself is barren, except for a full-size bed with a dingy blanket with questionable stains strewn across it and some furniture. There's a chest of four drawers next to the window and an open closet with a pull string light on the opposite wall. The floor is wood, scratched and worn from years of use. Various burn marks litter the floor and walls, where occupants used their surroundings as an ashtray.

"Nice place," I say, plopping down on the bed.

"Just imagine who else has been on that bed," Finnick quips.

"Ew. Stop. We're stuck here; I can't think about that."

Finnick grabs our duffle bag off the ground and tosses it on the bed. He takes out the blueprints of the main headquarters and the phone Abram set up so we could keep in touch with him and Solomon. He established a secure line directly to Abram's cabin, where he and Solomon were planning to hack into the matrix of the UFoA's security system to see what they could find. A couple of the board members headed out West to begin eliminating centers for the mark, and others stayed here in the East to do the same. Harry volunteered to lead the diversion in headquarters, while Finnick and I break into Alastor's office.

Finnick was able to contact the other group of resistors responsible for the burning of the Church of the Divine Truth, and they were eager to help. Several of them will be involved in Harry's mission. I'm about to ask Finnick if he thinks we should sneak over to the main headquarters to survey the area after curfew tonight, when there's two sharp raps on the door.

I jump slightly. "Who could that be?" I look at Finnick in alarm.

He quickly shoves the blueprints and phone back in the bag and pushes it under the bed. "I'll answer it." He takes three steps toward the door and puts his ear up against it. "Who's there?"

"A friend," a man hisses. "Hurry, I do not want to be seen." Finnick looks back toward me, and I shrug.

"Answer it, I guess." My words come out as more of a question than a statement.

With one hand on the revolver in his back waistline, he opens the door.

# 36.
## TWO YEARS EARLIER . . .

I stared at the clock centered on the front wall of my English classroom. The ticking of the second hand was reverberating in my ear. My leg was shaking, and I couldn't rid of the screaming in my head. How can everyone just sit here? Someone was just murdered!

Sergeant Barnes was droning on and on about the symbolic meaning of the intersex's ring in our assigned reading, *The Tryst*. I couldn't stop seeing Judah's face—the look of indignation when he had stood up in world history, his deflation upon realizing that no one had his back, his embarrassment in the cafeteria when everyone had stared at the sign, and his mouth, gaping open in shock and horror as he hung from the tree. I started trembling.

"You okay?" My friend, Lucy, to my left looked over at me.

"Fine," I muttered, keeping my head down. Don't talk to anyone. Don't trust anyone. I could feel my paranoia growing and the suffocation of it all around me. I raised my hand.

"Yes, Esther," Professor Barnes called on me.

"May I go to the nurse, please? I feel ill."

He examined me for a moment, presumably gauging whether or not I was telling the truth, before he nodded. "Write a pass and sign out."

I stepped into the hallway and took a deep breath. I still felt on the verge of a panic attack as I turned toward the nurse's office. But before I could make it there, I saw Ezra at his locker. I knew I should go to the nurse, since I told Barnes that was where I would be, but I was eager to know how things went with Mother Maura.

"Yikes." He looked up at me. "You look horrible."

"Thanks," I grumbled. "I'm going to the nurse to lie down. I just wanted to see how your meeting went."

"Oh, sorry, didn't realize you were actually sick. Stomach bug or something?"

I hesitated to tell him about Judah. I didn't know if I could say the words out loud. "Have you been outside yet or heard other kids talking about anything?"

He looked at me quizzically. "What? You mean the Judah thing?"

I was taken aback for a second. The Judah thing? I stuttered, "Uh, yeah, the, um, Judah thing. It's horrifying." But strangely, Ezra didn't appear to be upset or surprised. "Why don't you look bothered at all right now?" I asked, shocked by his reaction.

"I just saw it coming is all," he said with a shrug. "I mean, it's no secret that the UFoA hates Christians and Jews, especially those who are outspoken about their beliefs."

"So, that makes it right?"

"No, of course not." He reached for me, but I took a step back. "Esther, I'm not saying what they did to him, if they even did anything, is right. I'm just not all that surprised."

"If? You actually believe it could have been suicide? C'mon, Ezra!" I practically yelled.

"Shh! Keep your voice down," he hissed.

I lowered my voice an octave but continued. "I was there, Ezra, in world history, when he was humiliated in front of everyone and made to wear that ridiculous sign." I looked down in regret. "And I should have stood up for him."

"Esther, no. Do you want to be killed next? Keep your mouth shut and your head down."

"What's going on out here?" Sergeant Hall poked his head out of his classroom door, and I wanted to spit at him.

Ezra shot me a look that said, "Don't even think about it," as he quickly responded. "Sorry, sir, we're going to class."

"Now," he said in answer, staring at us both until we walked away in different directions. I looked back over my shoulder at Ezra, and he mouthed, "Keep your head down."

As I opened the door to the nurse's office, my mind still reeling from his calm reaction to Judah's hanging, I realized we never had a chance to talk about his meeting.

# 37.
## PRESENT DAY

Finnick is face to face with the front of a nine-millimeter revolver.

"Hands where I can see them," I hear a man command. I can't see his face behind the door. I pull the gun from my waistband and put it under the blanket next to me. He shoves Finnick into the room, pushing on his head with the gun.

"You there, stand up." I do as he says, standing slowly with my arms raised. "Against the wall," he orders. "Any sudden movements, and I shoot."

He keeps the gun trained on Finnick's head as he uses the other hand to frisk us. Finding Finnick's gun, he puts it in his coat pocket. "Thanks for the new piece," he says.

I force myself not to look at the spot on the bed where I hid mine.

"What do you want?" Finnick demands. The man, a heavily built machine who couldn't be more than thirty years old, smacks Finnick hard across the face.

"Did I tell you to talk yet?" he shouts.

I gasp. Finnick's lip is bleeding, but he keeps eye contact with the man, his gaze unafraid. He raises his chin slightly. The man punches him hard in the stomach, and Finnick doubles over, falling to the ground. I let out a soft scream.

"A cocky one, aren't you?" he asks Finnick, not waiting for an answer as he kicks him swiftly in the ribs. Finnick groans. I bite my lip to keep from saying anything. The man turns to me. "Nothing to add?" I just shake my head and look down. "Good," he continues. "Now if you'll both cooperate, this will end much better for you."

The burly man looks us up and down and gives a sarcastic laugh. "Your disguises are humorous. Did you think no one would know who you were?" he asks with amusement.

My mind is reeling. Who is this guy? Was Ezra tracking us somehow?

"I need some information, and you two are going to give it to me. You can give me the information willingly, and you won't get hurt, or you can try to hold out for as long as you can stand pain," our captor says with a smirk. "The choice is yours, but I admit that the latter sounds much more appealing to me."

"What do you want?" Finnick spits the words like venom.

"A little while back, the two of you were seen running out of a hospital in Lawrence. You had an older man with you who you claimed was someone he was not. Am I ringing any bells?" He sneers at us, his mouth twisting into a cruel smile. Out of the corner of my eye, I see Finnick twitch, but he regains his composure quickly. "You're going to tell me who that man is."

Finnick and I both say nothing. I shift uncomfortably and take a step back toward the bed.

The man's face slowly widens in a sinister grin. "Is that a no?"

We still say nothing. I can hear the loud pounding of my heart in my head. I take another small step backward. He comes toward me like a rabid animal, grabbing a fist full of my hair and yanking up, hard. I let out a wail, my scalp burning in pain. Finnick lunges for his gun, and the man strikes him with the back of his hand across his face. I'm still holding my head in agony, clenching my teeth to fight the pain, when I see him hurl Finnick against the wall. Finnick goes to stand up, but the man is there kicking him hard in the ribs, over and over.

I scream. *Get the gun.* I race to the bed, and the man turns; but I'm quick, and I am now gripping the cold metal of the revolver. I turn it toward him, and he lunges toward me.

Before I know what is happening, I hear a loud blast as the sound of the gun ricochets around us. My chest is heaving; tears sting my eyes as I look at the pool of blood spreading like fire. Our captor lies dead on the floor, his face twisted in a disparaging scowl, his cotton shirt drenched in the deep red of his blood. Almost as if in surprise, I drop the gun, staring down at my hand in confusion. I am a murderer—death tally: two.

Finnick groans from the corner. I hear him, but I can't seem to move my feet, which are becoming saturated by the puddles of blood. I hear him groan again. I will myself to walk toward him, stepping over the dead body to reach his.

"Finn." His name comes out in a croak; I don't recognize my own voice, the voice of a killer. He moans in pain, grabbing his ribs, his eyes opening to slits. "I-I . . . killed him, Finn; I killed him." He raises his head up and turns it toward the body.

"Callll Solomon," he moans.

I nod and force myself to step over the body again to reach our bag. I pull it out from under the bed, kneeling to unzip it and pull out the phone. My hands are shaking so hard, I almost drop it, but manage to catch it in a fumble. I take a deep breath and dial the numbers to Abram's cabin.

*Esther,*

*I shot a man once, killed him instantly. And I know I'm responsible for the deaths of others. You may hear about them if you pursue the path laid out for you. Try not to judge me, for you may find yourself in a situation one day where you have done the same. I'll give you the only light of comfort I found within the darkness of my own thoughts. God tells us in Ecclesiastes 3 that "there is a time to kill and a time to heal." In war, we must sometimes commit acts we would never consider in times of peace. This is the "time for war," and in the pursuit of salvation, not everyone can be saved.*

*I love you, Monkey. Be strong.*

*Dad*

## 38.
# TWO YEARS EARLIER . . .

The nurse, an older woman, pulled out a forehead thermometer from the glass cabinet behind her desk. I took in her graying hair and the creases on her cheeks and forehead. I wondered if she was someone's grandmother and imagined what it might have been like to have had a grandmother, who baked cookies for you or sat with you just to chat.

"When did your symptoms start?" she asked, pushing the base of the instrument against my head. Her words pulled me away from my thoughts.

At approximately 8:48 when I saw Judah's body swaying. I wiped sweat from my hands onto my jeans. But I only said, "Right before second period."

"You have a low-grade fever," she said as she cleaned off the thermometer and placed it back on the shelf. She took my pulse and looked at me curiously. "Why is your heart racing? Did something happen?"

Trust no one. "You know what, I'm okay. I shouldn't have come here." I got up and turned to grab my bag.

"Hold on for a second," the nurse said, placing a hand on my shoulder. I almost shrugged her off but thought better of it. "Let me at least give you some ibuprofen for your headache. And I'll write you a pass to get you out of class for the rest of the day. You can go back to your dorm and get some rest." She reached into a desk drawer and pulled out a large bottle of pills, shaking two into my hand.

"Thank you," I murmured, folding my fingers around them.

"I might be able to help if you'll explain," she said kindly. I couldn't meet her eyes. "Does it have to do with the boy . . . outside?" she asked with hesitation.

I willed myself to look at her, fighting the tears. "Thank you for the medicine." I turned around and walked out. I needed to find Finnick.

I knew he had world history third period because he had it right before Rachael and I did, and I always had to deal with seeing them fawn all over each other on my way into class. I was staring through the classroom door's window, waiting for the bell to ring and thinking how much I hated Sergeant Hall's smug face. The nurse's pass gave me the clear to get out of third period, but somehow, I needed to convince Finnick to skip with me. I thought of Professor Solomon and knew instinctively he would help us. Ezra would wonder why I wasn't meeting him at his locker, but he'd have to deal with it. He needed to know I was mad at his reaction to Judah's death. He needed to reflect on his flippancy.

The bell clanged loudly, and I jumped slightly at the sound. Sergeant Hall's door flew open, and kids came streaming out. He yelled, "Read section three!" But I doubted half of the students heard him. I caught sight of Finnick's dark hair and reached out for his arm.

"Hey," I said, pulling him toward me.

"Oh, hey, Es, what's up?"

"I need you. So, um, you're not going to third period, okay?"

"Judah?" he asked.

I was reminded of one of the reasons I liked Finnick so much. He knew my thoughts. I had a much harder time reading him, but when events unfolded, our reactions to them always seemed to be the same.

I nodded my head as I said, "This way," pulling him by the sleeve of his arm. I wanted to reach Professor Solomon's room before Rachael saw us. I didn't want her monopolizing all his attention.

I paused outside Professor Solomon's door, turning to face Finnick. Finnick had also been assigned Professor Solomon as a mentor when he started at St. Mary's, and I knew he trusted him as much as I did. But first, I needed to make sure Finnick knew what had happened. "Did you see Judah?" I asked him.

He nodded solemnly. "I almost threw up."

"Me, too." See? Same reactions. "But Ezra wasn't even phased when I asked him about it. It was so weird, Finnick. It was like he expected it to happen or something. How could he react like that?"

"Don't overthink it. Ezra has a tough skin. He isn't surprised by much after losing his parents."

"We lost our parents . . . " I trailed off.

He shrugged. "People are different."

"I guess," I said, but there was no sincerity behind the words. "Anyway, I have a plan. Come on." I pulled his arm toward me as I pushed open Professor Solomon's door. "Hey, Professor," I called out, poking my head into the room, "are you here?"

I saw his tall figure by the window, staring out in a daze. He turned toward the door. "Esther, hello, come in."

"You don't have a class this period?"

"No, it is my lunch hour. What can I do for you? Have you decided which philosopher to research for your paper?"

"Um, no, this is actually about something else. I have Finnick here with me, too, and if it's okay, we'd like to talk to you about something. It has nothing to do with class, though, is the thing . . . "

"Oh, well, yes, I suppose that is all right. Hello, Finnick,"

Finnick walked in behind me and smiled. "Hi, Professor."

"Have a seat," he said with a wave of his hand, and Finnick and I took seats next to each other in the front row. "What can I do for you two?" he asked, pulling his chair out from his desk and sitting down.

Finnick and I exchanged glances. I had brought Finnick there and didn't tell him exactly why, so I knew he was expecting me to do the talking.

"I want to do something for Judah, a memorial of some sort, and I was hoping the two of you would help me." My eyes danced back and forth between them. What I didn't tell them was that I felt like I was going to go crazy if I didn't do something, the image of Judah hanging torturing my mind.

Finnick sat up straighter and nodded enthusiastically. "I think that's a great idea, Es. Count me in. Though, I'd also like to find out what exactly happened to him because I'm not buying for a second that it was suicide." Finnick looked to Professor Solomon for an answer.

Professor Solomon looked uncomfortable, his eyes surveying the room as if it might be bugged. He went over to the door and peered out into the hall before closing it. "Just between us, I don't believe that it was either. There has been talk amongst the faculty. We are becoming very divided here at St. Mary's with all the recent changes."

"I can only imagine," I said, sympathetically. "Did Sergeant Hall say anything about what happened? I was in class the day he embarrassed Judah in front of everyone. I wish I would have done something."

"I understand your feelings, Esther, but it truly is best that you did not. St. Mary's is becoming a very dangerous place. And no, Sergeant Hall has kept mainly to himself since his arrival."

"Yeah, Es, stop beating yourself up about that. No one else said anything either."

"That's just it though, Finn. If no one ever says anything, this will only grow. I keep thinking about my parents . . . They would say how change only comes with courage."

Finnick smiled at me then and nodded. "I'm glad you're my friend, Esther."

The warmth of his words filled me with fondness. I knew going to Finnick was the right thing to do. "Me, too," I said, smiling back. "So, for the memorial, I was thinking a candlelit service tomorrow night by the tree. I can try to gather some pictures of him with friends and his former family. I'd also like to decorate his locker."

"You will have to run all of this by Mother Maura, but you have my full support." Professor Solomon paused a moment before continuing, "But you should try to gather as many students as you can, so there will be less of a backlash from those responsible for his death."

"We can do that," I said, my excitement gaining. "I'll talk to Ezra next period and get him on board." Professor Solomon's face twitched at the sound of Ezra's name. "What, Professor? You don't like Ezra?" I asked, a bit defensively.

"Oh, no, Child, it is not that. It's just, well, I . . . nothing really. I am only concerned that Ezra may not have the same core beliefs as you and Finnick."

"Why would you say that?" Finnick asked.

"His writing in class . . . " He paused, clearly troubled. "It is, um, very atheistic."

"Oh," Finnick and I said in unison. I thought about that for a second and realized that Ezra and I had never really had a conversation about our beliefs, at least not directly. That seemed absurd to me now.

"I guess I always assumed that he believes what I do," I said. How could I be with someone whose core convictions were so vastly different from my own? Maybe Professor Solomon was wrong. Maybe he had just misunderstood his writing.

"I'll broach the memorial idea with Ezra and feel him out. I'll also talk to my friends in choir and my lacrosse teammates. You can bring it up at art club after school today. Judah had a lot of friends in the art classes." *He did*, I thought, as I remembered the time we made a wall collage for world peace. Judah's portion had been the best part—a large peace sign he'd cut out from cardboard paper that he'd covered in various colors of paper machete so that it looked vibrant, tie-dyed.

"Okay," I agreed, nodding absently, my mind still plagued by what Professor Solomon had said about Ezra. "I'm sure those in art club will want to help with his locker, too. We'll make it look awesome." I smiled then. It felt good to be acting in some way against the horrors of what happened.

"Keep me updated, Children, and if you need further help, I am here for you. Otherwise, I will plan to attend the memorial tomorrow night." Professor Solomon stood up before continuing, "You better go on to class now. I'll speak with your teachers about you missing this period."

"Thanks, Professor," I said, wanting to hug him. I didn't think he realized how comforting it was to know we had an adult on our side.

"Yeah, Professor, you're the real deal, Man." Finnick beamed at him.

He blushed, and I smiled inwardly. "Yes, yes, thank you, Children. I will see you later," Embarrassed, he ushered us out the door. Once it closed behind us, I turned to Finnick.

"Do you think what he said about Ezra is true?" I asked, looking down.

"I don't see why he would lie to us, Esther . . . I'm sorry, though; I would be pretty upset if I had heard that about Rachael."

"Yeah." I kicked at the ground with the toe of my shoe. Considering who Rachael's parents had been, I'd be less surprised to hear it about her. But I kept that opinion to myself. "I'm just going to hope he was wrong—you know, a misunderstanding or something."

"Sure . . . that could be it," Finn said, looking at me sadly, both of us knowing that wasn't likely.

Finnick wasn't going to be able to give me the answers I needed. "I'll catch up with you later." I gave a quick wave and made my way toward the cafeteria for lunch. Ezra and I always met outside the wide oak doors and went in together. I was sure talking to him would clear everything up. He wasn't an atheist. He couldn't be.

# 39.
## PRESENT DAY

My fingers smear blood on the phone as I dial the cabin line. "Hello?" Abram answers my call.

"Ab—" I start.

He interrupts me. "Hold on for a minute." I hear scuffling and a clicking sound. "Okay, the line's secure. Is that you, Esther? Is everything okay?"

I'm gasping for air. "No-oo-o," I cry into the phone. "Finnick is hurt ... There was a man. Abram, we're in trouble." I swallow hard against the lump in my throat, wiping tears off my face. "I-I ... there's a body," I finish, almost choking on the words.

"Let me put Solomon on the phone." I hear him whispering to Solomon but can't make out what he's saying.

"Esther." It's Solomon's voice now, calm and reassuring. "Can Finnick move?"

"I-I-I'm not sh-sh-ure." My words come out in a stumble as my lungs struggle for air.

"I want you to go over to him and see. Check for major injuries."

"Okay," I respond, wincing as I walk over the body. The man's eyes vacantly stare up at the ceiling. "Finnick," I say softly, placing a hand on his shoulder and shaking gently. "Can you talk?"

"My ribs," he slurs. "I thin-k they're broken."

"It's his ribs," I say into the phone.

I look back at Finnick and ask, "Can you stand?"

He struggles to move, groaning in pain. My heart aches as I watch him suffer. He reaches out to me, and I put my shoulder under the pit of his arm to help him up. He leans against the wall and me for support.

"We're up," I say into the phone.

"Okay, I am going to have a car arrive for you at the back door of the house, by the kitchen, in ten minutes. Can you make it there?"

I look at Finnick doubtfully. "We'll try," I say. "What about the body, Solomon?"

"We will take care of it. Just get yourselves out. I want you both out of there before someone comes looking for him. And, Esther, check his pockets for a wallet and phone. We will need those to figure out exactly who he was and what he wanted." I don't tell him that *he* is what the man wanted.

"Okay," I say nervously. "I will."

"You can do this, Child. I know that you can."

"See you soon," I whisper, ending the call. I lean Finnick carefully against the wall. "Just relax for a minute while I get everything together," I tell him. He nods, grimacing in pain.

I grab the duffle bag from under the bed and go over to the man and collect both guns from him, his wallet, and a cell phone. I avoid looking at his eyes but can't dodge the pools of blood, my shoes now a proclamation of what I've done. I try to calm my heart rate by slowing my breath; but the amount of blood is dizzying, and it takes all my will not to pass out. I stuff everything into the bag and throw the strap across my body, so I'll have both of my hands free. I go back over to Finnick and help him put his arm around my shoulder. I wrap my arm around his waist, supporting as much of his weight as I can handle. We drag ourselves the few steps to the door, and I open it to peer out.

There's a couple to my right making out, and I divert my eyes. The left looks clear. "C'mon," I whisper. "This way."

Finnick nods, gritting his teeth. At the end of the hall is a door that leads to a stairwell that will open into the area by the kitchen. It's the way we came up earlier because we were less likely to be noticed. With each hobble, I remind myself to breathe, having held my breath since we stepped into the hallway. We reach the door to the stairs, and I struggle to open it while keeping Finnick upright. He moans in pain.

"Sorry," I whisper. "Just a bit farther." Each step downward is agony for him, but I force him to keep going. We're two steps from the bottom when I hear the door open behind us.

"Who's down there?" It's a woman's voice.

I don't recognize it. Nor do I say anything. Yet I all but push Finnick down the last two stairs, and we stumble through the door coming out into another hallway. I can smell the scents from the kitchen, a blend of garbage and this morning's breakfast, and I see the door to the outside.

"Just a little farther," I say, giving Finnick a smile of encouragement. "We're almost there."

"What happened to him?" A large man, who is bald and shirtless, walks out of the kitchen.

I think fast. "A little too much fun, if you know what I mean." I give a slight laugh and wink, smiling in a way that I hope looks coquettish and not grotesque.

He laughs loudly. "Do I ever. I'm in room 230, if you want to know what real fun looks like." He pushes his hips out in a perverse gesture, and I swallow the bile rising in my throat.

"Gotcha." I falter, moving us toward the door. "See you later, then." I give another wink to be rid of him.

I push the door open to the outside and give a sigh of relief at the sight of a black car next to the dumpsters. The driver gestures to us and pulls the car forward. I open the door and help Finnick in as quickly as I can muster, climbing in behind him.

# 40.
# TWO YEARS EARLIER . . .

The art club had been eager to help me decorate Judah's locker, and we assembled quotes and pictures that we taped onto the metal door; we even included some of his drawings from that year's art show. I had been trying to catch up with Ezra, but he hadn't been to our usual meeting spot or in calculus, which was the only class we had together. Never having found out what happened between him and Mother Maura, I hoped he was okay. Finnick had been able to recruit about half of the lacrosse team to help him spread the word about the memorial service tomorrow night, and last I had heard, there were about a hundred students planning to attend. It felt good to be doing something, while trying to keep the image of Judah hanging from a tree out of my head.

"How can I help?" Rachael came up behind me in the art room as I counted out candles for the service.

"Oh, hey," I said, distracted. "Um, you can place these wax holders onto the candles if you want and then put them in that box." I pointed over to a cardboard box Solomon had retrieved from his department's book room.

"Sure!" she said, a little too enthusiastically. "I think this is really great of you, Esther, just really great."

Her desperation for me to like her annoyed me so badly that I could barely choke out a thanks. I feigned concentration on counting.

"Hey, baby." Finnick came up behind Rachael, embracing her in a hug. She giggled and leaned her head back to kiss him. I looked away. "How's it going in here?" he asked me.

"Good," I answered. "We're pretty much all set after we finish these candles. Hey, did you ever see Ezra to talk to him?"

"No, I haven't been able to find him all day. I went to his dorm, and then I tried to catch him after fifth period, but he wasn't in class."

*That's weird. Why would he be skipping class?*

"I need to know what he learned about his parents. He's been so strange the last few days." I couldn't help but think he was avoiding me. "Do you think I should be worried?" I always asked Finnick these type of questions, like he had all the answers. I briefly wondered if it bothered him or if it made him feel needed.

"Not yet, Es." He smiled at me sympathetically. "If he's not at dinner, maybe we can go find Mother Maura and see what's up." I saw Rachael watching us as we talked, her face hard, and a quick flash of—what was it exactly, spite?—blanketed her eyes. But just as quickly as I blinked, it was gone. Surely, I had imagined it. Rachael couldn't possibly care about my relationship with Ezra.

"Okay." I sighed. I returned my attention to the candles. Rachael started humming a tune from the old Disney movie, *Beauty and the Beast,* and the other students, who were helping us, joined in. Before I knew it, we were all singing "Tale as Old as Time" and laughing at how terrible we sounded, until Sergeant Hall barged into the room.

"What's all this?" he demanded, his voice resonating in the small space. Immediately, the singing stopped, and I felt the air grow thick with fear. No one said anything.

"You!" He pointed at me, and I turned toward him, forcing myself not to look down.

"Y—?" I cleared my throat. "Yes?"

"Is this your doing? This little recognition put together for the Plaster Saint?"

"We have permission," I said firmly. "We just lost a classmate, sir."

His face twisted in disgust. "Well, if I were you, missy, I'd be careful about glorifying the death of an intolerant prude. Classmate or not." He turned and stormed out of the room, slamming the door behind him.

I swallowed hard against the lump in my throat, my eyes glued to the closed door. Everyone in the room was staring at me to see what I would do. I took a deep breath and started singing again, my voice a strangled whisper.

Rachael smiled at me, joining in. And it wasn't long until everyone was busy working, the fear of Sergeant Hall's threat temporarily detained.

# 41.
# PRESENT DAY

The driver of the car takes us to the west end of Headquarters, a sketchy area run down by the effects of deep-rooted poverty and the drug trade. These sectors have become so common, they're referred to as the ratholes, coined for their unsanitary appearance. I stare out the window as we drive by people sitting on rotting porches, their faces and hair dirty, track marks on their arms. A man is walking in small circles, his mouth moving in speech, but no one's around him. Dogs bark incessantly, and kids play on the sidewalks, wearing nothing but dirty t-shirts and worn jeans, despite the below-freezing temperatures.

Years of greed has spurred an opioid epidemic that's blatantly ignored by the government, and now people just lie dead on the streets. I've heard and seen what users will do for a fix, the agonizing shame people allow themselves to endure. I shudder thinking about it now and pull my sweater tighter around my body. I turn toward Finnick to see how he's feeling and find he's slipped out of consciousness again. Sighing, I look up toward the driver, a middle-aged man, with graying black hair.

"Will Solomon be meeting us?" I ask.

"Shortly. He said to give him an hour," the man responds curtly. I lay my head back on the seat, closing my eyes against the sights of the ruined world around me.

# 42.
# TWO YEARS EARLIER . . .

I knocked on Ezra's door about a half hour before we were supposed to meet Finnick and Rachael for dinner. I was hoping to talk to him alone first.

"Who is it?" he called through the door.

"Me," I answered, relieved to find he was in his room. I heard him shuffling around and what sounded like papers being jammed back in a drawer, then the lock being turned.

"Hey, what's up?" He pulled the door open with a thrust. His chestnut brown hair was disheveled, and clouds of worry bathed his deep gray eyes. I reached for him, but he flinched.

"You okay?" I asked quietly, hurt by his pulling away.

"Yeah, I'm good. Just busy, you know?" He looked right at me with his usual straightforwardness, but it was harsher now, more caustic. When I didn't answer, he continued, "Studying for calculus." I made a move to try to come into his room, but he blocked the entry with his shoulder. "I should get back to studying."

"Ezra . . . What is this? Talk to me."

"There's nothing to say." He kept his eyes on mine.

I suddenly felt queasy. I didn't understand what he was doing. "Okay . . . " I trailed off. "Are you coming to dinner?"

"Nah. Let them know I'm studying."

"Right. Studying," I said doubtfully. "There's a memorial for Judah tonight. I've been wanting to tell you about it, but I haven't seen you. It's at eight. Will you come?"

"I heard, and no," he answered, giving me nothing else. "See you around," he said as I found myself staring at the brown varnish of the door.

I lifted my hand to knock again, but then lowered it, trying to swallow the swelling sensation of my heart breaking in my throat. I replayed the events of the last few days to determine what could have possibly been making Ezra act that way. There had been Judah's death, of course, but he had also had his meeting with Mother Maura. If he wasn't going to talk to me, then maybe she would.

I walked straight to Mother Maura's office, which was located in a separate wing from the other nuns. She had her own secretary, who sat outside the office door next to a large aquarium of fish. It reminded me of my dentist's office growing up, and as I watched a black tetra fish swim through coral, I was filled with a longing for simpler days.

"Can I help you?" The secretary looked over at me, and I pulled my mind back to the present.

"Is Mother Maura available?" I asked.

"Do you have an appointment?"

"No, but I can wait."

She flipped through an appointment book before responding. "She has ten minutes free after the dinner hour. You're welcome to wait."

My stomach grumbled. "Okay," I said, taking a seat next to the fish. I looked around the waiting room to pass the time and noticed the signs from the UFoA plastered on the walls. If I hadn't been at St. Mary's prior to the takeover, I would have never known that it was once a religious institution. I thought about the Bible in the drawer of my nightstand

and my book of devotions. It was surprising that they hadn't been confiscated yet. I looked over at the table next to me to see what there was to read, but it was only brochures. The logo of the UFoA, the serpent with its feathered wings, stood out on the front. Underneath, it read, "Rules and guidelines for a better way of life." I heard the door open but didn't look up as I absently flipped the brochure open.

"What are you doing here?" It came out as a snarl, and I saw Ezra's feet over the brochure before I met his eyes.

"You won't talk to me, so I came here." I lifted my chin in defiance.

"You're relentless," he snapped in irritation. "And I don't have time for it."

"Wow, Ezra, really? Well, excuse me. Here I was under the impression that we actually cared about each other."

His eyes shifted down briefly. "Yeah, well, things change."

"In a matter of days? No. You're not getting off the hook that easy, sorry. You're going to have to explain yourself to me, or I'll find out on my own." The secretary had noticed our harsh whispering and was staring suspiciously. Ezra saw her from the corner of his eye and practically hissed at me.

"Fine," he retorted, his voice scathing. "Not here."

I looked over at the secretary and apologized for wasting her time. She nodded and appeared grateful that we were leaving. Ezra pushed open the door and held it for me, his demeanor still angry, like I was putting him out or something. He led me outside to a bench next to the playground. The pre-K kids were having recess. The air was filled by their laughter and chatter, a contrast to the tumultuous storm of my heart. I sat on my hands to keep them from fidgeting and looked to Ezra to start talking.

He took a deep breath and leaned forward, his arms resting on his knees. We watched as a child glided down the slide. "What do you want to know?"

"We can start with why you're being such a jerk."

"I found out some things about my family. It's changed my perspective." His tone was clipped, to the point.

"What kind of things?"

"Like the way some of them died, for instance."

"Okay . . . you realize that I want to be here for you through this, right? Did you forget that I love you?"

His face softened. "No, Es, I didn't forget. I just have different beliefs than you do, and—" He cut himself off. "Look, I just don't see how we'll get past it." It was funny he would bring his beliefs up after I had just had that conversation with Solomon. It must have been on his mind all along, but there had to be something else. I could sense it.

"What kind of beliefs do you have?"

"I don't believe in God, for starters."

I drew in a breath. "But why?"

"I could ask you the same thing. How can you possibly believe in a God Who took your parents from you? A God Who would allow such evil in this world that children can hang from trees and families can be . . . can be . . . " He stopped, swallowing a sob.

"Can be what?"

"Slaughtered," he finished, straightening his shoulders to hide his emotions.

"Is that what you found out happened to them?" I asked. "To your parents?"

"Yes, Esther, it is. And you know who was responsible? People like you. Those who follow your God. The hypocritical, judgmental frauds."

I swallowed hard. People like me? The anger and hurt was emanating off him, and I knew whatever I said wasn't going to neutralize his feelings.

"Not everyone who follows God is a fraud," I said softly. "And what happened to your parents is the result of evil, not good."

"Ha! It's funny you should say that, considering who killed my parents. And even if that is true, believing in God gets you nowhere."

"What do you mean who killed them? Do I know them?"

Ezra's face went blank, a shadow flickering over it as a cloud eclipsed the sun. "Forget it," he said.

"Ezra, if we don't combat the evil, who will? God is inherently good. It's Satan who is evil. If you don't choose to follow God, then by default, you follow Satan. Don't you see?"

"I make my own way. It's like I told you, Esther, I don't see how we get past this. I want us to stay friends and all, but we're fundamentally different."

I fought back tears, my insides feeling like they were on fire; my desire to fix it, to hold him, to make everything okay was so strong, I could scream. "Don't leave me," I whispered.

He stood up. "It's just how it has to be. I'll see you around."

I watched as he walked away, across the woodchips of the playground, never once looking back.

This conversation, the one that ended my relationship with Ezra, happened two months before he disappeared. We never talked again about what happened to his parents or about our beliefs, and we did stay civil. Some days, like the day we played Capture the Flag, the day he would leave St. Mary's forever, it even felt like we were friends. I cried into my pillow every night, but by day, I smiled at him and pretended like everything was fine. Finnick knew, but everyone else just saw it as the most amicable break up in history. If I had known that he would be gone so soon, perhaps I would have tried harder to break through to him, to get to the truth. But I thought I had time. People always think they have time.

# 43.
# PRESENT DAY

I learn that the man who's driving us through the ratholes is named Sam. He's taking us to one of those urgent care clinics with twenty-four-hour care. *And surveillance,* I think with concern. When we arrive, we sit in the parking lot waiting for Solomon before going inside. Finnick is still floating in and out of consciousness, and I can't keep him awake for more than a minute or two. He's talking some, but his thoughts come out jumbled. I try to give him water and speak to him soothingly. I pull the duffle bag up onto the seat from the floor and unzip it. I take out the phone and wallet of the man I killed. My mind flashes back to his cold skin and dead eyes, and I shudder.

"Cold?" Sam calls back.

"No, fine, thank you," I answer, fighting to stay focused. I decide to open the wallet first. His driver's license reads, "Gerald Mann." I whisper the name aloud, and the driver looks at me quizzically in the rearview mirror. I've never heard that name before.

I look through the rest of the wallet, but there's nothing else except a twenty dollar bill, an insurance card, and an ID for a gym membership. I pick up the cell phone next, clicking on the center button to see several text messages. I breathe in sharply upon seeing the name.

Jay Hawthorne: *What did you learn?*

Jay Hawthorne: *Report in, Gerald.*

Jay Hawthorne: *Are you hurt? Sending backup.*

I check the time of the last text. Fifteen minutes ago. Would that have been enough time for Solomon to dispose of the body? I don't know. I try to see past the texts, but there's a passcode, the need for a facial recognition. A face that no longer exists.

The Hawthornes.

My mind goes back to that day at the hospital with Solomon, and I remember their faces, the pain and loss that seemed to seep out of their pores. Now they want Solomon. Do they blame him for their daughter's death? I sigh heavily. Our list of enemies just keeps growing.

I wake with a start to a tapping on the car window. Solomon is peering through it. I push against the latch on the door and prod it open. "Hi, Professor," I say groggily, rubbing my eyes. I look over at Finnick, who is still asleep or unconscious and try nudging him. He groans.

"Hello, Esther, help me get him inside. I have a friend who will bandage his ribs and head." He looks tired, anxious.

We drag Finnick out of the car and enter the clinic through the back door. Solomon's friend, an older doctor named Elizabeth who looks to be the same age as Solomon, helps us carry him into an exam room. She waves smelling salts under his nose, and his eyes shoot open.

"What's going on? Where am I?" Startled, he sits up on the table.

"Everything's okay, Finn. We're getting help." My voice is soft; it seems to comfort him to see that Solomon and I are both there, and he lies back again.

Elizabeth hands Finnick an ice pack and tells him to press it against his ribs. She looks at the cut on his head. "He'll need stitches." She speaks directly to Solomon as if we're not there. Solomon nods, and she turns toward a cart next to the wall to retrieve the suture tray, gathering what she needs. We watch silently as she stitches Finnick's head, his teeth gritted in pain. I squeeze his hand, and he practically breaks mine in return. She finishes quickly.

"Remove your shirt," she commands, her tone one of efficiency, and he winces as he lifts his arms to pull the shirt over his head. I gasp softly when I see the bruising on his chest and stomach.

"I'm all right," Finnick says. He gives me a small smile, and I watch as Elizabeth swiftly bandages his rib cage, while avoiding both our eyes.

She turns back toward Solomon. "Be sure he applies ice packs for the next forty-eight hours. Here are two pain relievers. I apologize, but it's all I can spare." She places the pills into his hand, and he holds her hand in his.

"You have done more than enough. I can't begin to thank you, Elizabeth."

"Be careful not to be seen as you leave here," she advises, still clasping his hand. "And take care of yourself, Solomon." She turns to us then and nods before walking out and closing the door behind her.

## 44.
# TWO YEARS EARLIER . . .

"I think my parents might have killed Ezra's." Finnick and I were outside setting up for Judah's memorial. We were the first to arrive, but I knew Rachael would be there any minute, so I didn't waste any time saying what I needed to say.

"What?" Finnick's mouth dropped open in horror. "Why would you think that?"

"We broke up when you and Rachael were at dinner."

"Oh, Es, I'm sorry. I had no idea things weren't good between you guys."

"Yeah, neither did I. But he had that meeting with Mother Maura, and she must have told him some pretty heavy stuff because he's been super weird ever since."

"What does it have to do with your parents, though?"

"He said something about how his parents were killed—that they were murdered by people like me—and then I remembered this letter my mom wrote to me on my tenth birthday. She told me about this couple dying and how they had a young son. Ezra came here when he was ten, Finnick. We're the same age."

"But, Esther, come on; it's not like you and Ezra were the only ten-year-olds at the time. It could have been anyone."

"I don't think so, Finn. The way he looked at me—it was like I was responsible for their deaths. What if that's what he found out? How can I even blame him for leaving me?"

"Hey, guys!" Rachael's chirpy voice came up behind me, and I fought the urge to cringe.

"Hey." I forced a tight-lipped smile.

She looked from me to Finnick, confused. "Did I interrupt something?"

"No, not at all," Finnick answered, smiling and wrapping his arm around her waist. His eyes caught mine briefly, and we shared a look of apprehension.

"So, a lot of people are coming," Rachael said enthusiastically. "The whole cheer squad said they'd be here in support."

I forced myself to forget about everything with Ezra and tried to focus on the service. People had started gathering in circles, chatting quietly. It was a nice night, the warm, June air catching the last sun rays as they melted into the horizon. The first fireflies of summer popped into the increasing darkness, and there was a feeling of hope among us, despite what we had lost. I saw Professor Solomon mingling with a few students and silently worried that he'd be terminated soon.

"We should get started," Finnick said.

I took a deep breath and nodded. I was so anxious about talking in front of all those people, but the memorial had been my idea, so I just had to suck it up.

"Can you pass out the candles while I talk?" I asked Finnick and Rachael, pointing toward the large box by the tree. They nodded, and I cleared my throat to get everyone's attention. "Hey, everyone! I'd like to get started!"

The crowd's attention turned toward me, and I continued, "Thank you all for coming tonight to honor the life of Judah Daniel Brown." I waited a moment for everyone to quiet down before I went on. "Judah had just turned seventeen years old. He's been a part of our family here at St. Mary's since he lost his parents in a fire nine years ago. Judah was an active member of the art and drama clubs and played Iago in last year's production of Shakespeare's *Othello*. We have displayed some of his art tonight for you to see." I gestured with my hand to several easels we had set out with Judah's paintings.

"Judah's religion was very important to him; one might even say he died for it." There was murmuring across the lawn, but I went on. "From Judah's death, let us remember that, yes, courage is dangerous, but it is also the most honorable of acts." I looked around to ensure everyone had a candle. "I ask that you now light your candle in honor of Judah's life, a life extinguished far too soon." I lit a match and ignited my own candle before passing the flame on to those around me. Soon, there were over a hundred candles lit, flecks of gold glowing against the dark of the night.

Next to me, I heard Finnick begin to sing, "On a hill far away, stood an old rugged cross, the emblem of suffering and shame . . . " Slowly, students began joining in, and before I knew it, the whole crowd was softly singing the lyrics of "The Old Rugged Cross." The sound was so powerful and emotional. I wanted to take in the moment and reflect on what happened to Judah and celebrate his life, but I couldn't. As I was looking around at all those people and heard the beautiful rhythm of their voices, all I could think about was the gaping hole of Ezra's absence.

*Esther,*

*We just finished packing everything for the beach. It's the morning of your tenth birthday, and even though it's freezing outside, we're taking you to see the ocean. You won't know because your father and I will be doing everything we can to hide our emotions, but we are deeply grieving today. Something went horribly wrong last night, and people died. This couple, they wouldn't see reason . . . We tried to save them, but they wouldn't see . . . There's a young child, and my heart is breaking. I can't help but think of you, Monkey, and your innocence. It is hard some days not to question God amidst such evil, yet his purpose for your father and me is still clear. We must save as many souls as we can before the clock runs out. Evil grows, and the end is near. These are dangerous times.*

*I love you. Please understand.*

*Mom*

# 45.
# PRESENT DAY

The three of us are now alone in the room. I stare at the shut door where the doctor just left and pray she isn't harmed for helping us. "So, what now?" I ask Solomon as I hand Finnick a paper cup of water from the tap to take one of his pills. He downs the water quickly, and hands me back the cup.

"Well, Finnick is in no condition to continue with the original plan," Solomon states, looking at Finnick, who goes to stand, winces, and sits back down.

"I'll go alone," I say.

"You certainly will not," Solomon answers. "I will go with you."

"Professor . . . no offense, but do you think that's the best idea? You're not exactly sprightly these days," Finnick counters.

"I beg your pardon. I am perfectly capable. I will have you remember that I have seen far more than both of you and have a much better handle on the inner workings of the UFoA."

"Sorry," Finnick mumbles. "No disrespect. But that's just it—the inner workings are your area of expertise, not breaking and entering."

"I will go alone," I repeat. My face is firm, and I look at both in defiance, daring them to question me.

"Es—" Solomon begins.

"Shhh," I silence him. "I mean it. It's settled. I am not budging on the issue, and I am going alone whether or not either of you think I can handle it."

"I think you can," Finnick says, smiling at me proudly. "You're the bravest person I know."

My heart swells at his words, at the realization that his faith in me is growing.

"Well, now I feel bad, Child; it's not that I do not find you brave."

I laugh. "It's okay, Professor; you're just protective, and I do love you for it, but my going alone is the best thing for everyone."

"I will be beside myself with worry the entire time, but so be it. I have arranged a new hideout for us. I must warn you, though, the accommodations are a bit, um, unpleasant." Solomon's lips tighten in distaste

"We'll survive," Finnick answers. "It's important that we talk about what happened to us and who that man was."

"Not here. We can talk in the car. Come." Solomon motions for me to help him lift Finnick up off the table, and we each place one of his arms over our shoulders. We move quietly and cautiously through the door and outside.

Solomon takes the front seat next to the driver, and Finnick and I slide into the back seat. I hear Solomon give the driver an address not far from the clinic.

"We're staying in the ratholes?" I ask, making a face.

"I warned you it would be unpleasant."

"We'll fit right in. It's not like we shower anymore," Finnick jokes half-heartedly, his head laid back on the seat as he stares out the window.

"I'd like to discuss the situation at the brothel, now, Children," Solomon says earnestly. "Prior to arriving where there will be many ears to hear us."

"I looked through the man's wallet and phone already," I tell them. "His name is Gerald Mann, and he had three texts from Jay Hawthorne. There's a passcode, so I never got beyond that."

"I will have Abram break the code," Solomon responds.

"Hawthorne . . . I know that name from somewhere," Finnick reflects.

"Yeah, you do. They were the couple at the hospital who lost their daughter and then chased after us when we broke Solomon out."

"Oh, right."

"Solomon, I know that day is a bit of a blur for you, but do you remember anything that would give them reason to come after us? I mean, other than the obvious motive of their daughter trying to save you." I think back to what the doctor told them, how she had "changed her mind."

"I am sure they know we are in the Resistance and would have our names by now. There were plenty of witnesses that day who would be able to identify me." I'm about to suggest to Solomon that he needs a new look but remember how the man scoffed at Finnick's and my disguise.

"Anything else?" I ask. "I can't help but feel like we're missing something."

"Did the man say why he wanted to hurt you?" Solomon asks.

"He didn't want to hurt us, exactly," I say, hesitating. "He just wanted you."

# 46.
# TWO YEARS EARLIER . . .

Judah's memorial was over, and it was getting late. A canopy of stars shone in a sea of black, and the air was warm and pleasant. The perfect summer night. Everything was quieting down, and most of the students had returned to their dorms. There were still a few of Finnick's teammates helping to clean up as well as Judah's closest friends, huddled around his tree, struggling to let him go.

"I'm surprised we got through the memorial without interruption, honestly," said Judah's best friend, a tall boy named Timothy, to me as I finished folding up the last easel and placed Judah's paintings in a large box.

"Me, too. After that interruption by Sergeant Hall yesterday in the art room, I was expecting him to ruin this somehow."

"I'm grateful he didn't," Timothy said, smiling kindly. "Because tonight was really beautiful. Thanks to you, Esther. I know you and Judah weren't close or anything, so this was really cool of you."

"It's the least I could do. To be honest, I still haven't forgiven myself for not speaking up for him that day in world history. So, I guess this is my way of trying to make up for that, even though he's gone now, so obviously nothing can fully make up for it."

"Yeah, I get it," he said kicking at the ground. "Fear is the strongest motivator for silence in times like these. After all that happened in your world history class, I actually yelled at Judah for being so stupid and talking back to Sergeant Hall. Can you believe that? I yelled at him for doing what was right. Talk about being a coward."

I smiled at him sympathetically. "Hey . . ." I waited until he looked up from the ground. "We're all just doing the best we can, ya know? We're still just kids." He nodded, and I saw Finnick coming toward us, ready to walk back. "I should get going. Take care of yourself, Timothy."

"You, too, Esther. Thanks again." He gave Finnick a head nod and left to go join his friends by Judah's tree.

"Everything good?" Finnick asked.

"Yeah, we were just sharing a moment. I think Judah would have liked tonight."

Finnick pulled me into a hug. "He would have loved it."

## 47.
# PRESENT DAY

The car pulls into a back-alley lot overgrown by weeds that have sprouted out of the concrete at the same pace as the growing regions of ratholes throughout the country. Sam parks next to a fallen power line, and I have to carefully step over wires as I climb out. I make my way over to the other side of the car to retrieve Finnick. The cold, January air smacks my face.

Solomon leads the way as we hobble toward a basement door set in a sloped sidewalk of broken brick. He pulls open one of the heavy steel doors, the concealed hinges creaking as the door hits the ground. I look down to see several steps and an abyss of darkness.

"Do we have to go down there?" I ask pitifully.

Solomon pulls a flashlight out of his bag and hits it against his leg, the light flickering, then turning on. He doesn't answer me but instead begins to walk down the stairs. With my arm wrapped tightly around Finnick, we walk slowly into the darkness. At the bottom, I give my eyes a moment to adjust, and Solomon moves the flashlight around the floor and walls. No code word is necessary as no one here seems to be bothered by anything. Countless bodies, half-clothed, are slumped against the walls, heads down.

I remember a verse in the book of John stating how "the thief comes only to steal and kill and destroy." I look around and feel the power of the devil. These souls now lost to the darkness of this world. A deep cold settles into my bones. I pray silently for my own soul, pleading with God for salvation. I stand immobile, clutching Finnick and staring at the lifeless forms.

"This way, Children," Solomon whispers, gesturing with his hand to keep moving forward. He leads us over to a fairly empty corner at the far side of the basement. I begin to feel sick; the smell of human filth and dank mold fills my nostrils. I clasp a hand over my mouth.

"Here, use this over your face. It will help." Solomon hands me a handkerchief, and I tie it around my head to cover my mouth and nose. Finnick's forehead is screwed up in disgust, but he doesn't say anything, using my arm to support himself as he sits down.

Solomon gestures for me to hand him our duffle bag, and I push it toward him. He starts talking as he pulls out the blueprints for the main headquarters and the phone that links us to Abram. "This is where Finnick and I will hide out while you break into Alastor's office. I have my own phone that links me with Abram, who is in constant contact with the Resistance, so I want you to keep this one." He hands the phone to me and continues. "Abram will set up incoming and outgoing texts and calls to his and my phone, only, to ensure your safety. It will be very difficult for them to track this line, at least for now. He has also informed me that the Resistance's efforts have been successful thus far, having burned down several churches set up to distribute the Federation's mark.

"Three of those were out west, where the centers are rapidly increasing, and several more in the southern regions of the country. There are plans to hit this area hard, whenever we give the signal." He pauses and reaches for his own bag. He pulls out a woman's tailored suit, heels, and a pair of glasses. "You will need to wear these, Esther, in case you are stopped." He then hands me a badge with the name Susan Marks written on it under the title, Director of Commerce.

I take it from his hand, running my thumb over my own picture.

"Keep this around your neck. Susan has black hair and glasses and works on the other side of the building, so you should not run into her." He pauses. "Make sure you don't." I nod. "If you are stopped, tell them you are to set up an appointment with Alastor to discuss trade agreements with China. I doubt anyone will question it, but do what you need to do to get out of there if you feel they are on to you." He takes a deep breath, his eyes searching mine. "Are you sure you want to go through with this alone, Esther? It's not too late to change your mind."

"I'm sure, Professor," I say with assurance. "It feels like what I've been meant to do all along."

# 48.
# TWO YEARS EARLIER . . .

After Judah's memorial, Finnick and I started walking back towards the dormitories. The only light came from the solid, brass streetlamps and students' windows, a mist of glowing particles up ahead.

"Where did Rachael go?" I asked. Not that I wasn't grateful for the time alone with Finnick.

"Some of the cheerleaders were gonna study together for that calc exam tomorrow."

"Right . . . the calc exam. I haven't even looked at my notes. I'm gonna fail." I said the words like I cared, but I really didn't. Honestly, the calculus test was the least of my concerns. Finnick seemed to realize this.

"You want to talk anymore about Ezra?"

I didn't answer him right away. I just let the words fall into the air and enjoyed the silence of walking beside him. The number of people I could trust was diminishing quickly, and I was grateful to have him. I thought about his question, wanting to talk about it but, at the same time, not wanting to. I saw Ezra's face in my mind, the moment we first kissed, and I felt a lump forming in my throat. "It just really hurts, you know?" The lump having grown like a giant tumor, I choked on my next words. "He—he didn't even try." I swallowed hard, but the tumor had taken up residence.

"I can talk to him," Finnick offered.

"No, it's okay . . . It'll just make it worse if he knows I blabbed about everything to you. But thanks." We walked in silence for a while then, and I was about to bring up my concern for Solomon's job when there was a rustling from the bushes up ahead and to our right. "What is that?" I asked, squinting my eyes to see.

"Who's there?" Finnick called out. The rustling stopped. A boy and a girl sauntered out of the bushes, and I recognized them from my world history class. They were the ones who had spoken out against Judah that day. What do they want? I was confused as they walked toward us with confident, smug looks on their faces.

I took a step back as they came closer to me, but they kept walking. I thought they were going to pass us when I felt a sharp pain in the side of my stomach. The boy pulled his hand back, and I gasped as moonlight gleamed off the sheen of his pocketknife. "That's for tonight's little exhibition," the boy hissed in my ear. I put my hand down to my side, pulling it up to see blood. My mouth fell open in surprise. "Next time, you're dead. Change your loyalties," he threatened, his hot breath like fire in my ear.

"Get away from her!" Finnick shouted, barreling toward the boy. Finnick knocked him sideways, making him stumble.

He and the girl took off in a sprint, hooting and screaming, "Accept or die!"

# 49.
# PRESENT DAY

Solomon has arranged with the resistance to burn down two centers today within a ten-mile radius of the main headquarters over the span of an hour. The first center has been marking people for weeks, the ability to buy and sell becoming more and more dependent on UFoA symbology. Abram said there's a chip implanted in the eye of the plumed serpent that can be scanned to not only identify someone but to locate them as well. I remember when our veterinarian suggested that we chip our dog, Cocoa, when I was five. It was new technology then, and I thought how great it was since he was always running off. I thought, *We can always find him.*

Solomon looks over at me. His mouth is turned downward. Bags of exhaustion discolor his skin. He's been off and on the phone with Abram since five o'clock this morning.

"All right, Esther, the first burning will take place at 8:30 a.m., right before the morning's markings are set to begin. That way, not many civilians will be inside. We have eyes on the offices of main headquarters. Elden will lift the security clearance on the fire escape door closest to Alastor's office when the coast is clear. We will have sent you a code to punch in for entrance. Then you must be quick."

I nod. "How long do you think I'll have?"

"It is hard to say. The next burning is set up to begin at nine. We are, again, hoping that most civilians will be outside, though that one cuts it closer. It should buy you more time, though, and I estimate you will have about a twenty-to-thirty-minute window before you need to get yourself out."

"Okay, thanks, Professor. As always, what would I do without you?" I give him a small smile, and he embraces me in a hug.

"Take care of yourself, my girl."

I turn toward Finnick with an apprehensive smile. He fidgets with his hands before reaching to give me something. "Here, take this," Finnick says, lifting the engraved cross necklace from his neck.

"Finnick," I whisper, "I can't. It's all you have of your parents."

"And you need protection now and a reminder that people need you to come back. I want you to take it." He looks down, his shoulders slumped. "I feel so helpless, Es. I wish I was going with you."

I lift his face and meet his eyes. "Just get better. We're going to need your strength when we find out what Alastor is planning." I take the necklace from his hands and slip it over my head, tucking it into my shirt. "I'll guard it with my life."

He nods, and our eyes reflect the anger, love, fear, and loss we've experienced together.

"You're my best friend. Just come back."

# 50.
# Two Years Earlier . . .

"You're bleeding!" Finnick screamed, seeing the knife wound and a growing mass of red spreading across my t-shirt. He quickly tore off his own shirt, balled it up, and pressed it against my stomach.

"I feel dizzy, Finn," I murmured as my knees wavered. I blinked twice to stay conscious.

"I got you, Es, you hear me? I have you. Stay with me. We're going to the infirmary. It's not far." He pressed firmly against the wound again before lifting me up in his arms. I moaned quietly, the trees around me spinning.

The next thing I remembered was staring up at the white ceiling of the infirmary, the nurse taking my pulse, and Finnick clasping my hand. "Did I pass out for a little?" I asked.

"Yes, but you're okay. The nurse said you'll be okay." Finnick's words came out in a rush, like he was convincing himself that everything was fine, and I was filled with affection for him.

The nurse smiled at me kindly. "I'll be back to check on you shortly."

I squeezed Finnick's hand in mine. "I'm so glad you were there. What would I have done if you hadn't been there?" My mind filled with fear as I pictured myself bleeding out on the paved pathway, the only witness to my death two metal streetlamps.

"Shh. Don't think like that. You need to rest. The important thing is that you're okay."

"We have to report what happened." I sat up abruptly, remembering the boy's sneer and his hot words on my ear.

Finnick pushed my shoulders back gently. "And we will, but right now, you're healing. Let me take care of everything else."

"Oh no, what happened?" Rachael's voice rang through the room as she sprinted through the door, her face a painting of alarm. "One of the cheerleaders said she saw you carrying a girl across the quad toward the infirmary, and I just knew it had to be Esther. Are you okay?" she asked anxiously.

I took a sip of the water Finnick handed me and nodded. "I'm fine. We were assaulted. Well, I guess just I was assaulted, really. But I thank God Finnick was there."

"The nurse gave her five stitches and said she needs bedrest for the next few days, but she should be good as new in no time." He smiled at me encouragingly.

"Who did this?" Rachael demanded, and I had to admit that I was touched by her outrage on my behalf.

"Do you remember the boy and girl who spoke out in world history that day against Judah?"

Rachael thought for a moment before responding. "I think so. The girl has short, dark hair, right?" I nodded, and she continued. "And I think the boy's name is Victor. He's fairly new here."

"Well, he threatened me to change my loyalties and ran off screaming, 'Accept or die.' The message was pretty clear." My body tremored slightly, remembering the ruthless look in his eyes.

"Oh no, that's exactly what I've been afraid of," Rachael said, her eyes wide. "I think students are starting to take sides. This thing with Judah is stirring up a war." She lowered her voice, ran a hand through her hair, and looked around to make sure we were alone. "Chloe was telling me at cheer yesterday that they're planning a book burning."

"Who's they?" I asked.

"The officers here, I guess—those representing the UFoA. They want to get rid of all the Bibles and publications that promote the Christian and Jewish God."

As I took this new information in, I thought back to the day I first arrived at St. Mary's. I had stepped out of the car and looked at the sizable, brick building with hope—not hope for happiness, my parents' deaths having stolen that from me, but hope that I would be safe. It seemed funny to me now that I thought St. Mary's could protect any of us from what was out there. I should have known that nowhere was safe.

"Well, I guess we need to come up with a plan," I responded, looking from Rachael to Finnick. The three of us sat in silence, the sterile air of the infirmary suffocating as we realized what our lives were becoming. In that moment, we had no idea that it was only the beginning.

# 51.
# PRESENT DAY

Walking briskly, I pull the lapels of the suit jacket tightly around me, but it does little to combat the cold. My new look clearly didn't fool the man hired by the Hawthornes, but hopefully, it'll help my anonymity today. I step out into the street; the dew of the morning is wet on the windows of the row homes and office buildings. The temperatures are below freezing, and while we were in the confines of the rathole, a fresh snow descended like a blanket over the cold, hard ground. The beauty of it fools me for a moment, and I almost forget that I'm living in an apocalyptic nightmare.

I keep my head down as I walk. I take side streets, dodging the surveillance cameras the Federation's been placing throughout major cities and towns. The key is to blend in, to not draw attention to myself. The truth is, I'm glad to be going alone. If I mess up, at least it won't cost Finnick his life.

Shouts of confusion and disorder ring out from across the street, and I look over to see flames rising beyond the buildings adjacent to me. The first burning . . . I pick up my pace.

Less than a kilometer from Alastor's offices, the phone in my pocket vibrates. I pull it out of my suit jacket and straighten the material to try to make it more comfortable before pushing the glasses up farther on my nose. My legs are wobbling in these heels; I can't even remember the last time I wore heels.

The winter dance at St. Mary's, maybe? I see Ezra's face, his gray eyes swimming with love and hope as he leaned in to kiss me. I struggle to repress my emotions. Focus, Esther. I look down at the phone, which reads, "0891," the code for the fire escape entrance. I need to hurry now.

The main headquarters is ahead of me, the silver blaze of the sea of windows shining underneath the curve of the wind turbines, strung like beads atop of the building. People are flocking toward the billowing clouds of gray smoke rising east of the capital building, and just as I hoped, I'm lost in the shuffle. I slip out of the crowd and approach the side of the building. The alley of the fire escape is mostly empty, but there's two uniformed officers standing around, smoking cigarettes. I keep my back against the wall, out of sight. I need to get rid of them.

Straightening my shoulders, I take a few steps forward, my head held high in authority. My hand is already on my badge, ready to brandish it.

"Officers," I command, "You're needed on the corner of West Third and Elm; there's been another fire started by resistors."

The officers look at each other, confused. One tosses his cannabis down, the smell wafting through the air, burning my nostrils. He crushes it out with his boot as he answers, "On whose authority? We were told to be here. We can't leave this door unguarded."

"President Alastor gave the order for all military units to report, but you're right about the door," I answer, keeping my tone even. "I'll stay here and call in for a security guard. But we need military representation over there, now. It's mayhem."

They look at each other and shrug. "All right," the one still smoking says as he looks at my badge. "Ms. Marks."

I nod curtly and stand my ground as they walk off down the alley. I wait until they're well out of sight and allow myself to breathe normally again. I can't believe they bought that. I look at the steps along the concrete wall up to the door before looking around. With no one in sight, I glide up the steps. The panel for the keycode is against the side of the metal doorway. Glancing around once more, I lift the plastic casing, punch in the four numbers, and slip cautiously inside.

## 52.
# Two Years Earlier . . .

After the stabbing, they kept me in the infirmary under observation for twenty-four hours. Finnick never left my side once. I was watching him sleep now, his body slumped in the chair, head bobbing up and down. I let my mind wonder to what it would have been like if Finnick had asked me to the winter dance that day instead of Rachael, how different things might have been.

Ezra had come by once while I was sleeping, dropping off flowers and a note that simply said, "Feel better!" I was sure he meant the gesture as genuine, but it only came across as hurtful, the two words a chipper reminder that I was no longer worth his time.

Rachael had been wonderful—annoyingly wonderful. She had borrowed the key to my room to retrieve my favorite blanket, collected all my homework from my teachers, and even brought me ice cream. I again found myself questioning her motives. What was she trying to prove?

Professor Solomon had come by, too, his face grave. He had taken copious notes of the incident and wanted every last detail. His plan was to meet with Mother Maura and Sister Margaret later today.

"All right, careful now," the nurse said while lifting me gently from the bed to the wheelchair. She looked over at Finnick as she lowered me into the chair. "She needs rest and fluids. Don't let anything overexcite her if you can help it." Her eyes shifted over to me. "And not too much movement until that wound completely heals." I nodded slightly, already thinking about how I could save books from the burning tonight. "I mean it, Miss Warder. You do not want to wind up back in this bed, do you?"

"I'll be careful." I tried to sound assuring.

"I'll be sure she rests, Nurse Judy. Thank you so much for everything." Finnick flashed his award-winning smile, and the nurse's face flushed.

I slit my eyes at him, and he shrugged. The nurse handed him a bag with my bloodstained clothes and a bottle of painkillers before walking out.

"Do you want your blanket over you or anything before we leave?" he asked.

"Finnick, it's like eighty degrees out. I'm not elderly."

He laughed. "Okay, then, I thought we'd make a pit stop at Rachael's before I take you back to your dorm. I think we should talk about tonight."

"Sounds good," I said with a nod. "It's all I've been able to think about. I feel like I'm living in Nazi Germany or something."

"The similarities are scary. Next, they'll be trying to gas Christians."

I shuddered. "Please don't say that, Finn."

"I just think we need to be prepared for the evil we're dealing with is all."

"God won't let something like that happen again," I said more confidently than I felt.

"If this is the beginning of the end, the devil gets free reign for a while."

I tried to stifle my fear. "Why couldn't we have lived in a simpler time?"

He reached down and squeezed my shoulder, wheeling me toward the elevator. "At least we have each other."

It was a slow trek across campus to Rachael's room, I had to practically beg him to let me walk and not use the wheelchair. Finnick knocked on the patterned wood. I noticed Rachael had decorated her door with pictures of her and Finnick and some inspirational quotes. I silently read one by Vernor Vinge: "The heart of manipulation is to empathize without being touched." What an odd quote to have on your door.

"Hey, guys, come on in," Rachael interrupted my thoughts, holding the door to her room open with a smile.

Finnick's arm was around my waist, and I had a crutch under my right arm. We hobbled inside, where there were a handful of people sitting on the floor talking and eating snacks. I recognized Judah's best friend, Timothy. We made eye contact and exchanged a smile.

"Sorry, did we interrupt something?" Finnick said, confused.

"No, not at all; we're here to help," said a mousy girl, no taller than five-one. She jumped up from the floor and held out her hand. "I'm Lizzie," she said.

"Finnick," he answered, shaking her hand. He tilted his head toward me. "This is Esther."

"We know who you are," Lizzie said with a laugh. "You guys are earning a reputation pretty quickly around here. Everyone's calling you the avengers of truth."

I was touched by her words but also a little surprised. When we had planned Judah's memorial, I had never expected it to start a resistance.

I gave Lizzie a small smile. "We just wanted justice for Judah. He didn't deserve to die, especially not like that." There was a moment of silence as everyone thought about what had happened to him and the lies surrounding his death.

"Judah would want us to stand up for what's right, starting with the book burning tonight," Timothy said, the first to speak up about the UFoA's most recent agenda. Everyone in the room nodded in agreement. "I've been thinking about it all day, and I think we should refuse to go—as many of us as possible," he suggested.

"I ripped up the floorboards under my bed to store Bibles and any other religious books you guys want to keep," Rachael said.

"That's an awesome idea," I responded warmly, forgetting for a second who I was talking to.

Rachael was also startled by my praise, and her face lit up in surprise. Finnick looked between us and grinned. I fought the urge to take it back, hating that she was so hard for me to dislike. I tried to swallow my feelings for Finnick. They were just rebound feelings. Normal after a break-up.

"I'll nail them back down for you in case they do room sweeps," Finnick said.

"They're definitely doing room sweeps," Timothy told us. "I overheard Sergeant Hall discussing it with Sergeant Barnes earlier today. They're happening in the morning. Those who show resistance tonight will have their rooms swept first."

"That'd be us, then," I said, thinking aloud. "How many people do you think we can convince to join us?"

"At least the same number who were at Judah's memorial," Timothy answered. "Maybe more."

"Maura and I can start going door to door," Lizzie offered. Her friend, Maura, gave a nod of agreement.

"We'll take the dormitories on this side if you take the ones across campus," Timothy offered, gesturing to two of his friends, who quickly agreed.

"Since I can't really walk, I can stay here to make signs for a protest. We can form a rally march at the same time as the burning," I suggested.

"Good thinking, Es," Finnick responded. "Rachael and I will go see what Professor Solomon has learned from the inside." The room grew weirdly silent, and Finnick looked around, confused. "What'd I say?" he asked.

"Nothing . . . it's just we thought you'd have heard." Timothy peered around uncomfortably and realized no one else wanted to tell us. "They fired Professor Solomon last night for his part in the memorial. They said he was 'encouraging rebellion.'" He shook his head. "So ridiculous," he finished quietly.

"They did what?" I practically yelled, standing up, only to remember that I couldn't stand and was about to fall when Finnick caught my arm.

"It's true," Lizzie confirmed. "He has to be off campus by the end of the school day."

I looked over at Finnick. "We need to go see him. Now." I picked up my crutch from off the floor and stood up. "We'll see you all for the rally tonight. Meet out front at seven."

There were murmurs of agreement, and Finnick kissed Rachael goodbye, the boys giving low whistles. My frustration compounded, and I pulled on his arm to leave. He placed his arm back around my waist to keep me upright, and we walked into the hall, shutting the door behind us.

## 53.
# PRESENT DAY

I'm blinded by the iridescent overhead lights as I slip inside the building. I quickly press my back against the wall, blinking several times to adjust my sight. There are voices coming from the hallway around the corner.

"The center on East Market . . . "

"Yes, send backup . . . "

"Resistance . . . any means necessary . . . "

I swallow, my throat dry, and wait until the voices have moved away from me. When there is silence, I tentatively step into the hall. President Alastor's office is only thirty feet away. As planned, the secretary is away from her desk.

I can see the door behind a table that holds a coffee maker and a basket of fresh muffins. My mouth waters at the thought of biting into freshly baked bread. Ensuring no one is around and taking no chances, I walk with purpose toward the door. My hands are shaking as I turn the metal lever and slip inside. The hallway surveillance cameras will have picked up my presence, but I'll deal with those consequences if I even make it out of here alive. I pass by the muffins and head back toward his office, encased in large panels of glass. I know I don't have much time now. I stay low in case anyone looks through the windows from the hallway. Crawling on hands and knees, I glide to the drawers of his desk, passing a framed portrait of Alastor on the wall. Of course, he's a narcissist. The first drawer is filled with mundane office supplies. I quietly shut it.

I look on the surface of the desk and shuffle the papers on top. There's one on gender identity reform. I snap a photo with my phone. Another on a world currency. *Snap.* Facial recognition technology. *Snap.* I pull open the bottom drawer, and it's full of files. *Bingo.* I rake my fingers through them. There's many with names of places—one on last year's world leaders' summit. I'm overwhelmed. I want to take the whole drawer.

My hands skim across a file entitled, "Euphrates." Knowing the significance of the river, I pull it out. I open it onto the floor. The first page is puzzling. It seems to be some kind of code. I take a picture. My eyes skim the next page, reading that "NASA studies indicate the river is drying up." Yes, yes, I know that.

I keep turning through pages, looking for anything significant. I gasp when I see it, my hand flying up to cover my mouth. The words *YOU'RE DEAD* flash back into my mind. Bile rises like a snake in my throat. I gulp, forcing it down.

I stare down at the file of the man in my parent's photo—the man who was protesting with them, who was likely the one who threatened them, who may have even killed them. I stare at the name at the top of the file. David Knapp. "David," I whisper the name. My mom's last letter. I take in the picture of his face that's been paper-clipped to sheets of information. Trembling all over, I fold the papers and jam them into my pocket. I don't care if they see they're missing. I quickly take pictures of the other documents in the folder and shove the file back in the drawer. My phone is vibrating. Finnick. I'm about to answer it but hear a voice outside the door.

"Hello, yes, the president would like you to arrange a meeting with the leaders of each major region."

Oh no, the secretary is back.

"Uh-huh, Thursday, yes. I will email you the agenda."

Oh no, oh no, oh no. How am I going to get out of here? I scan the room from my spot on the floor behind his desk. There's a coat closet to the right. If I can make it there, I can stay until she leaves again—could be hours. I groan inside.

"Hello, sir."

"Yes, sir, three messages. And I made the call regarding Thursday's meeting."

*Alastor.* Beads of sweat form on my head and lips, and I taste the salt as it falls into my arid mouth. I scurry like a mouse to the closet, slowly pulling it open from the bottom. I barely make it inside as I hear the lever of the door turn.

I hug my knees tightly to my body, terrified I'll make a sound. Easing my phone out of my pocket, I see a text from Solomon stating, "R u inside?"

I quietly type out a response. "Trapped in the closet."

Outside, I can hear Alastor on the phone. "The gender mainstreaming exercises are not optional, Robert. They are compulsory. Our largest problems can be conquered through this reform. We must institutionalize gender beginning with daycares. We start young and gradually transform society. I will not have these people defying the new laws. You know what to do." He hangs up.

There's a quiet knock on the door, and then I hear the secretary's voice. "Sir. Ezra Lodge is here to see you."

My heart jumps into my throat. Ezra.

"Send him in."

"Uncle," Ezra says, and his voice conjures so many feelings, my mind's floodgate shatters, and years of emotions rush in. I haven't seen him since that day Finnick and I watched him shoot a man.

I've shot a man since then, too. How am I any better than him? The familiar pang of guilt washes through me as I picture the man's bloody face, his body a limp mass on the floor.

"My dear nephew. I hope you're well and that you've brought the briefs."

"I am, sir, thank you. There are some issues we need to address, but I have our plans here."

"What issues?"

"Well, there's been more instances of burnings throughout the country, two this morning just a couple miles from here. It's becoming a much larger problem than we had anticipated."

"Curse those resistors," Alastor snaps. "Let's push up the date of Agenda 47. Put Hawthorne on it."

"Sir, I don't know that we're ready. Things aren't in place."

"You will make it happen," he answers, leaving no room for question in his tone. "You must make your father proud. Remember, that it was those resistors who stole him from us. They took his life away as if it meant nothing. I will hold you personally responsible for the results of this mission."

"Yes, sir."

"I'll have Caroline working on the agenda around the clock. See her on your way out."

"Yes, sir," Ezra answers.

"And, Nephew? "

"Yes, sir?"

"Don't mess this up."

I hear the movement of feet, the door opening and closing, and I let out the breath I've been holding. Oh, Ezra, why did you do this to yourself? Why do I care? As much as I've tried to fight it, I still worry about Ezra. I worry about him all the time. I fear there's no turning back for him now; he's in it with the devil himself.

"Caroline! The press release, please," Alastor shouts out to his secretary.

"Yes, sir," she answers, and I hear her feet scurry into the room. "Here you are. There are reporters waiting for your statement outside, sir."

There's a shuffling of papers. "These resistance groups are growing, Caroline. They must be stopped."

"Yes, sir." A moment of silence passes. "The reporters, sir."

"Yes, yes, I'm coming." I hear his chair push back as he gets up and moves toward the door.

It shuts behind him, and I relax my shoulders in relief. I wait a minute to make sure he's not coming back, then inch the door open. I send a quick text to Solomon, telling him I'm going to make a run for it.

Seconds later, the phone vibrates with a reply. "Be careful."

# 54.
# TWO YEARS EARLIER . . .

"We can't do this without you," I whined to Professor Solomon as he pulled shirts out of his closet and placed them into a suitcase.

"You will not have to, Child. I will not be here at St. Mary's, but I am not permanently leaving your lives."

"But what does that mean, Professor? Where will you go?" Finnick asked.

"I have friends I trust who will take me in. They are part of the growing resistance. I can help them fight."

"Let us come with you," I said, my voice urgent. "There's nothing for us here."

"On the contrary, Esther. There is much need for you here. I was privy to the upcoming changes at St. Mary's; and they are not only going to compromise your beliefs, but they will be gravely dangerous for those who resist. You must stay and help the weak. You both must save who you can. There will come a time when St. Mary's will fall away. Much like the cities of the Old Testament, the institution is mounting in its corruption. But that time is not now."

The gravity of his words frightened me, and neither Finnick nor I could respond. There were several minutes of silence as we took in what he had said, the only sound that of Solomon as he carefully placed toiletries into a small canvas bag.

"How will we reach you?" Finnick finally asked.

Solomon moved over to his desk and pulled a piece of small, white paper off a tablet. He wrote down an address and a phone number. "Do not lose this paper. Only use it when St. Mary's falls."

I looked down at the paper. "This isn't that far from here. But, Prof—" I started, but he held up a hand to silence me.

"We will meet again. This is not goodbye. It may be months, or it may be years, but you must not contact me until you leave here. Do you understand?"

I wanted to protest but swallowed the words, a sob rising in my throat. Finnick and I nodded quietly.

"I will miss you, Children," Solomon said softly, reaching his arms out to us, and we embraced him in a hug. Warmth surged through me as I hugged the only two people in the world I trusted, and the three of us stayed clasped together, afraid to let go.

Later that evening, when Finnick and I were standing outside the dormitories with our signs, waiting for everyone to join us to start marching, the thought of that hug and Solomon's promise that I'd see him again gave me hope. With Solomon leaving, there was only one teacher left who was willing to help us. Professor Darci was coming toward us now, a sad smile on his face. I gave him a wave, distracted by my surroundings. I'd been super paranoid since that kid, Victor, stabbed me. I kept looking over my shoulder every few seconds.

"What's your deal?" Finnick asked, looking at me strangely.

"I just don't want someone creeping up behind me." I leaned hard on my crutch as I looked around.

"You're losing it, Es."

"Tell me about it," I muttered.

"Hey, kids," Professor Darci greeted us. He was a big man, muscular and tall. He looked like he belonged on a football field, not in a classroom. "Great signs," he said nodding toward the large signs I had spent the last two hours making.

I looked down at them proudly. In large, block letters, one read: THINK FOR YOURSELF, DON'T CONFORM. Another said: WHAT HAPPENED TO RELIGIOUS FREEDOM? And my personal favorite: HYPOCRITES CLAIM ACCEPTANCE FOR ALL.

"There will be repercussions," Professor Darci said.

"We know," I answered solemnly. A wave of fear rushed through me as I remembered Judah's swaying body, but I shook it off. The alternative was to do nothing, which really wasn't an alternative at all.

"Hey, guys," I said to Timothy, Lizzie, and about five others, who were coming toward us, carrying more signs and waving.

Seeing them gave me some relief, and my sense of security only grew as more and more resistors showed up. Some were carrying signs; others were wearing t-shirts.

One had the slogan, GOD BROUGHT YOU INTO THIS WORLD. HE CAN TAKE YOU OUT." I smiled, thinking of my mom, knowing she'd have found humor in it. There was a general buzz of excitement in the air that helped alleviate some of my fear.

"Are we ready?" I shouted, feeling like I should let out a battle cry and pound my chest or something.

"Ready!" The group returned my sense of eagerness.

"Let's march!" Finnick yelled.

# 55.
# PRESENT DAY

I sprint in front of the large wall of plated glass lining Alastor's office before looking out into the foyer. I then press my back firmly against the door. My heart feels like it's going to detonate and blow up the whole room. I turn to peer out at the secretary's desk, but she's still sitting there, typing away on her computer. I need her to leave.

I send a text to Solomon. "Can you get the secretary out?"

It takes a couple minutes, and it feels more like half a century; but my phone buzzes, and it says, "Yes. Expect Elden." I sigh. Poor Elden. What if they figure out he helped me from the surveillance videos?

Abram's words ring in my ears: "He has two children." Before I can text back that I'll figure something else out, I hear a voice through the door.

"There's an issue with a security breach, and I need your help. It can only be cleared with Alastor's facial recognition, but he's at the press conference," a man's voice, which must be Elden's, is telling Caroline.

"I'll need to see your credentials, please. Then I'll come with you and perform an override," she answers him.

"Of course," he says, and I watch through the glass as he pulls his security clearance from his wallet and shows his ID.

"Soon, we'll have the chip recorder in here, and it will be much more efficient," she says apologetically, taking his papers.

"I don't mind," Elden replies. I bet he doesn't.

I wonder if Elden will have to quit his job. I'd imagine that would be better than him having to tell these people he won't receive their mark.

"Thank you," she says, handing him back his papers. "I'll just follow you, then."

Elden nods, and they turn and walk out of the room. I force myself to count to thirty before opening the door. I step out and am about to make a break for it, but I pause at Caroline's computer screen. What the . . . I stand there, blinking my eyes in horror.

Caroline left open a document, the words now blurring before my eyes. At the top of the page, in clear black letters, it reads, "Agenda 47: Seven Year Liquidation Act of Christians and Jews."

*Everyone's haunted by something. In my dreams at night, I see Rachael. Her beautiful mouth is open wide in horror; there's blood on her face. She reaches for me, but I can't quite grasp her hand. The sound of screaming ricochets like echoes in a void. I think it's my voice or maybe hers, but then I realize it's Finnick's. I wake up sweating, reminded that I failed him, that I've failed God. This life, the one we're living now, where evil creeps in and snatches virtue, has ripped through me, slowly removing my innocence. People love newborn babies so much because they're a reminder that there's still good in the world, that purity still exists. It's what so many of us long for—another chance, a cleansing of spirit, a way to start new. In this fight against evil, there's only one fear that torments me endlessly. It's not death, and it's not even pain or loss. What I'm most afraid of is that I've destroyed my soul.*

# 56.
# TWO YEARS EARLIER . . .

As we marched toward the book burning that was being held in the square behind the gymnasium, I could already see the black smoke rising. I kept looking around for Ezra, hoping he'd show up to join us. I had stopped by his dorm after Finnick and I left Solomon's, but he said a protest march "wasn't really his thing."

There were at least a hundred of us who had shown up, and Professor Darci was leading the march. I admired him. Surely, he knew the risks of being the only faculty member helping us today. And sadly, I realized he wouldn't be with us much longer. I thought about Mother Maura and Sister Margaret, their power becoming less and less influential in the direction of our school. I worried for their safety. I'd miss Solomon, but at least he had gotten out alive. I silently prayed that Professor Darci would, too.

We approached the square, and my palms grew sweaty as I struggled to reposition my sign, holding it high above my head. I looked over at Finnick and Rachael, marching side by side, and felt another flicker of jealousy. I shouldn't have had to be alone. Ezra should have been with me. I tried to shake off my sadness, but it was looming over me like a storm cloud. It was why I didn't see it at first—the burning cross.

"Dear God, help us," a boy next to me cried out, and I followed his eyes, mine growing wide in disbelief.

What was this? A KKK rally? The cross had been placed next to the large flames of a bonfire. I recognized its form from the front of our chapel, the three bars lighting up the darkening sky. How many times had I prayed at the foot of that cross? How could they desecrate something so sacred? I thought I was going to be sick.

"Stand up for religious freedom," a girl next to me screamed out. The students around me quickly followed and began chanting religious slogans, like "Hosanna in the highest" and "No God, no peace!"

Armed UFoA officers were throwing books from large bins into a roaring fire. I cringed as I watched the pages of a Bible disintegrate in the flames. There was a mass of students, larger than our group, watching and cheering—some even participating. I heard a student shout, "May His name be obliterated," and my eyes filled with tears. God, where are You, I prayed.

I saw Timothy, Lizzie, and some of the other kids pulling books out of the flames and stomping the fire off them. An officer came over, and using the barrel of his rifle, he cracked Timothy over the head. Timothy fell to the ground like a marionette. I stifled a scream, dropping my sign and looking around frantically for Finnick. I spotted him and Rachael with their signs raised, and I hobbled over.

"Timothy—he's . . . he's hurt," I stuttered, my head on a spindle to make sure we were not hit next.

"Take him out of here if you need to. I'm not leaving yet," Finnick said firmly, raising his sign high and shouting, "Saved by grace! God promises a new day!" He marched off circling the fire, and I turned to Rachael.

"You'll help me get Timothy out of here? I can't let him die—not after Judah." A sob strangled my throat, and I tried to swallow, my mouth bitter.

"I'll help you," Rachael said, taking my hand. "Come on." She led me like a child to where Timothy was lying on the ground. Lizzie was kneeling next to him, sobbing.

"He has a pulse, but it's weak," she whispered, her fingers on his throat, tears streaming down her face.

"Let's try to get him up," I said, ignoring the pain in my side as I knelt next to her to hoist him forward.

Above us, I heard someone say, "Leave him."

I looked up to see the cold eyes of Sergeant Hall. I couldn't speak. I had unconsciously started shaking my head no. Sergeant Hall reached between the three of us, all hovering over Timothy's body, and shot him in the head.

The sound of Sergeant Hall's gun ricocheted in my ears. His cruel eyes assessed us defiantly before he walked off into the crowd. My body shook as I stared down at the blood on my clothes. Seconds turned into minutes, and Lizzie's ear-piercing screams continued. I began to rock back and forth on the ground, holding my knees tightly against my body. Rachael was cradling Timothy's head, her hands and arms covered in his blood. We didn't move for what felt like hours.

The people spun around me like ghosts, the smell of burning pages obstructing my nostrils, the smoke filling my throat. I kept rocking. My mind left the present.

*I was a little girl, and my parents were ahead of me walking up the steps of a large church. It was the day of my baptism. My dress was pink tulle, my hair curled in ringlets. My mom turned around and smiled . . . but the smile dissipated, and I was staring at her corpse, lying in a coffin next to my dad's.*

*There was a procession of people, kind words, pats on the back. I nodded; said thank you, "kind of you to come," "yes, they were wonderful." I was in Ezra's arms now. We were lying on a blanket under a vast sky of bright stars. He whispered, "I love you," and I pulled him into a kiss...*

"Esther! Esther!" Finnick was screaming in my face, shaking my shoulders. "Where are you? Snap out of it!"

I shook my head and blinked. "Finnick?" I looked over and saw Timothy, remembering where I was, and suddenly, I was screaming, too.

Lizzie's and my screams connected together like two streams converging. Finnick's eyes widened as he looked down at Timothy in horror. Rachael sat in silence, still cradling what was left of Timothy's head, sobbing, her body heaving.

"Enough, Girls. We have to get out of here, please. It's growing worse. We have to leave. Now!" Finnick screamed the last word, pleading for our attention. He looked at all three of us, gauging who was the most mentally stable to try to see reason. The fear in his face snapped me out of my shock, and I made an effort to stand.

"We'll come back for his body, Rachael. Set down his head." My words came out monotone, like they were someone else's.

Finnick picked up Lizzie off the ground, her screams having died down to moans and whimpers. Her face was blotched red from her tears. Together, the four of us hobbled away from Timothy's body and the flames. There were officers and students still jeering and shouting at the fire as they tossed books into the air. My eyes blurred as I noticed more bodies dead on the ground—students I recognized, their faces twisted in surprise, agony, anger. I thought back to that morning when I had been sitting in English, and I couldn't make sense of that night having been part of my earlier day. Evil had emerged from monotony like a creature in darkness, forever taking from us the last hope for peace.

# 57.
# PRESENT DAY

I push open the door to the fire escape exit of the main headquarters. The cold air is like a slap in the face. I look to the sky, dark despite it being midday, the sun a foggy glow in a sea of mist. The officers I sent away are back now, and I draw in a breath. I pull my suit jacket tight around me, ensure that Susan Marks' ID is visible on my chest, and push the fake glasses up on my nose. I keep my head high and try to walk with purpose. The street adjacent to the alley is chaotic. People are running away from the locations of the burnings, and there's a general atmosphere of disorder and confusion.

"You again!" the first officer snaps at me. "We went where you said, and there was no record of our presence being requested."

The other officer walks toward me accusingly. "Who did you say gave the order?" he asks suspiciously.

I swallow hard before speaking, hoping my voice doesn't convey the sense of panic rising in my throat. "President Alastor himself," I answer. "Obviously, it is chaos right now, so if protocol is taking longer than usual, it is of no surprise."

"That may be." The first officer's face softens slightly. "But I can assure you that I will be asking the president about your orders."

"I would expect nothing less from two of our best officers." Their bodies relax at the compliment, seemingly pleased that a superior would commend them. I give a brief nod to indicate that our conversation is finished and move swiftly toward the street.

As I step foot into the mayhem, I breathe a sigh of relief. I just may have gotten away with it . . . for now. I walk swiftly toward the ratholes catching bouts of conversations.

"My brother was in there, about to receive his mark . . . "

"Did you see how those officers grabbed that dude?"

"President Alastor gave a statement."

"I'd hate to be a resistor right now."

"Hawthorne was furious, man."

Hawthorne. I almost pause to ask why but catch myself and keep walking. I see the side street leading to the nest of ratholes and break off the main street to the right. An old man in rags, heating his hands over a barrel fire, whistles toward me. I pick up my pace and avoid his eyes.

"C'mon, girlie, spare some change?"

I feel my pocket vibrate and reach for my phone while keeping my stride. "Hello?"

"Esther!" It's Finnick's voice, fearful and anxious.

"I'm all right, Finn. Coming back now."

"No, we're leaving here. We'll come get you. We're going back to Abram's."

"Good. I have so much to tell you guys." I look up briefly for a street name. "I'm turning on Bristow Street, about a quarter mile from our previous location."

"Gotcha," Finnick responds. "See you soon."

The same black car we rode in after our stint at the urgent care peels up next to me. The door swings open, and Finnick yells, "Get in now!"

I slide quickly into the seat next to him, confused. "What's with the yelling?" I ask, shutting the door of the car.

"It's Solomon!"

"What do you mean, *it's Solomon? I just talked to you, like, five minutes ago." I look up to the driver. "Hi, Sam." He nods and gives me half of a tired smile.

"I know. Solomon had been talking to some people in the rathole while I was on the phone, just some addicts he was trying to save. I only had my back turned for, like, two minutes." His hands cover his face, and he run his fingers through his new buzz cut, searching for his old hair. "They took him, Es; they took him." He chokes out a sob.

"Who took him?" I demand.

"I don't know what to do . . . " His sob has turned into full-out crying, and he's gasping for air. "It's—" he says between breaths—"my fault."

"Finnick, come on now. It is not your fault. We're going to figure this out. Did you talk to the people he had been talking to?"

"Yeah." He looks over at me, his eyes rimmed in red. "They said two men took him; one called the other Jay."

"The Hawthornes," I whisper.

He nods, his eyes downcast. "They'll kill him, Esther. They'll torture him; then they'll kill him."

"We don't know that." But I had been thinking the same thing. I think back to the man who assaulted us and how desperate he had been to gain Solomon's whereabouts. How did they find him? "Does Abram know yet?"

"No, I—I was gonna call him, but I just couldn't."

"He'll know soon enough, I guess," I say, looking out the window, my brow furrowed in worry. "Until we get there, we should strategize, so we can help."

"Strategize? Esther, we have no idea where he is or where they would take him. How do we strategize?"

"Actually, we might be able to figure out where he is. I overheard Alastor talking about an Agenda 47. I was going to wait to tell you this, but with Solomon gone, we can't waste any time. They're planning to exterminate Christians and Jews. I think Hawthorne's working on it."

"I'm not even surprised by that, Esther. It's where their movement's been headed all along. They hate those who oppose their ideals, and those who oppose their ideals are largely evangelicals. So, yeah, it's no surprise."

"I was still shocked. I never imagined after Hitler that the world would come to this point again. How could it? How could we let it?"

"Because people are as inherently evil as they are good, and right now, evil is winning." Finnick pauses, then continues, "At least, Abram will be able to look into this Agenda 47."

"Yes, he will. And we will find him, Finnick."

"I just hope he's al—" But he can't finish his thought, his throat choking up again. He turns away from me toward the window.

His wish finds the fears in my mind, and I force his words away. I can't allow myself to think of losing Solomon or to imagine what they might be doing to him.

"Yeah," I say, the words heavy in my throat. "Me, too."

## 58.
# ONE YEAR EARLIER . . .

Several students had died the night of the book burning. In the aftermath of their deaths, life had become surprisingly normal, given the circumstances. We were following the same routines by attending our classes, eating our meals, and hanging out with friends. No one in administration said anything about the book burning or the students' deaths; it was like the night had never happened at all. Though, of course, it had. And the reminders were there, in the day to day, like the sweep of our dorms, two officers briskly striding in and tearing my room apart, or in Sergeant Hall's look of repugnance when I would come into class.

And just as we had predicted, Professor Darci lost his job. At least, that was what we assumed happened when he disappeared from campus. All the teachers were now UFoA officials, with a few nuns as the only remaining members of the original faculty of St. Mary's. So, life for those of us in the Resistance had become difficult in subtle ways. But other than those changes, I could almost have convinced myself that Judah's and Timothy's deaths hadn't happened. I could almost have made myself believe that things would go back to the way they had been. Almost.

"I miss us," I told Ezra as we walked together to calculus.

He looked at me sadly for a moment before responding. "I miss us, too, Esther."

"It doesn't have to be like this," I continued. "We can figure out our differences if we really want to."

"You know that's not true. The truth would continue to push us apart. Eventually, we'd hate each other. It's better this way. We can remember the good." His tone was final. His decision made.

"What truth? If you would just tell me what you learned about your parents, we could work through it together," I pleaded, hating the sound of my own voice. He didn't say anything, and his silence hurt more than any words. I wanted to fight for us, but you can't fight for something that was lost to the other person. "Us" was in the past for Ezra now, and I was just going to have to accept it.

"Mr. Lodge. Just who I was looking for," Sergeant Hall said, smiling and putting a firm hand on Ezra's shoulder. He looked at me strangely. "Miss Warder," he said, his tone changing to one of dislike. "I'm surprised to see you two together. I wasn't aware you were friends."

"Yeah, well, we are," I said, my eyes defiant, daring him to do something about it.

"Esther," Ezra said gently, "I'll catch up with you later, okay?"

I moved my eyes from Sergeant Hall's face to look at Ezra, forcing my face to relax. I didn't want to leave him alone with Hall, but he seemed anxious for me to leave. It made me uncomfortable that they were so familiar with each other. "Yeah, sure, okay. I'll see you in class."

But they were already walking away from me, and my words fell empty into the hallway. I wanted to know what Sergeant Hall could possibly want to talk to him about, but there was no one for me to ask anymore with Professor Solomon and Professor Darci gone. I stood there for several seconds, not sure of my next move, when the bell rang, and I realized I was late. I was already failing calculus after my spell in the infirmary and my preoccupation with the book burning, so I couldn't afford to miss any more lessons. I raced down the rest of the hallway, slid through the doorway, and slipped into my seat.

"Nice of you to join us," the new teacher, Sergeant Barrios, snipped. She was young and rather striking, certainly nothing like Sergeant Hall with his pug face. Her Hispanic descent gave her a beautiful olive complexion, and she had long, dark hair that she had pulled up into a professional bun.

"Sorry," I mumbled. I looked over at Ezra's empty chair.

"Come up here and write last night's homework on the white board, so you can remind yourself of the importance of this course."

There was no way I had gotten last night's homework right.

"Um, okay." There was a current of laughter and a few looks of sympathy as I walked slowly toward the front with my newly issued electronic tablet. Where the nuns had never wanted us to have technology, the officers were all but shoving it down our throats. I picked up the black dry erase marker and wrote out the problem. I hesitated before writing my answer, which I was one hundred percent sure was wrong.

"The answer, too, Esther," Sergeant Barrios said smugly, crossing her arms.

She was making an example out of me. I thought about Judah and the sign he had to wear, this being only a fraction of what he must have felt. I wrote out my wrong answer and just stood there, still facing the white board. My palms were so sweaty I almost dropped the marker.

"Not that anyone here is surprised, but that's wrong. I'm going to assume the rest of your answers are wrong as well and that you writing them would be a waste of our time." There was silence, since I was unable to speak. "Take your seat," she said finally.

I didn't look at her but turned back toward my desk and walked, my head down, ignoring the snickers from other students. "And, Esther?" She waited until I turned and faced her. "Don't be late for my class again."

Her eyes glared into mine with the fiery look of a serpent, and I knew she knew who I was and my part in the Resistance. I gulped and sat down.

# 59.
# PRESENT DAY

Sam stops the car on a dirt road that's about a two-mile walk from Abram's cabin. Finnick and I climb out and give a small wave as he pulls away. My concern for Solomon is a tightly gripped hand on my heart, making it hard to breathe or think. Based on Finnick's facial expression, his anxiety exceeds even mine, and I know he's still blaming himself.

"It's not your fault," I say to reassure him, but part of me is upset with him for not keeping a better eye on Solomon. He starts hobbling forward, and I rush to help him, putting his arm around my shoulder.

"Thanks, but it is," he says, catching his balance as we start walking. "You would blame yourself, too, if you had been there. I shouldn't have turned my head for even a second. I knew they were after him. How could I be so stupid?"

"He's a grown man. You couldn't watch him every second."

"Why not? He would never have let anything like that happen to us. If he dies, Es, it's on me. How do I live with that?" As soon as the words are out, we both hear the irony of them, my having had to live with Rachael's death on my conscience for months. The familiar chasm of betrayal and angst resides like the Grand Canyon between us. "I shouldn't have said that, sorry," Finnick mumbles.

I try to shrug it off and hide the pain from my voice. "I don't know how we live with any of this."

I think back to everything I've done since all this began: not standing up for Judah but then defending his death, which led to the starting of a resistance. Then protesting book burnings, resisting the Federation's mandates, running for months that turned into years, just trying to stay alive, to keep Finnick alive. Rachael's murder. The murder of a man in a brothel. Having to lie in order to break in and enter a federal building. Will it never end? I can't stop to think about all that I have had to do to maintain survival, or I won't be sane anymore; and if I lose my ability to think, to keep fighting, then I might as well just let the enemy win.

We walk the rest of the way in silence, each relishing the quiet solitude of the woods, allowing our minds a chance to recharge. I pray for what I've done since I last talked to God, for the sins on my soul that I worry He won't forgive, that He won't understand. And by the time we reach the cabin, I'm exhausted and hungry, but I feel better, somewhat redeemed.

I knock on the door of the cabin before softly pushing open the door. I see the back of Abram's head above his wooden chair. It's the kind of chair you'd find in a mountain lodge, sitting atop a large, brown area rug with faded prints of grizzly bears. He has headphones in his ears, typing furiously at his computer. He doesn't even look up when we enter, not realizing that we're there. The thought of how vulnerable he is here alone flashes through my mind. I try to think of an alternative, but it's his loneliness that allows us to continue the security breaches that give us so much of our information. I tap him lightly on the shoulder, trying not to scare him. He still jumps.

"Sorry," I say. "I was trying not to sneak up on you."

"Esther! Finnick! It's good to see you. I've been so engrossed in this matrix of the main headquarters' underground. Did you know there are labs where they are altering babies' genders? Babies!" He shakes his head in disbelief as he lowers his headphones from his ears. He sees our faces and realizes there's something wrong. "Oh no, what's happened?"

"It's Solomon," I whisper.

"I'll tell him," Finnick interjects, putting a hand on my upper arm and pushing me back slightly. "We were in the ratholes, Solomon and I, waiting for Esther to finish the break-in to Alastor's office. I just turned my back for a second—one second to talk to Esther on the phone—and he was gone. I—I went to ask the people he was talking with, some addicts, and they said one called the other 'Jay.'"

Abram gasps. "Not Hawthorne?" he asks.

"You know him?" Finnick says, surprised.

"Only by his name. He's the commander of the Secret Forces, whom the police designated to complete the missions Alastor doesn't want to be public knowledge. I've read things about him, seen footage of what he's done. If he has Solomon . . . " He trails off, silence filling the room like a suffocating gas. "God help us," he finishes in prayer, as he sits down at his desk and puts his head in his hands.

I fill him in then on what happened at the hospital and how the Hawthornes' daughter had seemingly saved Solomon from death, how she had somehow changed her mind and began to believe in a God she was always taught did not exist. Abram is nodding as he talks.

"Yes," he affirms, "Solomon has that way with people. He likely knew her somehow and helped her find salvation."

I realize then that we never got the full story from Solomon. He always played off what happened at the hospital, treated it as insignificant in correlation to our other problems. When it obviously wasn't.

"What can we do?" I ask Abram, my eyes desperate. "I thought of some places on our walk here, places he might be. I did learn a lot from the documents I saw at headquarters. I need to share them with you. I took pictures."

"You got rid of the phone, though, right?" Abram asks.

"Yes, of course, immediately."

"I am sure they know that you were there by now and must be furious," Finnick notes. "I so wish there was a way for us to see news broadcasts."

"I can do that," Abram says in response. "Give me a moment."

He turns back toward his computer and quickly types different codes that look like gibberish flowing like tributaries across and down the screen. But a moment later, there's a flash of a reporter, a couple glitches, and we can hear the news report like I'm sitting in someone's living room. It's the Mock-Up News channel; Solomon and I used to joke about the name, its accuracy to what the news has become—merely a prototype, a barely functioning system that used to bear truth.

"Several more burnings have spurred up across the country, and the UFoA is not taking them lightly. We go to Bruce Walker live at the main headquarters for the story."

"Thanks, Denise. As you can see behind me, there are masses of people protesting their right to refuse the mark the UFoA is mandating, and it has turned into an all-out brawl. This mandate comes on the heels of new legislation that will require that people be chipped in order to buy or sell property, bypass building clearances, and even buy food. Those protesting claim that their rights as individuals have been taken from them. Let's hear from one of these protestors," Bruce finishes, walking up to a man, who looks young, maybe twenty or twenty-five, holding a sign with the words: WE HAVE RIGHTS!

Bruce turns the microphone to him and asks, "What brought you out here today?"

"My rights!" the man screams into the microphone. "They have no right to force this piece of metal into my body without my consent!"

"What will you do, sir, when you are unable to purchase food or find a job without the chip?"

"We'll burn this whole city to the ground!" the protester screams as he runs off into the crowd. "We have rights! We have rights!" An officer cuts him off at the knees with a swift swing of his nightstick, and we watch the screen in horror as he falls to the ground.

"There you have it, an angry resistor who is not accepting these new terms lightly. Let's hear from the UFoA next," Bruce says as he walks up to an officer who has his hand gripped tightly around the arm of a resistor. Seeing the reporter, he pushes the man to the ground hard and kicks him in the side. Bruce and the cameraman are taken aback, and the screen wavers to the ground before coming back up on the flushed, angry face of the officer.

"What is your take on those resisting the new mandate?" Bruce looks shaken now, holding the microphone out to the officer. The officer rips the microphone from his hand, his face twisted in fury.

"I'll tell you my take! This is a message to all those resisting: you will lose. Do you understand me?" He spits the words. "The harder you fight us, the harder you will fall." He throws the microphone on the ground and spins back toward the crowd, barreling toward two resistors who have somehow escaped the brawl and are holding their signs high. The camera finds the ground momentarily again before it's back on Bruce, who is pale and clearly unnerved.

"As you can see, the violence is increasing here at the main headquarters. It may be best to stay home tonight and follow the curfew. Stay safe out there, fellow acceptors. Back to you, Denise."

The camera cuts back to Denise, who is behind her desk in the station, her composure more intact than Bruce's, but I see a slight shake of her hands as she reaches for a document.

She clears her throat before speaking and looks straight at the camera. "These uprisings come at the same time as the recent announcement by Commander Hawthorne, who is planning a public execution on Friday at twelve p.m. Eastern Standard Time. This will be the first execution of its kind and broadcasted live throughout the United Federation. Stay tuned for more details. Here's the weather with Mock-Up's News' weatherman, Charlie Downs."

The feed cuts to the weatherman, and Abram clicks it off, shutting his screen. The three of us look at each other, our mouths open in disbelief. No one dares to speak in case our words will add truth to what we saw, what we heard. A live execution.

"We need back up." Finnick speaks first, and his voice sounds odd, distant, as I try to make sense of what this all means. Abram doesn't answer, only nods, and turns back to his computer, the sound of his fingers on the keys filling the silence of the room.

# 60.
# ONE YEAR EARLIER . . .

It was late August at St. Mary's when a man came for Ezra. The day after he left, I refused to pull myself out of bed for breakfast, and I missed my first period class. Finnick and Rachael banged continuously on my door, but I couldn't move, my body curled firmly in the fetal position. I hugged myself tightly as tears streamed down my face. I kept replaying a conversation Ezra and I had a week before his disappearance—a conversation where he had told me he was scared, like he had felt something was coming, something he couldn't avoid.

"Where is the fear coming from?" I had asked him, but he wouldn't tell me more, his mouth clapped shut like a clam. There was this gap between us, this wide polarity caused by the information he refused to tell me. What was even more maddening was how often I had started seeing him talking with Rachael. Sure, they tried to be low-key about it, but more than once, I had run into them together on campus or seen Ezra standing by her locker. What could they possibly have to talk about that he couldn't talk about with me? For weeks, I had to deal with nothing but confusion. And now, I was here, depressed, anxious, unable to accept he was gone, and no one would answer any of my questions.

My mind went back to the conversation Finnick and I had heard through the door of Sister Margaret's office last night. I knew if anyone could tell me who took Ezra, it was Mother Maura. Who was this "he" that they had said "had every right under the law to take him"? This question is what finally forced me to pull myself out of bed. I was going to plod to Mother Maura's office and plead with her for answers.

"Esther, hello," Mother Maura said in surprise. "I wasn't expecting you." With merely a nod, I moved past her to sit, slumped, in front of the desk. She raised her eyebrows before taking a seat herself. I forced myself to sit up, careful to maintain direct eye contact, so she could see just how important this was to me.

I stared into her eyes, my own a sea of fading hope. "Mother Maura, I know that you know who took Ezra away from us," I pleaded. "Please, I'm begging you. Ezra is my friend."

My legs shook, causing the chair to quiver with them. As I waited for her response, my eyes scanned the room, noting that her office had changed. Once a shrine to Jesus's crucifixion, the walls were barren now, the only decoration a framed copy of the UFoA's creed.

"Esther, dear, I can clearly see that you're upset. And I want to help you through this sorrow. But there is nothing else that I can tell you. He had family who claimed him, and he is gone now."

"It can't be that simple, though. He would want to be able to talk to us. You must have a phone number or an address or some other way to reach him?"

"I'm sorry, but no. You need to let this go now, Esther. Asking too many questions about Ezra's whereabouts will not end well for you."

Tears burned my eyes, and I couldn't move from the chair. "I can't let it go, Mother Maura. I—I love him." The words were hot as they rose through my throat, and I cringed at Mother Maura's look of pity.

"Sometimes, we love the wrong people," she said gently. "The best you can do is allow that love to make you a better version of yourself and try to release what you're unable to change." I reached for a tissue from the box on her desk and wiped my eyes. I knew I looked pathetic, but I couldn't even bring myself to care. "I'm going to suggest to the guidance office that you begin therapy again."

The tears dried up quickly. "No, Mother Maura, that's not necessary."

I knew that they had replaced our old counselors with UFoA officers, and I had no interest in being brainwashed.

"Just a few sessions, Esther; it will help,"

"But, Mother—"

She put a hand up to silence me. "It's not up for debate, Esther. You'll go, starting next week."

I sighed and nodded. Looks like she had known how to get rid of me after all. "May I be excused? I have an English essay due."

"Of course, dear. I hope you'll find some peace."

I didn't answer her as I reached for my bag and hoisted it over my shoulder. I turned to walk toward the door but paused, my hand on the knob. "Just one last thing, Mother Maura."

She looked up from her desk. "Yes, dear?"

"Why did you teach us that we should always do the right thing when you don't?"

I spent the next three days in detention.

# 61.
# PRESENT DAY

Abram put out an all-call to resistors throughout the nation, notifying them of Hawthorne's plans. We had three days until Solomon's execution, and by now, we had contacted members of the Resistance in all six territories of the United Federation. Those in the most western province arrived in stolen convey trucks filled with weapons. They used all their resources to travel here, disguised as UFoA officers with false papers. I worry about the day when everyone that isn't a resistor has been given the opportunity to be chipped. Travel will be nearly impossible. We're meeting in an abandoned warehouse forty miles outside of the main headquarters. It was a furniture warehouse at one time, but now stood empty, its windows cracked from age and stones once released by the hands of unruly children.

An old, ripped sofa reminiscent of the building's former life lay forgotten in the desolate yard, weather-damaged and soiled. The rigid, iron-clad roof of the building provides shelter for scurrying rats and nests of birds and insects, and as I slide open the large metal door, a spider crawls onto my hand. I shake it off roughly, watching as it hits the ground and scurries through the dirt.

"Gross," I mutter, rubbing my hands on my jeans.

"Remember that time at St. Mary's when Ezra put a fake spider on your pillow on Halloween?" Finnick asks, laughing. "I almost died of laughter that day. Your face was so good." He laughs again at the memory. "You screamed for, like, thirty full seconds, and Sister Margaret came running in like someone had died." He's laughing so hard now that he's bent over, his hand clutching his ribs in pain.

"That's what you get for making fun of me," I tease, but I'm laughing, too. "You okay?" I ask when his laughter slows. His eyes shut briefly in pain.

"Yeah, I'm good. They're healing. Slowly." He lifts his shirt to show me the bandages, and I slowly unwind them to get a closer look. The bruising is still there, but its coloring has faded into hues of a pale yellow.

"I keep thinking how if that man could do that to you, then who knows what they're doing to Solomon."

"You can't think about that, Es; you'll make yourself crazy. We have to focus on what we can do. We have to move forward."

I'm glad to see he's stopped blaming himself, and I know he's right, yet it's impossible for my mind to not think the worst after everything we've been through. There are worse things than being dead, and I don't want to lose Solomon, but I would if it meant he could be spared that kind of pain. I try to shake the thoughts out of my mind as I look around.

The inside of the warehouse mirrors the outside, full of cobwebs and dust. There are a few old pieces of furniture that had never been sold or stolen after the place was deserted, some lone chairs, an old sewing table, a bookshelf. We're the first to arrive, but everyone should be gravitating here shortly. For now, it's just Finnick and me—and our thoughts.

"Finn, do you ever think about what's next?" I ask him tentatively as I wipe the dust off two chairs with my hand and move them together for us to sit down.

"You mean, like, the afterlife?"

"Well, yeah, but more like our judgement," I answer, not quite meeting his eyes, the sins of my soul bearing the weight of an elephant on my chest.

"I think God understands this is a war."

"I don't mean that. I just . . . I . . . "

"You're worried because you've killed people. You think it's your fault." I nod softly, looking at my feet. "I get it, Esther. And I'm not saying you're blameless. Because you're not." He puts his hand to my chin then and forces me to look at him. "Particularly when it comes to Rachael. You are not blameless."

Tears fill my eyes at the harsh reality of his words. Of course, God will punish me. I deserve it.

"But," Finnick continues, "I think you are genuinely remorseful, and God forgives those who repent. He'll forgive you."

"Do you forgive me?" The words slip out before I even realize I was going to ask them. But once they're in the air, I know I want an answer. I need to know if Finnick can forgive me. If he does, perhaps I can begin to forgive myself. Perhaps I will wish things had been different, that Rachael had lived. Perhaps the horrible fact that I don't regret her death will change. There's so much Finnick doesn't understand about me, so much that I won't let him see. I have these demons, so much rage, jealousy, anger. Emotions that eat me alive.

"I'm trying," he answers.

The tears are like a current down my face, and I swipe at my eyes. "I understand," I say. "Of course, I understand."

"That will just have to be enough for you for now."

I want to say more to him, to justify what I did somehow, but we're interrupted by the metal door as it slides back, a parade of resistors, armed and angry, filling the space.

I have a memory of being outside with my parents. I was ten, maybe eleven. The sun was scorching, and my dad had set up a make-shift waterpark in our backyard, complete with a slip 'n slide, a sprinkler, a blow-up swimming pool, and these bazooka-looking water guns. We ran in circles around the outside of the house as he shot at me with one of those guns. My dark purple bathing suit was soaking wet, my braided hair dripping, and grass was sticking up the sides of my legs and feet. I screamed as I tried to escape him, but he caught me, wrapped his arms around my waist, and pulled me into the pool with him, laughing. My mom had come running outside, confused, asking what was going on, telling us to knock it off. So, we turned the water guns on her.

I think about that memory a lot now, the innocence of water in contrast to the bullets that ripped their lives away from me. I think about what my parents felt when the gun that killed them was aimed at their heart. I think about what their last thoughts might have been and whether or not they suffered. I wonder if they had regrets, if they worried for their souls the way I worry for mine. But what I think about most is turning a gun, my finger slipping across the trigger as I stare into the eyes of whoever stole them from me. I think about the pull of the trigger as I finally take my revenge.

# 62.
# ONE YEAR EARLIER . . .

On the third day serving my detention, I was cleaning the surfaces of the lockers with cleaning spray and an old rag when Finnick came up behind me.

"Did you hear the news?" he asked, seizing the rag and spray from my hand and taking over.

"Finnick, let me. It's my responsibility," I said, grabbing for the rag back, but he shrugged me off.

"They're holding a school-wide assembly this afternoon. Mother Maura's been dismissed."

"What?" My mouth opened in disbelief. "But why?"

"Sergeant Barnes said they'll explain it all at the assembly today. That there are additional changes . . . " He trailed off, lowering his voice. "I heard Sergeant Hall is taking over."

"No." My voice came out like a breath. I thought of what it would mean for the school, for us. The weight on my chest returned, the feeling of being trapped, like I was encased in this tomb where everything around me kept mutating into something worse. I imagined monsters that encircled me as I clawed futilely at the walls. How could we stay here? What would become of our lives?

Finnick's words brought me back to the present, and I tried to focus on his face. "A few of us are planning to meet after to talk. You'll be there?"

"Yeah, of course. Sit with me in the assembly, though, if you can?"

"Sure. Rachael and I will wait for you."

Rachael. Of course. Why was she everywhere? "Thanks, Finnick," I said, my hand stretched out for the cleaning spray.

"Bogus deal on the detention," he offered sympathetically, handing me back the bottle.

"Yeah, but it was worth it. Bunch of hypocrites," I muttered, but I immediately felt guilty when I thought of Mother Maura being dismissed. She might not have been as straightforward with her beliefs as I had thought she should have been; but she was still a good person, and I was sorry to see her go. I thought of Sister Margaret then, her small stature, her encouraging words whenever we felt unsafe. "Sister Margaret's still here, though, right?"

"No, Es, they're all gone. We're under full-blown military regime now. But I gotta go. I'll see you at the assembly."

"Okay, yeah, see you."

I gave half a wave and turned back toward the lockers. I couldn't shake the image of the school run by Sergeant Hall. His cold, empty eyes haunted my mind as the lockers blurred, the metal transforming into a grotesque fog. My nostrils filled with the smell of gunfire, and I was back on the ground with Timothy, screaming. I tried to refocus on the present, to concentrate on spraying the bottle and wiping the locker, but my thoughts were so jumbled. Beads of sweat spread like a rash over my body. I slid down to the ground, chest heaving, as I waited for the panic to pass.

# 63.
## PRESENT DAY

A burly man, who looks to be in his early thirties, leads the pack of resistors. "Name's Mikey," he says, roughly shaking my hand, then Finnick's. He gestures to the people behind him. "We're from out west, used to be Kansas before this territory nonsense."

"It's nice to meet you," I say, smiling politely and beckoning everyone to come inside.

"Not much in the way of furniture, is there?" Mikey asks, looking for a place to sit down.

"No, I'm sorry. This location is secure, though, which seemed much more important than comfort."

"Right. Right. Of course," Mikey agrees. People begin pouring in, and some sit or squat on the ground, forming a circle around us.

We had told Abram he should stay back for his own safety, not to mention how lost we would be without his skills. He tried to fight the idea at first, but realizing we were relying on him to breach security the day of the execution, he relented. He tried to hide it, but I could tell from the hollow look of his eyes how worried he was about Solomon. My thoughts are interrupted by the sound of engines revving outside.

"What the . . . " I look over at Finnick, who races with me out of the wide metal doors.

My mouth flops open at the sight of fifteen, maybe twenty, motorcycles. Sitting on the bikes are men and women in black leather vests, their bodies covered in tattoos. I look for the wings of the serpent, my eyes searching their arms, their legs.

"You won't find that on us, Girlie," a gruff, older man with a beard like Santa Claus calls out to me. "We're God's people." I let out a breath, feeling guilty that I assumed the worst of them. The effect of years of stereotypes that have been pounded into my mind.

"Sorry," I say, "of course. I'm Esther Warder. Please, come, join us inside." I wave my arm behind me, and they shut off the engines on their bikes. Some take off their helmets and hug them to their side.

"Tobias Stone," the man responds, shaking my hand.

"Where are you guys from?" Finnick asks the woman next to him. She has a shaved head and a tattoo of a cross on her neck.

"We're from the Peaceable region, used to be Montana," she says, smiling, and I see she's missing a canine tooth. "Far from peaceful there, though. I'm Ruby, by the way."

"It's nice to meet you, Ruby. I've never been out to Montana," Finnick says. "Did you have any trouble getting here?"

"A bit. Had to take back roads, so it took twice as long as it would've. But we was only stopped once, told the men we was going to get our mark with family back East. I think because we look the way we do, that's why they bought the story so easy," Tobias tells us.

"Well, we really appreciate you taking the risk. We need the support, and it means a lot," Finnick responds.

Ruby smiles, revealing the gap of her teeth and two dimples. "You bet. It's getting bad back where we are. They're openly shootin' people who won't be chipped, and people just shoot 'em back. It's chaos."

"Ruby's right. The UFoA is a bunch of idiots. Who starts a war in a country where guns are hidden under every mattress and in every closet?" asks a man with a green mohawk and the tattoo of Ephesians 4:1 up his arm, joining in the conversation.

"They've been raiding people's homes here. Cleared out any weapons they could find. There's a lot of fear circulating. We watched them tie people to trees and assassinate them in public. People just watched from their office buildings. There has been some pushback, but mainly in the form of the burnings of the centers, though," I tell them.

"This Solomon guy," Ruby says, "he's a friend of yours?"

At Solomon's name, the crater of anxiety is back in my stomach. "He—he was our professor at the orphanage where Finnick and I were placed when our parents died. He's been the only adult who's stood by us. He's—he's our family." My voice cracks, and I clear my throat. "Sorry, I'm still struggling a bit with his being taken."

"Oh, I understand, hon. Lost my momma during a protest. An officer shot her dead right in front of me. Had the gun at my face and said to me, 'You want me to shoot you, too?' I couldn't even speak, my lips were quiverin' so much, and I just shook and fell to the ground sobbing. I must've laid there for hours 'cuz when I woke up, the sun was set, and it was just me and my dead momma lying in her blood." She stops talking then, looking through me like her mind's stuck back in that day and she's living it all over again.

"I guess we've all been through a lot," Finnick responds. "They'll just keep taking from us, too, until there's nothing left." Everyone around him nods.

"It's why we're here. We're gonna fight. Save your man Solomon, your family," Tobias says, raising a fist.

My eyes fill with tears as I look around at all the people who have come to help. It restores my soul to know there are people who still believe, people who want justice and morality restored.

"All right, then," I say smiling. "Let's get inside and make a plan."

# 64.
# ONE YEAR EARLIER . . .

The assembly was being held in the old chapel—the only place large enough to accommodate the entire student body. My heart ached when I saw the younger students, some only five or six, as they wandered in behind their teachers and took a seat. They would be the most affected by the UFoA's propaganda, their minds having not yet established what was fully right and wrong. The officers stood ready to pounce, to force their ideas, their objectives into their minds.

"Esther!" Finnick called out above the rumbling chatter from a pew a few rows from the front, waving his hand in the air. Rachael was sitting beside him, her hair placed perfectly in a tight bun on her head, emerald studs in her ears that matched her eyes.

Of course, she looked perfect. I ran a hand over my own frizzy, blonde hair, my hands still emanating the smell of the cleaner.

"Ugh, you smell like bleach," Finnick groaned as I sat down.

He placed a hand over his nose and mouth, and I saw Rachael's little nose scrunch up. Ignoring the comment, I was about to ask where Ezra was when I remembered he was gone. The recollection of his leaving hit me like a punch in the stomach, and I leaned back against the seat.

"What?" Finnick asked. I just shook my head; there was no point saying his name anymore. He was not coming back.

"You doing okay?" Rachael leaned over Finnick to ask me, her large eyes reflecting concern. "I was sorry to hear about Ezra."

"Fine . . . and thanks," I mumbled, slipping further down in my seat, feigning interest in my fingernails. Out of the corner of my eye, I saw Finnick shake his head at Rachael, signaling her not to press it, before taking her hand.

The seats were filling up quickly, and even with the chapel's vast size, I wondered if everyone would fit. There were two horizontal lines of men in military uniforms lined up on either side of the podium, like a bridal party at a wedding. Their faces were cold and stern, conveying no emotion as they stared straight ahead. The flag of the UFoA with the protruding feathered serpent, had been raised high, the Christian flag having been taken down long ago.

The hum of the anthem played in the background; the words, "No one will defeat us, our union is strong, hold tight, conformists, equality is ours" rang loudly in my ears. I heard hard footsteps coming up the aisle and turned my head to see Sergeant Hall approaching. He looked taller somehow in his full military regalia, new medals clipped on the front of his jacket. He marched with authority up the steps to the podium. His face twisted in an arrogant sneer. Tapping the microphone once, I nudged Finnick to signal we were starting, and he stopped his conversation with Rachael. Our eyes all turned to the front, and an uneasy quiet fell across the room.

Sergeant Hall looked around the room before speaking, taking in everyone's face; his own remained in the same arrogant sneer. He cleared his throat and began, "Hello, Students, and welcome to the dawn of a new age." I anxiously shifted in my seat as he continued. "You are bearing witness to what will be a new empire. The time for scientific knowledge and advancements, gender reform, sexual equality, and a prosperity like this country has never before seen is upon us. You must now ask yourselves, 'Will I be a part of this journey? Will I be on the edge of innovation? Can I be brave enough to defy the laws of a God Who has failed me, a God Who, if He does exist, has created a world of judgement and pain?' Wake up, Students, and be our ally!" Groups of students let out cheers and catcalls.

I looked over at Finnick, whose face and neck were growing red with anger, his fists clenched at his sides.

"How are people buying into him?" I asked, feeling as infuriated as Finnick looked. But he just shook his head angrily, his eyes on the front of the room. Sergeant Hall had projected the new mandates and expectations onto the two screens on either side of him.

His tirade of intended inspiration continued, his voice reverberating in my head. "St. Mary's will now be under new guidelines. These guidelines will be enforced. So, let me be clear. Your compliance is not only expected, but the consequences for non-compliance will be severe."

I tried to ignore the growing pit in my stomach as I silently read the list:

1.  The unisex uniform of the United Federation will be pressed and worn daily.
2.  You will recite the UFoA's creed with your class before first period begins.
3.  You will maintain a behavioral profile that adheres to UFoA's guidelines.
4.  Your rooms and social media will be inspected periodically.
5.  You will read only literature and sing songs approved by the Federation.

"Do not be discouraged by the new mandates. Through these guidelines, we are creating a life for you that will embrace equality and freedom. In fact, exploits of all kinds are encouraged. The Federation's Academy of Science has approved the latest technology allowing our health center to offer gender reassignment surgeries that will be open to all students of any age. You are also now permitted to use all technological devices and social media platforms. In fact, we highly encourage that you engage yourself in technology as much as possible under our supervised watch.

"This brings me to my next point. We are implementing another new program where we will be observing your daily activities and contributions to St. Mary's. Through this program, you will be able to access your behavioral profile. The actions found within your profile will determine your status here at school and the opportunities provided to you after you leave these halls. For we are all equal and must accept everyone, and in failing to meet the expectations of the Federation, one is defying such acceptance of this order. We will be holding competitions and selecting the most advanced students to aid in experiments within the new synthetic biology and bio-robotics programs. Your achievements here at St. Mary's will be fully up to you; today, you begin on an equal playing field, and your actions when you leave this room determine your success. Isn't it wonderful to know you will no longer be discriminated against for your gender, your class, your sexuality?" He took a deep breath and surveyed the room with a proud grin. "Welcome, Students, to your freedom." Cheers broke out again throughout the room. Finnick, Rachael, and I looked at each other with growing fear.

"How is it freedom to watch our every move?" A girl stood up, screaming the question, her arms pulled back from her body in defiance, her chest pushed outward. I recognized her from the book-burning rally; she had been one of Timothy's friends. I watched in terror for Sergeant Hall's response.

But he just smiled at her, his teeth clenched, his upper lip curling with mirth. "You're only being watched so that we can commend you on your contributions to our growing, new world."

"Okay, well, I opt out. I don't want to be commended. I just want to be left alone," she retorted.

"I'm afraid that won't be an option." He passed a look to the guard next to him, who marched with little urgency toward the girl. The guard made his way through the students until his hand gripped her upper arm.

"Don't touch me! Get off!" She kicked him hard, and flinching in annoyance, like swatting at a bug, he quietly pulled both her arms fiercely behind her back. She yelped. Everyone just stared. A couple of her friends made feeble attempts to grab her but shrank back at the officer's glare.

Sergeant Hall watched, his smile never faltering, his eyes dancing with malignity. "Would anyone else like to contest the new orders?" He stared out into the crowd, his face imperious.

But no one dared say anything else as Timothy's friend was dragged out of the room screaming, "Don't give up! Please don't let them win!"

# 65.
# PRESENT DAY

I look around and can't believe how many resistors have come. There must be three or four hundred people here. Despite how isolated this warehouse is, I know that this many people must have drawn attention from the Federation's surveillance. They're watching closely, and I'm certain they'll be here soon.

Abram had spent the better part of a day preparing me on what to say. I try to make Solomon proud as I yell out loud enough for everyone to hear me. "We do not have much time. The live broadcast of Solomon's death is scheduled for noon on Friday. The plan is to raid the event. I do not want you to take unnecessary lives, but if your own is at risk, defend yourselves. Make no mistake, my fellow resistors, we are now in a civil war to win back our country!" There's a cheer throughout the warehouse, and the cries surge my confidence.

"We will find Solomon, and we will rescue him alive. I will count on your team, Tobias . . . " I look over at him, and he meets my eyes. "To distract and detain the officers within his range, so that Finnick and I can free him. Can you do that for us?"

"Yes, ma'am," he answers, raising his gun in the air.

"Mikey." I turn to find him in the crowd. "I will need your team to make statements to the media about the evils of the UFoA. You'll need to witness, give testament to Christ on camera. Can we count on you?"

"We would be honored," he answers, nodding.

"The rest of you will be maintaining crowd control, which will be a feat in itself. I am counting on us being highly outnumbered; but we have God behind us, and we won't fail. Are you with me?" The cry of David defeating Goliath circles around the room. Chills run through my body as small goosebumps appear like freckles across my arms. "As you leave here, watch your backs. The enemy is coming. Stay low. Keep to the woods and hide the best you can. I will see you all on Friday. God bless you and keep you safe."

# 66.
# ONE YEAR EARLIER . . .

A blend of excited and outraged conversation surrounded us as we filed out of the assembly, the student body torn in their allegiances.

"The dawn of a new age, huh?" I asked Finnick with a mix of sadness and disgust.

He kept his head down, walking angrily beside me. I could almost feel the indignation radiating off his skin. I touched his shoulder lightly, but he flinched.

"We're gonna have to watch our backs constantly," he spat. "No doubt our names are already on the top of their list."

"We can't just comply, Finnick. I . . . I can't. I feel like I've already betrayed my parents by not finding out more about their murders. If I give into this system I might as well have killed them myself."

"I'm not suggesting that we comply. I'm just so angry because I feel helpless. That's the thing with this new system; it forces people against each other. It's wrong. It's like if I don't condone every action someone does, then I'm somehow an anarchist or a plaster saint." My heart dropped at the truth of his words as I thought of Judah and his sign, his body swaying from the tree.

I looked around uneasily, like there's a spy cam on my back. "It's not our place to judge people's hearts; it's God's. But where do we draw the line on what we allow and condone in a society? They're making clinics where one can freely change their gender at any given time or age. That just feels wrong to me."

"I know," Finnick answered, sighing. "But I don't know how we fix this." We were outside, walking beside each other toward Rachael's dorm to meet up with everyone.

"I will not fear though tens of thousands assail me on every side."

"Psalms, right?"

"Yeah. Psalms 3:6. One of my mom's favorites."

"You been thinking about them a lot lately?"

"Yeah, and it just makes me feel weak . . . " I trailed off, my mind on my mom's last letter—the haste in her words, the undertone of fear. I couldn't help but feel that she had known death was imminent, that they had been coming for her. But why? What had my parents done to get themselves murdered? I thought back to the picture they left for me to find, the other couple in the photograph—were they killed, too? Or were they the killers?

"Earth to Esther." Finnick nudged me with his elbow. I shook my head and looked toward him vacantly.

"What if all this—the rise of this new Federation—has actually been going on for much longer than we know about?" I asked. "What if this is not the beginning at all but the escalation of an old order that's gained ground?"

"What are you saying? That there are people who knew what was coming and didn't stop it?" He looked skeptical.

"Maybe they tried . . . "

"Are we talking about your parents now, Esther? You can tell me."

"Yes. I believe they were murdered by members of Alastor's organization for resisting, but I think they were important, or they did something to Alastor and his cronies that they couldn't forgive. The letters they left me—especially the last few—they were infused with fear, incoherent at times . . . and their bravery amidst all that . . . I just feel so weak in comparison."

He looked at me sympathetically. "They sound like they were amazing people." I didn't say anything, still lost in my own thoughts. He frowned, nudging my arm with his elbow again and trying to meet my eyes. "Hey . . . I'm sorry you have to live with all that—about your parents—but you can't tell me for a second that you aren't brave. You are one of the bravest people I know. Look at what you have already done for the Resistance. You even wound up in the hospital!" He took my hand, then, and I finally looked at him. "And I'll try to help you figure out what happened to them, okay?"

I gave him a half-smile before looking away. "Yeah, okay, thanks."

He kept looking at me, but I didn't say anything else. It wasn't that I didn't appreciate his being there for me, but there were some things I had to figure out on my own. I couldn't help but think my parents left me those letters so that I would find the answers for what happened to them. And maybe they had even wanted more than that. Maybe they had wanted me to save the world.

# 67.
## PRESENT DAY

I bolt upright, my body in a cold sweat. My eyes dart around like a frantic rabbit, my breath slowing after finding I'm safely lying on a blanket in the corner of our tent. We are deep in the woods awaiting the morning's raid of headquarters. My sleep had been fitful, filled with frantic thoughts and dreams. The most recent was of my parents—again. They were running in what looked like a scene from Armageddon, a conglomeration of beast-like dragons and robots spitting fire at the buildings and roads. My mom's long hair cascaded behind her as she ran, her head turning back, mouthing a word I couldn't make out. I could see them, almost reach out and touch them.

Hot tears burn my cheeks. I sit there, hugging myself, and let them fall. I allow myself to feel everything I've been fighting over the last weeks, months, and years since I lost them. How can I do this? How will I not fail them today?

I look over at Finnick sleeping beside me, his features soft in the early morning light, his arm stretching lazily over his head. I'm transported back to simpler times, fleeting moments of happiness in the orphanage, when Finnick, Ezra, and I would race among the trees or build blanket forts in our rooms. We were still children then. Children who had already lost so much but were not yet aware of just how much more we could lose.

Finnick groans softly, opening his left eye a crack to see me staring at him. "What is it?" he asks groggily.

"Nothing. Just a bad dream." My eyes fill with tears again when I see the concern in his eyes. "I'm sorry, Finnick, for all of it, for letting you down so many times, for not being who you thought I was or who you wanted me to be." I pause, my voice catching on the next words. "For Ra—chael."

My chest rises and falls now in heaves, sobs choking my throat. I rock myself a few times, trying to regain my composure, to make the pain stop. Finnick sits up beside me, scooches over, and places a hand around my back, rubbing his eyes groggily with the back of his other hand.

"You're right not to forgive me," I continue. "I don't deserve forgiveness. I can't even tell you that I would take it back because I don't know that I would." The words come out rushed, mangled, my admittance of this guilt, this idea that I would do it again, released into the air for the first time. "Rachael was a liar. But I was also jealous. It's inexcusable, but I was jealous. I loved Ezra. I loved you, too. I—I love you, too."

Despite that I am the one saying the words, I can hardly believe that I'm hearing them, having never fully acknowledged the truth to myself. But today, I might die. Finnick might die. I can't go on and carry out the acts of violence we'll certainly have to commit in the next few hours and not tell him how I feel. That's a weight I'm not willing to take to my grave. If this is the end, then I need him to know. Despite the resentment, trauma, and betrayal of our past that we'll likely never be able to escape, I still love him, all of him.

He doesn't say anything for a few moments but hushes me soothingly while rubbing circles on my back. His voice is soft when he finally speaks, tentative, like he's handling glass. "You need to come to terms with your sin. But Rachael wasn't who I thought she was, or maybe she partly was. I honestly don't know. But I knew that day why you did what you did. I could see it in your eyes—the love, the hurt of being deceived, the envy, the realization of the horrible thing you had done. It hurt me so much—not only to lose Rachael or to be blindsided by her betrayal, but also that you would do that. I knew things could never be the same, that any future we may have had together was at risk. I love you, too, Esther—perhaps I always have—but that's tainted now. I'm not sure that I can forget."

I nod in response, and a sob escapes my throat. We sit there, and for a minute, we're just two people wondering why things had to happen the way they did. I let the tears fall down my face because of course he's right. Of course, I knew this might be too much for him. But now, there's a sharpness in my chest, a tightening at the realization that we might never have our chance.

I start in again, trying to make him understand. "I just needed you to—" But before I can finish the sentence, Finnick's lips are on mine, and he's kissing me with such fierceness, the entire world stops moving. I pour every emotion I've ever felt for Finn over the last five years—everything I want and hope for us—into the kiss. And when he does finally pull away, I'm panting, breathless.

"I know," Finnick whispers against my lips. His own chest is rapidly rising and falling. He pushes his forehead against mine as he continues. "I think about that day with Rachael all the time. How I didn't see what was happening. How it's possible that I could have been so dumb, so blinded by love. But I also think about you and the love you've shown me through everything—through the betrayal brought onto both of us."

Finnick pulls back from me. There's confusion, fear, and affection dancing in his eyes. "Do you think Rachael ever really loved me, Esther?" There is so much sweet innocence in his question that it takes me a moment to respond. I watch this battle play out in his eyes—the need to reconcile what I did and the love he felt for Rachael with the love he feels for me now.

"I do. I think, like all of us, she felt a loyalty to her parents' beliefs. But her sense of loyalty was destroying her. Ultimately, I think it led her to be unfaithful to God, to you, to our cause."

"I've had similar thoughts," he answers, looking down at his watch. We must need to move out soon. "It's nice to hear you affirm them, though." He pauses. "I need you to know, Esther, before whatever goes down today . . . I'm grateful for you, for us. I could not do what we are doing alone. And I will always love you, whether or not we ever have our chance. I need you to understand that."

I swallow the lump in my throat, forcing myself to nod. I know this is another one of those moments when I must take a deep breath and move forward. I must take Finnick's hand and fight for good with everything I have.

He gives me a sad smile. "Let's go and take inventory. It will help to take our minds off of things. There's not much time before we'll need to wake up the others." He again grazes my lips with his own, and shivers disperse over my arms and legs.

I watch him stand, his long legs cracking with the movement. I want to make him stay, to go back in time, to change the course of our fate. But, of course, I can't. Instead, I must rise with him and walk together toward whatever lies ahead.

# 68.
# ONE YEAR EARLIER . . .

I sat at the desk in my room, staring vacantly at my Spanish book and trying to make sense of how to conjugate a verb. I looked up at a quick knock on my door and saw Rachael's face emerge around the side of it.

"Hey," she said, hesitating. "I just wanted to let you know we're all meeting in Lizzie's room about what happened at the assembly today."

I looked up and set down my Spanish book, which was a useless distraction, anyway. "Okay, cool, thanks."

She paused, and I felt the awkward cloud of tension that rolled in whenever it was just the two of us. Fortunately, she decided not to say any more, opting to just leave and shut the door. I stared at the engrained wood of the closed door, my mind spinning. I had been in panic mode since my conversation with Finnick about my parents. The extreme measures they had been capable of taking in order to change the course of the world's events was ever present in my mind. And I already knew what the meeting in Lizzie's room would be about; they'd want to think of ways to combat the new mandates and try to fight back.

But I didn't see how we could ever win a war against the officers. We were largely outnumbered by weaklings who followed blindly and by officers who were armed. We'd only end up getting ourselves killed

. . . or worse. No, the answer was much simpler. The idea had brewed in my mind over the last hour. The St. Mary's all of us had loved, the haven that had given us comfort and friendship during times of great loss, was gone. It was time to move on, to take the next steps, to be adults. The home we once had at St. Mary's was merely buildings now, buildings that housed evil and corruption. Buildings that should be burned down.

# 69.
## PRESENT DAY

We move into headquarters like bullets on water, barreling through security and taking out whoever tries to stop us. There are hundreds of us, and with stolen tanks and convoy trucks, we're prepared for a fight. Finnick and I are riding together; he's driving, with a gun secured in the belt around his midsection, a look of determination drawn on his face. I find that I'm asking myself once again how it could have come to this. How did it get this bad?

That's the thing about life, about our society. We go through the day-to-day like mindless drones until something happens that slaps us out of our daze. We allowed the same atrocities to continue for years, making excuses for people's actions or just being too lazy to really do anything about it. Mankind is the only one to blame for where we are; the original sin at its fruition.

My parents' pleas within their letters resound in my mind, asking me not to judge them for what they had to do. I wonder what they would think of me and how far I have had to come. Up ahead, I can see the gathering crowd, the media's cameras, the heavily armed UFoA officials. I try to catch sight of Solomon, but there's too many people, too much commotion. My breath's shaky as I check my own gun to ensure it's fully loaded. Finnick and I are both wearing protective vests in the likely chance we're hit by a bullet. Everyone is counting on us to retrieve Solomon while they create a series of violent diversions. I look over at Finnick, and he nods, reading my thoughts that we've driven in far enough and should take the rest by foot. He pulls the truck into a side alley and waves on the rest of the crew. I catch sight of Tobias and Ruby and silently pray they're protected.

"Keep low against the buildings. The longer we stay out of sight, the better advantage we have," Finnick whispers, tightening his belt, his fingers grazing the gun. I nod in agreement but prefer to keep the cold metal of my own gun in my hand. "Let's see if we can get eyes on Solomon." He looks back at me to ensure I'm ready, and we move forward. I follow him toward the edge of the alley and look out into the crowd. The Federation's anthem is blasting through loudspeakers, and people are staring anxiously at the platform where Commander Hawthorne is about to address the audience. I try to see past him, but I can't make anything out but a blur of soldiers.

"I can't see him," I murmur, standing on my tiptoes.

"We have to move up," he answers but pushes me back when I step forward. "No, not until Hawthorne starts." My heart's beating so loudly, I barely hear him. I try to take steadying breaths, but it only leads me closer to hyperventilating. "You okay?"

"Fine," I quip. *Get it together, Esther.*

"Here he goes . . ."

I squint my eyes to see Hawthorne straighten the lapel of his jacket and clear his throat into the microphone. Silence dispenses through the crowd, and the cameras are all aimed toward the stage. His voice, firm and poised, disseminates over the mass of faces. "Today, we are here to demonstrate the consequences of betraying your nation, a nation who has done nothing but offer each of you acceptance, the opportunity for equality, and the chance to grow on the cutting edge of modern technology. To betray your nation is to betray one's self, for you are allowing yourself to live with iniquity. You are allowing yourself to not embrace all people and move toward a new age, an age where there is no wickedness or judgement but only pleasure and free love. Those who still choose to judge and adhere to the old ways—ways that ostracize and discriminate others—need to be eradicated. With us today is a man who represents the very judgement we want to remove. Let his death serve as a symbol to a new era, an era without condemnation of supposed sins."

"Let's go." Finnick places a hand on my wrist, and we shift into the crowd.

# 70.
# ONE YEAR EARLIER . . .

Lizzie's room was down a hallway and up a flight of stairs from mine. As I walked there, I thought about how I could broach the idea of burning down St. Mary's to Finnick. I would need his full support if I was going to gain everyone else's. My only concern was that he wouldn't be ready to give up on St. Mary's yet, that he would think there was still something worth saving. I just needed to convince him that there wasn't.

I reached the top of the stairs and turned toward the door of her room. I could hear the arguing inside before I was close enough to knock.

"If we do that, they'll just do to us what they did to Judah or Timothy, or even worse." Lizzie, usually soft-spoken, said louder than I had ever heard her talk before.

"I'm with Lizzie. I'm not gonna die. I'm only sixteen," said Timothy's friend, Isaiah. I heard murmurs of agreement throughout the room, and I couldn't help but think that I might have more support for my idea than I had thought. Maybe it didn't matter whether or not I could convince Finnick if everyone else agreed with me. After all, no one wanted to fight an enemy they couldn't beat. We were outnumbered here. We could do more somewhere else.

"Well, what do you all suggest then? We do nothing? Because I'm sorry, but that's just not an option for me." Finnick's voice boomed through the door, and I took the opportunity to knock quickly before entering.

"I have an idea," I said with resolution as all eyes in the room looked toward me. "What do you say we burn this place to the ground?"

# 71.
## PRESENT DAY

I was eight the first time I ever went to see a concert, and it was a rock band. My parents had insisted we rush to the front, wanting me to have the best possible experience. As I hold tightly onto Finnick, forcing our way through the crowd to the platform and Solomon, I'm reminded of that feeling of powerlessness among so many bodies. The crowd here, though, is far from joyous and exuberant like the one that day. No, these people are incensed, fearful, some with a self-righteousness that borders on instability.

"Stay close," Finnick whispers back in my ear. I link a finger through his back-belt loop and press my body to his.

"Hey, watch it," a man hisses in my ear as I trample his toe. Another man elbows me hard, and I try to shove past him.

"Ouch," I grunt. I try to fight past the clouds of suffocation invading my head and lungs. Any moment, Tobias will set off pipe bombs to spur the crowd's attention away from the platform. As people push against me, I fear being trampled before even reaching Solomon.

We've made it a few more feet, and I can see him now, his hands tied behind his back, kneeling as if in prayer behind the commander. I study his face, a mix of stoicism and grit. Only those closest to him would recognize the gleam of angst in his eyes. *Hang in there, Solomon; we're coming.*

There's the sound of a loud explosion. Before anyone can react, the sound of another one echoes not twenty feet from the last. A flash of fiery light discharges upward. It's time. Finnick pulls my hand hard, and I crush up against him. There are screams around us as everyone tries to determine what is going on and where they should run. Smoke infiltrates the air. Finnick and I both fall against the platform, my pants ripped from stumbling, my knees a bloody mess.

I look upward at the sound of Hawthorne's voice. "Hang him, now!" he yells to an officer who's standing guard by the noose.

My mind conjures images from my history books as it recognizes the irony of the world's advancements, which have come so far but also have not moved at all.

The next few moments happen at the speed of light as Finnick and I crawl onto the platform and rush toward the scaffold. Finnick uses the barrel of his gun to crack two guards in the back of the head. I watch as Hawthorne's mouth drops in anger and recognition.

I hesitate only a moment before running to untie Solomon's hands. "We're here now; you're okay." My voice is a shaky hush.

"My dear girl." Solomon looks back at me, his face badly beaten, tears in his eyes. With my help, he stands. We barely move before Hawthorne barrels us to the ground.

I reach for my gun, but his fist meets my face first. Crying out in pain, I grasp my right cheek. Solomon grabs Hawthorne's leg, and he falls forward, but not before he reaches back and pulls Solomon down with him. There's scrambling on the ground, and I go for my gun again, this time retrieving it. A guard makes his way toward me, and I shoot him down. My heart's beating like a procession of drums. My hands are clammy, shaky. The guard falls in a heap of blood at my feet. I turn toward

Solomon, hold my breath, and shoot Hawthorne in the side. He cries out, and I look toward Finnick, his face mirroring my own shock and horror.

He picks up Solomon, never taking his eyes off mine. Hawthorne moves, trying to stand up.

"Run!" Finnick screams to me, and I stumble forward.

I look back only a moment to ensure they're behind me. Finnick's arm grips Solomon's waist, and they're running as quickly as their injuries will allow. I notice the pool of blood growing on the shirt sleeve by Finnick's shoulder and know he's been shot. Chaos has descended over the crowd like vultures on corpses. People are fighting with whatever they can find.

I watch as a looter shatters the windows of a nearby store. It's impossible to tell who is part of the Resistance and who supports the Federation. Leaping over two bleeding bodies in the street, I lose my footing and fall on my marred knees. I struggle to pull myself up and turn to check for Finnick and Solomon. Our eyes connect, theirs crisp with fear and pain. I'm still assessing the volume of their pain when it happens. It's a sole gunshot, a sound as familiar to me as rain. I watch as it connects to the side of Solomon's head, whipping it back with the force of a tide. The pupils of his eyes momentarily absorb the heat of the wound before he collapses against Finnick and onto the ground.

"Solomon!"

My arms reach forward as I search for where the shot came from. There's a ringing in my ears, blood rushing to my head. My feet stumble over each other as I stagger and fall against Solomon's body. I look up, searching for help. "Someone, help us!"

I cry into the chaos that surrounds me, my words lost in the mayhem. My eyes dance the perimeter frantically until I see the shooter's face. But no. I blink several times. Hot tears blur my sight. My mind's playing tricks on me. But he's staring at us, the hint of a smile on his lips, his gun falling casually against his side.

My ears ring louder now, the sound deafening. Images are clouding around me as though I'm falling through space, a pendulum of time. I can see the photograph of my parents, the file in Alastor's office. The man is mouthing words to me. I can't make them out. *Focus. These are the words of your parents' killer, the murderer of your professor, your friend.* I reach my hand out to grasp the words, but the world is slipping into blackness, the people swaying mirages around me. The shooter transforms into the beast from last night's nightmare, a hazy image, an exaggerated shadow.

"Esther, climb in," Tobias demands as he pulls up his convoy truck. He sees Solomon and cringes in pain. "Put him in the back," he tells Finnick softly, jumping down to help lift him.

Ruby gets off the truck when she realizes I'm not moving and lifts me carefully, my body convulsing in silent heaves. She places a comforting hand on my arm, but I can't look at her, not able to see anything but blackness, the void of loss.

Tobias takes off through the mass of disorder, honking loudly and waving his gun to clear a way. I watch Finnick apply pressure to his shoulder. I make an effort to help him, neither of us speaking. A tarp covers Solomon's body, the shape a shadow of death against the fading light of the day. I had come here to save him. Not only did I fail, but with each life I took today, I forfeited another portion of my soul. I allow the numbness to take over, to consume my psyche and barricade the pain. There's no room for regret in this world. The decay of society drips around me as my mind slips further into the depths of Hell.

# 72.
# ONE YEAR EARLIER . . .

The plan to burn St. Mary's had taken days to organize. The goal was to save as many lives as possible while ensuring St. Mary's would never house children again.

"This way," I whispered, motioning with my arm for Isaiah to follow me.

It was three o'clock in the morning, and the halls were eerily silent, the only sound the occasional click of the heater as it reverberated through its cycle. We had decided to start the fire in the kitchen, the room farthest from the dormitories. We wanted people to have time to escape, but the evil that lived there had to be destroyed. And we needed to move on. There was a bigger battle out there calling us.

"Shh," Isaiah breathed as I opened the kitchen door, its old hinges creaking with the pressure. We walked cautiously toward the stove where I cranked the gas and forced a leak. I heard a hiss as the fluid substance dispersed into the air. I checked my watch: 3:10. Finnick would still have been with Rachael and the others. They had been evacuating people silently out of the side doors of the building. We had agreed to give them until twenty after three before I lit the match.

I looked at Isaiah nervously. "Do you think we're doing the right thing?" I asked, the hesitation in my voice clear.

"Of course, we are," he affirmed. "We're doing something that really matters. We're destroying a place filled with evil, a place that is brainwashing children. Trust me, Esther, this is right." His eyes on mine were steady, genuine, and I nodded to let him know I heard what he was saying.

If not now, when? It would only grow worse. I checked my watch again: 3:16. I paced a few steps in anticipation. The plan was to start the fire and then make a run for it ourselves. We wouldn't have long before the room engulfed in flames. I had told Finnick I'd meet him and Rachael behind the school at the bottom of the hill. The tree line of the forest began a hundred feet from the school's caged yards, and we'd be able to make our journey through the woods from there. We had spent the earlier hours of the night packing food and blankets to help us through the long days ahead. Once everything had settled down, Finnick and I would break from the group and try to find Solomon.

I was dreading the journey, but I was anxious to leave and see Solomon again. My mind darted to those at St. Mary's who wouldn't make it, but I quickly erased the thought. I couldn't dwell on the negative outcomes of the fire, or I wouldn't be able to go through with it. I reminded myself that we had no choice. They would persecute and eventually kill us if we didn't leave.

"It's 3:21," I told Isaiah, checking my watch again. "It's time." We exchanged a look of apprehension and fear, but he merely nodded. I took the matches I had stolen from the chapel's podium out of the pocket of my jacket. "Here goes nothing." Taking a deep breath, I pulled out a match, striking it against the box. "Go, now," I told Isaiah as I leaned down to the ground and tossed the flame. I watched as the blaze hit the gas, disseminating like the rush of a stream. Then I turned and ran.

I looked back over my shoulder for only a second, thinking of Sodom and Gomorrah, fearing I'd turn to salt.

"Esther?" a first grader invaded my thoughts, and I turned to see the little girl I had been tutoring in science. She stared at me with wide eyes, and my shoes squeaked against the shiny linoleum of the hall. Her hair was disheveled from sleep, and her bare feet stuck out from the bottom of her pajamas. "What's going on?" she asked, confused.

I swallowed what felt like my heart in my throat as I tried to focus on her face. "Get out, Sara. Get your friends, whoever is left, and get out." Her eyes filled with tears, and I knew that I had terrified her, but there was no time for comfort now. "Go!" She jumped at my demand but turned around and ran toward her dormitory hall.

I raced through the other dorms, knocking on doors and screaming for students to get out. A few sleepy heads emerged, rubbing their eyes, terrified as they realized what I was telling them. I made my way through the residence halls toward one of several fire escapes. I could smell the smoke now, and I knew the fire was spreading. Frightened screams resounded; the cries of students ricocheting off the walls like pebbles skipping across water.

*Dear God,* I prayed, *what have we done?*

# 73.
# PRESENT DAY

The morning of Solomon's funeral is overcast. The darkness of the clouds juxtaposed with the dismal horizon makes the mood suitable to the sentiments associated with funerals. There is no funeral home to assist us, and we spend hours preparing Solomon's grave at the bank of Barron Creek, next to Rachael and so many others since. Finnick is taking it even worse than I am, his silence a brooding reminder that the darkness that lies ahead will supersede any joy within this world. I wipe the sweat from my head with the bottom of my soiled t-shirt and look to the dark sky.

"There'll be hail for sure," Tobias says, meeting my thoughts. He places his callused hands atop the handle of his shovel. I don't answer him right away, then stare at him vacantly. His words float in the air between us. "Ya all right?" he asks kindly.

"Hmm," I try to register his face. "Oh yeah, just lost in my mind, I guess. I think you're right about the hail."

He nods, his eyes conveying sympathy, maybe even a little pity. "Very sorry about Mr. Solomon. He was what we call a rare breed back home. Ya don't meet too many like him these days."

The water in my eyes burns with the truth of his sentiments. I try to smile, but I find that I can't lift my lips. Like the rest of me, they feel numb. Solomon's death has ripped away the ability to feel anything but desolation; even the fond memories of those I loved feel empty. I search for Finnick, finding him standing by the rushing water, covered in mud from digging. He's still so handsome, despite everything. His hair has grown back even fuller, and it contrasts beautifully with the pallor of his skin. Cautiously, I walk to him and stand by his side in silence.

A few moments pass before he says anything. "How did we get here, Esther? How is it possible that he is gone?"

The tears glide off my face, leaving streaks through the crust and dirt caked on my cheeks. "Somehow, it's part of the plan. We . . . will see him again." The words come out in a croak, my throat dry from emotion, the poor quality of the air, and a lack of drinkable water.

"Where we will go now?" he asks, turning to me, his uncertainty setting me back.

I'm used to his leadership, his ability to know what to do even in the worst situations. His face conveys to me now just how much of the Finnick I love has been lost, the parts of him that now lie dead, here, with the others. I stare off, unable to give him an answer, unsure of what the future will hold and the pain that awaits us.

I think back to the night after I had killed that man in the brothel. I couldn't sleep. I knew I had been protecting Finnick, yet I still felt the guilt of what I'd done eating at my soul. Solomon had heard my sobs and come to console me. I sat up next to him as he reminded me that God views our actions in war differently, showing me the verses in Jeremiah when Babylon falls. Jeremiah 51:20 says, "You are my war club, my weapon for battle."

As a soldier of God, am I justified to commit murder? Solomon seemed to be telling me that I am, since it's my duty to rise against evil. The idea gives me some comfort as Finnick and I stare out at the fading horizon. I know that life isn't black and white, and the day will come when I must fully face the gray area of what I've done. The familiar pang of guilt stings my chest as I'm reminded of the one death neither God nor I can justify.

I struggle to clear my throat to speak. "We move forward, Finn, the way we always have."

I think of Rachael as I watch the darkness roll in, draining the last bit of light from the clouded sky.

# 74.
# ONE YEAR EARLIER . . .

The sky was dark on the day Rachael died, almost like the atmosphere had been prepared to mourn. There was a density in the air that signified another bad storm, a common occurrence within this culminating apocalyptic world. St. Mary's had fallen, by our hands, and the future was unknown. The scent of smoke was everywhere—permeating the air and covering our bodies and our clothes. Still reeling from my part in St. Mary's destruction, I was not in a healthy state of mind. There were so many unanswered questions, the confusion about our existence amidst chaos, the guilt of what we'd just done weighing on my heart. There were a lot of ways I could try to justify my actions, but when forced to look hard at what I did, I knew there was no one else to blame but me.

"This way," Finnick beckoned, his hand gesturing for the rest of us to follow. "I want to try to make it to Barron Creek before this storm hits. We can set up camp under the bridge and try to ride it out."

"I hope it doesn't turn into a tornado." Rachael spoke softly, her eyes searching the sky for signs of what was to come. The rest of us remained silent, some nodding vaguely, all lost in our own ominous thoughts.

The walk was strenuous. We were tired, having not slept since our evacuation of the school. The emotions of leaving that world behind were a plague on our minds. No one knew how many hadn't been able to find a way out. The screams of children echoed through the air, reminding us over and over that their blood was on our hands. I shuddered, praying to myself that God would forgive us.

"What have we done?" I whispered. The question was continuously on my lips. It was only Isaiah who heard me, and he placed a comforting hand on my arm.

"What we had to," he answered.

The rest of the walk was silent, like the march of the dead; and as we approached the creek, I saw that the water was close to flooding.

"This storm will push it over the edge," I said. Everyone nodded in agreement, realizing we couldn't post there for long.

"I'm going to take Lizzie and Isaiah with me to find firewood. I'd like to get a fire going before the rain starts, so we can cook something to eat." Finnick looked to me and Rachael as he talked. "Esther, can you and Rachael assess our food rations and set up shelter under the bridge? There're some blankets in our packs. I don't know that our tent would survive the storm, so I wouldn't bother with it."

"Of course," I told him, eager to do something useful. Rachael went to him, embracing him in a hug.

"I love you," she whispered. He returned her embrace, enfolding her in his arms tightly, and I looked away, uncomfortable, envious, at the show of their affection. She pulled back to stand beside me, and we watched as the three took off into the woods, just as the first crack of thunder filled the air. Rachael turned toward me timidly. It was strange for it to just be the two of us; I was rarely alone for very long with anyone those days, and the solitude of it was unsettling.

"Let's go open the packs," I said, breaking the silence, averting my eyes.

"Okay," she agreed, following me under the bridge to the wide stretch of muddied, hard ground, sheltered by the immense concrete slabs of the overpass. Water rushed next to us, swiftly cascading over the large rocks that barricaded its smooth passage downstream. I absently unzipped the first pack I set down, not paying attention to whose it was, my mind still lost in the day's events. Later, I would think back on that moment, wondering what might have happened if I had opened another pack and not seen what I did that day. But it had been Rachael's pack that I selected, and as I unzipped it and reached in to see what was inside, my fingers laced around a note.

I looked down at a folded piece of paper in my hand, sitting atop a scrunched-up blanket and a large storage bag of food. I was about to push the note downward, acknowledging that whatever it said was none of my business, when my eyes recognized the handwriting on the top.

There was merely a scribbled, "Rachael," addressing who it was for, but I would know that writing anywhere. Ezra.

*My parents taught me CPR when I was only five years old. They had made sure I kept up with the skill, having me practice on a dummy doll they kept in our house. I always thought it was so weird. Why were they so obsessed? There was no one dying. There was no one I needed to save.*

I tried to bring her back. I cradled her bleeding head in my lap and gave her CPR long past the time she stopped breathing, past when her pulse faded from a slowing throb to the stop of her existence. That was how the others found us, me sitting on the bank, covered in Rachael's blood, her beautiful head of dark hair a misshapen mass on my thighs.

Finnick's screams superseded anything I had ever heard. I had thought it would be the screams of those left in St. Mary's that would resound in my nightmares, but that new tragedy, that fresh horror, was what would haunt my nightmares in the days to come.

It was Isaiah who spoke first, his voice a shaky, confused stutter. "Wh-what happened to her?"

My eyes were hot with tears. I knew he was talking to me. Everyone was looking at me. I had to respond, to say something.

"She hit her head." The words peppered the air like poison. I reached out my finger to point at the rock her head had slammed into. There was dark red on the whitewash of the stone, a marking, a reminder of how easily life was lost. Lizzie gasped. Finnick's moans grew louder. He was a ball at my feet, grasping Rachael's legs, his own head down, his body moving back and forth.

"Bu—" Lizzie went to speak but struggled to find the words. After seconds that felt like hours, she finished. "How?"

Everyone was looking at me again. I was supposed to say something. I felt the note, damp but solid, in my hand under Rachael's head. An instinct of survival washed over me. I was like a rabid animal who must protect itself.

"She slipped," I whispered. It was logical enough.

The water was cascading down at an increasing speed. The others took this in. They looked from the rock to Rachael, trying to make sense of her beauty fading into the darkness of death. They all seemed to buy what I was saying. They don't know. My mind was consumed by self-loathing and relief. Then Finnick looked up at me. His eyes were unrecognizable, the blood of the veins like that of a maniacal fiend.

I saw the doubt there, the unanswered questions circulating. I couldn't meet his eyes, my own turning away. I had to get her off me. I couldn't breathe with her there. The blood, her hair, his eyes as they searched mine for truth. I pushed her head off my legs gently and vomited into the water, my hand clutching the note.

"Come and find me, Rachael. Join us."

I gagged on the words, the thought of them renewing my anger, my inability to understand. The emotions of his leaving me came back like a tidal wave against my heart. She was why he left me. She was responsible for all of that pain.

Wasn't having Finnick's love enough for her? Did she have to take Ezra away from me, too?

Lizzie put a gentle hand on my back. "That must have been so horrible for you to see, Esther; I'm sorry." Her words stirred the bile of my shame, and I leaned down to put my head between my knees. When I looked back up, my eyes met Finnick's.

"What else?" The question was asked calmly as though the dependency of the answer wouldn't ruin us, destroy who he thought I was, but his face conveyed his wrath. He already knew.

I couldn't respond, only shaking my head over and over again until he was shaking me. He had his hands gripped firmly on each of my shoulders, and I could smell the angst, the turmoil in his breath, like hot fire that burned my face. My fingers loosened, and I let the note fall at his feet. He loosened his grip, looking down at the paper on the ground. His eyes widened as he leaned to pick it up, then the wave of understanding, of disbelief, when he read the words. His head unconsciously shook left to right, not allowing himself to believe what he was reading.

*Dear Rachael,*

*When you came to me that night with the letter from Esther's mom, I admit it was difficult to accept. But you were right to show me. One should always know who is responsible for the murder of their parents, their source of life. To hear that it was Esther's parents who killed my own broke me in a way I will not come back from, and this hate and loss will fuel my decisions to come.*

*I will not make her pay for the sins of her parents, but I cannot look at her and love her knowing that she is a part of them. I'll be forever grateful that you made copies of the letters. I can't begin to tell you how useful they'll be. We can do this together, Rachael, you and I, as it should be, as our parents would have wanted it. Yours deserve retribution as much as my own. Leave them behind and find me, Rachael. Join us.*

*Ezra*

I remembered the words, empathizing with Finnick's pain, and saw the look of dismay that had transformed his face. I could see he hadn't known, that he was battling with the fact that Rachael hadn't told him and may have been planning to leave him. I had been right not to trust her. The realization gave me no comfort as I unfolded the truth.

"I'm so sorry. I—I was so angry. I pushed her, but I didn't think she . . . she . . . " At my words, he turned away from me, a look of disgust cloaking his face as he shoved the note deep in his pocket. My mouth dropped open to say something else, but nothing came out. I couldn't defend what I'd done. How could I? There was no justification for murder.

"Hey, Finnick, I know this is rough, man, but don't take it out on Esther." Isaiah, not having seen the note or our exchange, came to my defense.

Finnick's eyes glazed mine with loathing. "We bury her here," he snapped.

"With . . . with what?" Isaiah asked, taken aback by Finnick's conversion from grief to rage.

"Esther will go find us shovels, won't you?"

"Finnick, that's crazy. A storm's coming . . ."

"No," I said quietly. "I'll go."

"Then I'll come with you," Isaiah said. "But I think it's crazy." He followed me then, shaking his head at Finnick but fearing to push the issue.

I couldn't look at Finnick, shame consuming me. I wanted to process what Rachael had done—when she had been able to steal and copy my letters—but the loathing I had for myself was clouding my thoughts. How would I ever get past this? This wasn't self-defense. It was not killing for the purpose of the cause. Accident or not, I was a murderer.

# 75.
# PRESENT DAY

There are about thirty resistors gathered around Solomon's final resting place, the only survivors who got out with us that day. I know that this war is far from over. All I can continue to do is save as many souls as I can. Prophecy tells me this world will fall away, and as I look around at the despair around me, I long for the joy of the next life. Yet I know that God isn't done with me yet. I may never entirely forgive myself for what I've done, particularly when it comes to Rachael, but I find hope in the good I've done in this life, in the promise of redemption.

It's been almost forty-eight hours since Solomon's death, but the pain is as raw as if he had just collapsed. My mind replays the horror on repeat like a song stuck in my head. Pellets of hail bounce off my jacket, and I watch as they roll over Finnick's feet. The wind's picked up and whips around us, blowing my ponytail hard against my face. My eyes burn from the tears of the wind and the grief.

"We'll need to seek shelter soon. Before it gets worse," Finnick says.

"I want to say a few words first," I answer, taking a step forward. I clear my throat, and waves of emotion roll over me. I prepare to yell over the deafening sounds of the wind and the hail.

I look around to make sure everyone realizes I'm going to speak and raise my voice several degrees. "When I first met Solomon, I was lost. I had no understanding of who I was or who I was supposed to become. He not only helped me, but he changed me in every way. When others judged me, gave up on me, or left me, it was he who stayed. He became my voice of reason in the darkness, a beacon of hope in a world of despair."

I pause to swipe at the torrent of tears on my face. I'm about to begin again, but a movement by the trees on the other side of the bank stops me. I blink a few times and squint in that direction, trying to make out what it is. My eyes land on a sole figure leaning plaintively against a tree. He's clearly watching us, arms pushed deep in his pockets, a shadow of my past. I swallow hard.

Seconds turn into minutes, and the silence is becoming awkward. No one is sure why I stopped talking. Finnick lays a hand on my arm, bringing my mind back to my surroundings, to the people who are waiting for me to continue. With eyes still locked on the figure in the distance, I take a deep breath, forcing myself to go on. "That is the kind of man he was, a man who lived with more honor in one day than many men achieve in a lifetime. I celebrate that he is with God; I am honored to have known him; and I am forever indebted to him for his kindnesses." I look down then as I hear murmurs of agreement throughout the crowd, mingled with whispered blessings and prayers. A few place a comforting hand on my shoulders and arms. I will my eyes upward to look back at the tree in the distance. Are there others? I must have been seeing things, my grief generating hallucinations. I squint through the storm, crying out as I see more shapes form, at least a hundred soldiers moving through the trees. The figure by the tree raises a hand to stop them, locking his eyes with mine.

"Ezra," I breathe.

I grip Finnick's hand and run.

# THE END

For more information about
**Christy Dietz**
&
*Serpentine*
please visit:

www.christydietz.com
Twitter: @DietzChristy
Instagram: @christydietzauthor
www.facebook.com/dietzchristy


For more information about
AMBASSADOR INTERNATIONAL
please visit:

*www.ambassador-international.com*
*@AmbassadorIntl*
*www.facebook.com/AmbassadorIntl*

*Thank you for reading this book. Please consider leaving us a review on your social media, favorite retailer's website, Goodreads or Bookbub, or our website.*

# More from Ambassador International

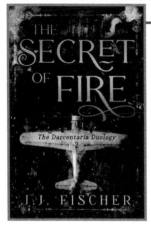

Darcentaria has been invaded by the Outside. El of the Outside has been captured, and Torsten Eiselher, the once-formidable warrior-has been injured and is lost in the woods. Will he ever be able to find his way back to El and discover the true Way? Or will the darkness and his thirst for revenge swallow him whole? El has her own choices to make between the man she loved from the Outside and the man she loves now. Will her heart make the right choice?

Polar opposites, pretty girl Willow Rysen and humble nerd Christian Blythe, find themselves forced to work together on a project for their science class at Bethel Private School. As the two work together, Miss Popular finds her world turned upside down after a night of partying, made even worse when Christian is the only one around to rescue her. Will she find that the grace of God can overcome her past failures or will she allow the lure of the world's ideologies to keep her tight in its grasp?

Seventeen-year-old Adaliah is the warrior and Lady of Targe, but when she wakes up in the Kest River, presumed dead by the world, she has lost her memory and is being hunted by unknown forces. Injured and alone, she must put together the pieces of her broken past and shattered kingdom.